THE LOST

THE ALCHEMY OF TREASON

PETER NEALEN

THE LAND of ICE & MONSTERS

THE TEETH
of WINTER
GRICHENCOS'
CITADEL
POHLOJA
SUMNOTH
MENNINKAI
VAHAVA
PAYKHAH
N
W
E
S

WARGATE

An imprint of Galaxy's Edge Press
PO BOX 534
Puyallup, Washington 98371

ISBN: 978-1-949731-83-5

www.forgottenruin.com
www.wargatebooks.com

CHAPTER 1

CRAWLING forward on my belly, Bowie in hand, I stalked the Avur sentry through the tall grass.

It wasn't nearly as dark as I might have liked, but time was against us, and the darkness was only ever going to be a mixed blessing in this place, anyway. We didn't think this particular band had a shaman with them, just from the scouting we'd done over the last day or so, but we also knew from experience that these foothills were almost as haunted as the plains we'd just re-crossed.

I'd been crawling for a couple of hours. Back in The World, that might have seemed like an awfully long time, but we were getting used to the old ways of doing things. There were no arbitrary timelines set by operational or training schedules here. There was only the light, the weather, and the necessities of survival.

On a stalk like this, stealth and slow, careful movement were necessities of survival.

I inched forward a little bit farther, trying not to watch the Avur too closely. Let him start to feel like he was being watched, and I'd be blown, and this entire attack would fall apart before any of us were in position.

Of course, I had no way of knowing where Santos, Rodeffer, or Farrar were right then. My world was limited to the dirt, the grass in front of me, and a slice of the darkening sky that the Avur sentry was currently silhouetted against. I couldn't hear that much, either, though the scrape of my cammies against the dirt and the grass still sounded deafeningly loud with each movement, despite the whisper of the wind through the rocks, grass, and windswept, gnarled trees.

I paused behind a rock, small enough that I probably wouldn't even have looked at it as cover, once upon a time. Down in the prone, low-crawling with no gear on, though, I could get a lot smaller than I might have imagined in a conventional warfare environment.

We were learning, not only from the Tuacha and the other allies we'd met since coming to this strange, haunted world, but from the need to adapt to circumstances and the environment. We were steadily becoming more and more like the Apaches and Comanches some of us had read about back in The World.

We were adapting in different ways, too, but one thing I'd learned from the Galel, a few of whom were still riding with us, currently sheltered in a gully down the hill, was that even the honor-bound knights of this world weren't so rigidly wedded to one form of warfare that they wouldn't learn all the others.

Peering around the rock, I listened carefully as I scanned my surroundings. I could hear the Avurs' horses moving around, but none of us had spooked them yet. We'd carefully approached from the opposite side of the camp in order to avoid just that.

Low voices murmured near the fire. It wasn't a large fire, but oftentimes in this place, the risks of a corporeal enemy seeing your fire were outweighed by the need to keep spookier foes at bay.

My target sighed and shifted his weight. His armor creaked slightly with the movement. The Avurs were great horse warriors, and we had plenty of experience with just how savage they could be, but they were still men, and subject to many of the same weaknesses. Few men enjoy holding security, and if they are warriors with the sort of thirst for action and glory that we'd seen from the Avurs, that just made it worse. Old boy would much rather be sleeping or out hunting than sitting there, watching the dark.

I fully intended to use that discontent to my advantage.

The Avur sentry had his helmet off, but he still wore his lamellar breastplate. Sitting on the ground with his legs crossed, he had his saber across his knees and his spear stuck into the ground by its backspike. He was watching his sector, but he wasn't happy about it, and he wasn't expecting anyone in their right mind to be coming from this direction.

After all, the frontier between the Empire of Ar-Annator and the Galel Kingdom of Cor Legear was barely five miles away, over the crest of that ridge to the west. That was where the threat lay.

They had to know that we were out there, somewhere. It had been over a month since we'd broken out of the ruins of Gremman, and word had to have spread to the Avur tribes that roamed the wilderness of the northern marches of the Empire that we were still loose, somewhere. We'd already had to go to ground and evade at least three warbands just in the last week.

We *had* avoided contact, though, which was why this guy was staring off into space and hating his life, instead of keeping watch the way he was supposed to.

I carefully scanned what I could see of the terrain around me, looking for the next leg of my route. While I was trying to sneak up on the sentry, I wasn't going to try to crawl right up to his face. That's not how stalking works.

There. I got as low as I could and continued my inch-by-inch skull drag, moving into a slightly lower fold in the ground, shielded from the sentry by several stands of nearly two-foot-tall grass. I still had to move very slowly—even more slowly than I already had been for the last two hours. I was a good twenty yards away from him, but that was plenty close enough to get spotted or heard if I wasn't careful, even in the deepening dark.

I might have heard something off to my right. Maybe a grunt, suddenly cut off. Santos was supposed to be over there. Maybe he'd moved faster than I had.

The last of the faint remaining glow in the west had faded and the stars were glittering in the black sky overhead when I finally rose to a low crouch. Firelight glinted faintly off the dark, satin steel of the Bowie in my fist as I quickly scanned my surroundings before padding as silently as I could toward the sentry, his back now to me.

The fire still flickered, though most of the Avurs were now proned out and snoring. A couple were still up, sitting by the fire, one of them staring into the flames. That one almost gave me pause. There was something about him that bothered me. I couldn't put my finger on it immediately, but something told me he was more dangerous. He wasn't staring into the fire because he was a boot who didn't know any better. Any man who had any experience in the wild wouldn't look directly at an artificial light source at night. It would ruin his night adaptation.

I'd have to watch that one.

Rolling my feet carefully, almost wishing I had moccasins on instead of combat boots, I crept toward the sentry, planting each foot slowly and smoothly before putting my weight on it. It was achingly slow movement, while every nerve screamed at me to get up and rush the guy, take him out before he turned and saw me, or one of his buddies noticed something.

It felt like it took forever to get barely ten feet from him. I hadn't made a sound, careful to breathe through my mouth so that I didn't give myself away with a nose whistle, but his head started to turn as I got closer.

Close enough. I lunged.

I hit him hard, with all one hundred seventy-odd pounds I had left on me after close to a month of ever-shorter rations and long days on foot or in the saddle. With him sitting on the ground the way he was, there was only so low I could get, but I put a knee in his back and knocked him hard onto his face, catching myself with one hand before I went over his head. Putting my weight on that knee, I shoved his face down into the dirt and the grass as I brought the Bowie plunging down onto the back of his neck.

The blade cleaved through skin, muscle, tendon, and nerve, and he stiffened, then went limp. His head was still attached, but I'd just severed his spine. He wasn't getting up ever again, nor was he going to make any further noise.

Unfortunately, I was one of the lucky ones.

I heard a strangled cry off to my left, where either Rodeffer or Farrar were closing on their own targets. A moment later, the noise increased, as a hand-to-hand fight really started to get going.

A shout rose from near the fire. I spun around, just as the man who'd been staring into the fire threw something into the flames.

The fire flared up suddenly, the flames turning a sickly green. There were a couple of chemicals that could do that, but generally speaking, borax or copper sulfate don't result in a small, disproportionately long-limbed fire goblin leaping out of the flames.

Under different circumstances, I might have shot it, even though it wasn't coming for me right at the moment. However, the needs of stealth, not to mention the fact that I had a whopping three mags left for my M110, meant that I'd crawled up to the Avurs' perimeter with only my knife. I'd left my rifle—and the Sword of Iudicael, which had been a pang, let me tell you—back at the main body with Gunny.

The man I'd just killed hadn't been unarmed, though, and necessity had already led us down some training paths we wouldn't have expected a little over a year before.

Snatching the spear out of the dirt, I flipped it around in my hand, reared back, and cast it as hard as I could at the shaman who'd just summoned that fiery little goblin.

Throwing a spear isn't nearly as easy as it looks in the movies. I'd discovered that while practicing on Mathghaman's manor, back on the Isle of Riamog, months before. You can't just grab it and throw it. You need to find the balance point, shift your hand back slightly, and grip it kind of like a pencil, rather than just wrapping your fist around it. It takes practice. And I hadn't practiced in several months.

Still, even if I just hit him with the haft, it might buy us a few moments. Sorcerers and shamans had to have a certain degree of investiture and concentration in a summoning, or else—unless the darker power they'd called upon had a vested interest in their objective—it could rebound on them, to their eternal chagrin.

Somebody up there was looking out for me. Maybe even the glowing, mysterious guardian I'd seen in my dreams, and occasionally out of the corner of my eye in waking moments. The point ripped through his shoulder and buried itself in his chest, transfixing at least one lung.

Probably the best throw I'd ever managed.

As blood sprayed from his mouth and he slumped into the fire, another Avur warrior nearby let out a yell, drew his saber, and started for me, even though he probably couldn't see me all that well. Three more quickly joined him, two with spears, one with a short, wickedly curved axe.

I had two options at that point. I could shift the Bowie to my off hand, snatch up that Avur saber from under the dead body at my feet, and fight, or I could fade into the darkness as quickly and quietly as I could.

I wasn't much more than bone, rawhide, and meanness by then, but meanness only goes so far against four men with spears, sabers, and axes. They were moving cautiously, but I wasn't nearly as far away from that fire as I would have liked. I probably never could have hit that shaman with the spear if I'd been only a few paces farther back.

As much as I wanted to carve them up, since that was why we had closed in on this bunch in the first place, I knew what I had to do. I still pulled the saber, but I moved back into the grass and down the hill as I did so.

At least the little green fire goblin had vanished into sparks as soon as I'd killed the shaman.

Fortunately, even as it looked like I was going to have to throw stealth to the winds and just run for it, the rest of the operation kicked off.

There was no stabbing flame, no thunderous roar. Everyone was running suppressed, be they Recon Marines from a time and world far from this one, Tuacha warriors who are somehow more than human, or Menninkai auxiliaries trying very hard to become Recon Marines. Everyone was also being extremely careful with what little ammo we had left.

With a series of sharp *crack*s, bullets sped out of the dark and knocked both spearmen off their feet. The axe-wielder staggered, but he didn't go down right away, and a second bullet smashed through his skull from not all that far away. He collapsed limply to the dirt.

The man with the saber was the luckiest of the four. Whoever had shot at him missed, at least at first.

He was no coward. While the Avurs had limited experience with firearms—and most of those who had that experience were dead—he'd grown up in a world teeming with the spooky and unexplainable. He didn't cower, didn't run. He charged me, knowing only that the spear had come from my direction, so he was going to shed blood before he went down.

One on one, I was much more confident in my swordsmanship. I surged to meet him, though the Avur saber was balanced differently from the Sword of Iudicael, and I wasn't sure I liked it. I'd fought with worse, though.

I didn't wait for his opening swing, but slashed at his knee, forcing him to arrest his momentum as I loomed out of the dark. He went up on tiptoes as he stopped abruptly, barely getting his own saber in the way to parry mine. I rode the parry, quickly swinging back in a shearing cut aimed at his head.

You learn pretty fast when swordfighting not to just swing with all your might. Balance, speed, and the ability to quickly redirect the point of your blade are far more important, not to mention footwork. Unfortunately, this guy was easily as good as I was, and quickly swayed back from my cut, almost making me overextend. He was ready for it, too, as his point almost tore a hole in not only my camouflage blouse, but also the flesh underneath it.

I'd shed my mail for the stalk, and right then, I was regretting it. Still, he only had his saber, while I had my captured saber in one hand and my Bowie in the other. It gave me a little bit of an advantage.

I got the saber inside his own blade and batted it aside, even as I thrust for his groin with the Bowie. He was still wearing his lamellar breastplate—none of the Avurs seemed to have taken their armor off to rest—so trying to stab him in the heart or the guts was out. He jumped back, almost doing a wrestling splay, even as he grabbed for my knife wrist, desperately trying to keep that razor-sharp blade away from his nuts and his femoral artery.

That threw him off balance, though, and while I can't say that I'd completely planned for it, I was still on my game enough to take advantage.

Rather than try to push with my knife, I sidestepped and pivoted, yanking him forward by his grip on my wrist while putting myself offline from his saber. His dodge suddenly threatened to throw him onto his face.

He wasn't a pushover, though. He let go immediately, and while he couldn't quite arrest his fall, he hit the ground with his suddenly freed hand and practically bounced, quickly rolling away as he tried to bring that saber back up to cut at me.

I didn't give him a moment's breathing room, though. If I'd thought I'd been hard before we'd come through that strange fog bank to this eerie place, the long miles and constant fighting since had made me into something almost atavistic. I was on him in a half a heartbeat, and even as he spun to face me, that saber coming up to cut at my head, the point of my own transfixed him through the mouth, punching up through the palate and into his brain.

Blood welled around the blade as he stiffened and spasmed. His fingers tightened around his saber's hilt for just a moment, then it slipped from suddenly nerveless fingers.

Then Gunny was next to me, holding out my rifle, as the rest of the platoon flowed into the campsite, weapons up and searching for targets. The gunfire had died down, though I thought I heard hoofbeats somewhere out in the dark. Hopefully, that was our guys mopping up any squirters, but in the dark, sometimes you never knew. Especially without my NVGs.

"Gear up." Gunny was on a knee to cover me as I took my rifle from him and moved to my horse, not far behind, where my chest rig, mail, and everything else was tied to the saddle. "Even if we got them all, we need to move."

Even after hours of crawling, and with my heart still pounding and my breath heaving in my lungs from two close combats in almost as many minutes, I didn't object. I didn't say anything. There was nothing to be said.

We'd been out in wild, haunted lands for months. There were no friendlies outside of the platoon, and nothing could be taken for granted. Everything out there was trying to kill us, and had been since before we'd first crossed that ridge to our west. We had become attuned to that constant threat, and it had become as natural as breathing to act accordingly.

We'd consolidate and fade. We still had a long way to go, and there was no guarantee that no one—or no*thing*—had heard the gunfire.

CHAPTER 2

FIVE miles doesn't seem that far when you're used to driving. When you're on foot or even horseback, worn down and hungry, staying off trails—such as there are—and moving over increasingly rough terrain, it gets a lot farther than it used to appear.

Especially when you also have to worry about threats natural and preternatural, without any overwatch beyond what you can provide between teams.

Furthermore, the dark was as much a threat as it was a shield. Things that weren't human stalked the night here, and we weren't always in a good position to fight them. Those things dwelt in an arena that often went beyond the physical. An arena that mortal men dipped their toes into at their peril, no matter how strong they believed themselves to be.

We swept through the remnant of the Avur camp quickly and quietly. My team ended up in the rear simply because of the necessity to gear up and rearm, though we left our armor on the horses for the moment. It felt good to have my rifle back in my hands, not to mention the Sword of Iudicael at my side, along with the buckler affixed to the scabbard. I looked a little like a heavily armed gypsy wagon sometimes, but every weapon I carried had its role to play.

Though sometimes it felt a little like I had a role to play as well, when it came to the Sword.

"Looks like a typical scouting band." Bailey knelt in the center of the clump of trees where we'd consolidated, the Sword of Categyrn on his hip, as Gunny joined him along with the other team leaders. Gunny Taylor was on his left, Gurke on his right. Mathghaman and Orava flanked me where I crouched down facing him.

Voices were low, barely murmurs, and while most of us had some hearing loss from years of gunfire and helicopters, after the last few months, we were more attuned than we'd ever been in our lives.

"We can't be sure of numbers, but Baldinus thinks that one of them ran for it, heading south along the ridgeline." Bailey's voice was a little hoarser than it used to be, but we'd been almost as short on water for the last few days as we had been on food. "That means we can expect company soon, probably by morning."

Mathghaman shook his head. The months in the wilderness had made us all shaggy, but the towering King's Champion of the Tuacha da Riamog was now nearly as leonine in his profile as Bearrac, who had always been massive and hairy. It didn't take away from his sheer presence. Nothing I knew of ever could.

"They will not move in the dark. These hills are not as haunted as some, but even among the Peruni, their fears of the night run deep." He might have laughed, though there was no sound in it, and almost as little humor. "They pride themselves on their dismissal of the old fears, even as their rulers treat with the powers of the Outer Dark, and render even that pride a lie, from the greatest to the least."

"So, we've got a little bit of breathing room." Gunny glanced up at the ridgeline above us, still some distance away, over several hills, through patches of forest and a lot of rocks. We knew what it looked like, even though it was practically invisible now, as the clouds moved in and began to eclipse the stars. "Still, I don't want to go to ground here. Let's put some distance behind us before we lay up for the rest of the night."

There were nods all around. There were a few reasons for that. The noise would have attracted attention, and again, not only from the Peruni or their auxiliaries. Even back in The World, we wouldn't want to consolidate and set in in hostile territory that close to the site of a firefight. Not without a lot of support on call, which we definitely didn't have here.

That wasn't all, though.

Not only had we killed men on that ground, which would attract more than a few preternatural scavengers and predators, but that shaman had summoned *something.* That little green imp or whatever it had been might have disappeared, but sorcery tends to cling to places where it's been used.

I was starting to gather that there was a hierarchy in the Outer Dark, one that was variably acknowledged by those who duped themselves into believing they could dally with such forces without bringing down utter destruction on their own heads. Whatever that thing had been, it was small enough that there was probably something a lot bigger and nastier that it served, and that thing would know that someone inimical to it was out here.

We needed to make tracks.

With that decided, we spread out to our teams and got ready to move.

Less than two minutes later, we had vanished into the night like ghosts.

* * *

We probably moved farther than we needed to, and by the time we stood to as the first light glowed in the east, under the lowering cloud cover, I don't think any of us had gotten more than three or four hours of sleep.

It wasn't an unfamiliar feeling. When you're out in the bush for a long time, sleep becomes more of a luxury than it really should be. We weren't at patrol phase level yet; nights like this last one hadn't been the rule on the way. It still hadn't been a journey of nice, restful nights.

It took a few minutes' planning, but we decided to proceed on foot, leading the horses. It would be quieter and give us a lower profile. Staying in the trees as much as possible, we kept moving up toward the pass, hands on weapons and reins tucked into belts and chest rigs. It wasn't the ideal way to lead a horse, but those that had survived this far were almost as attuned to us as we were to each other.

I hadn't especially liked most of the Galel horses I'd been loaned once we'd set out on this expedition. They simply hadn't had the hardiness or the stubborn courage of my Menninkai horse, Myrsky. Over the last month, though, Allon, the big dun that was the only mount I had that had survived the whole trip, had seemingly found his foothold, and he and I had developed a bond that I hadn't thought would ever happen. He followed me almost without needing the reins, and Darrick, my packhorse, followed him.

I'd just ducked under the low-hanging branches of a big, bushy pine when I saw Rodeffer ahead of me with his fist up. I froze, though not before passing the signal on to Farrar and Santos, behind me. Allon stopped dead as soon as I did.

Eoghain and Diarmodh had been on point, and now Diarmodh came quickly back down the column, whispering urgently to each man as he passed. Slender and quick, with pointed features and blond hair and beard that always seemed to nearly stand on end, Diarmodh had been one of the Tuacha we'd rescued from Taramas's catacombs.

"The Peruni have moved faster than we thought they could." His whisper was almost quieter than the dawn breeze. "They stand between us and the pass now."

"How many?" I wasn't in a position to see over the finger ahead of us, but clearly Diarmodh had.

"At least a hundred. Cataphracts and spearmen both." He seemed to sense my next question. "No Dullahans. Not yet."

That was a relief. We'd faced the headless horsemen that the Emperor of Ar-Annator had dug up to lead his armies a few times, and while I'd hurt at least one, we still had no idea how to kill one. They were ancient sorcerers, old enough and powerful enough almost to make the Fohorimans of the north look like rank amateurs, and that meant trouble. Knowing that we weren't going to have to face one with only a handful of mags left before we were down to swords, axes, and sharp sticks was a good thing.

A hundred Peruni cataphracts and their supporting infantry, however, was still bad news.

Diarmodh gave my shoulder a squeeze, then he was gone, flitting down the slope behind me toward where Gunny and Mathghaman were moving with Cailtarni and the six other Galel knights who were still with us. We'd lost a few, including Galan, whom I'd truly begun to think of as a friend, along the way.

I kept moving, then, pushing up to join Rodeffer. Tying Allon and Darrick to a nearby tree, well below the military crest, where I could be sure that they wouldn't be spotted from the other side, I joined my pointman, a bit lankier than he had been—and Gene Rodeffer had never been a big man—as he moved up toward the crest, where Eoghain was still set up, watching our adversaries.

We got low as we moved out of the trees and up toward the windswept, rocky crest of the ridgeline. While there were patches of woods all through the foothills that led up to the mountains which formed the eastern boundary of the Galel kingdom, for the most part it was still pretty open country this far down, so we'd had to get inventive with our route to stay in the shadows of the trees. Now, to spot our enemies, we were going to have to leave that overhead cover, taking the chance that the Peruni might have a wizard of some sort with them, one that could summon creatures that essentially acted like UAVs back in The World.

Someday, if I was willing to carry the extra weight, I might ask the *Coira Ansec*, King Caedmon's mystic cauldron that had provided us with our M110s, ammo, and various other weapons, for some small UAVs. It could probably turn out stuff far superior to anything the Marine Corps would be using for a long time.

Eoghain was up near a boulder, under the shadow of a tree that was so flattened and gnarled by the wind that it might as well have been a bush. In the prone, huddled against the rock, peering over his engraved, almost musket-looking rifle, his cloak spread over him, he was almost invisible, but his horses, about ten paces down the slope beneath him, were not. We got low as we moved up to join him.

He didn't turn to look as we got closer. He probably didn't need to. My guess was, the Tuacha being what they are, he'd heard us and identified each of us by gait and breathing, if not different heartbeats.

They can be spooky, the Tuacha da Riamog.

He pointed as I crawled up alongside him, then he faded around the boulder so that I wouldn't be sticking my head up over the crest of the ridge, but could peer *around* the rock. It's harder to get spotted that way.

I eased myself up to where I could see down into the valley beneath us, a valley we'd passed on the way out toward Gremman and the Sword of Categyrn. There wasn't any sign of the Avur camps we'd hammered with long-range rifle and mortar fire. Whatever traces the tribesmen might have left had been swept away by the elements in the two months since then.

What was there, however, was a force that I didn't want to tangle with, not with a reinforced platoon, low on ammo, and without the mortars that had been such a force multiplier before.

The Peruni hadn't set up camp so much as they had deployed in such a way that they could switch off on security during the night. The cataphracts were gathered in the center, though they had stripped the armor off their horses for the time being, and now stood, armed and armored, looking up toward the pass while their attendants strapped that armor back on. Two squares of spearmen had stood to on either flank, while archers just sort of milled around behind them, cooking their breakfasts. It seemed that the archers might have been auxiliaries rather than regular Peruni troops. Their armor was different, and their discipline was noticeably laxer than that of either the cataphracts or the spearmen.

Their attention mostly seemed to be directed toward the pass that was our only really viable route back to Cor Hefedd and the Galel lands, but the spearmen were still watching the flanks.

Not closely enough, though. My eyes narrowed as I studied their deployment. These men were ready to fight, certainly, but they were still all in the low ground, relatively speaking. If I were in charge…

I drew back from the rock and looked around. A hawk circled overhead. The clouds were scudding off toward the east, dimming the rising sun but leaving ragged gaps in the west, over the mountains. I turned to Eoghain.

He was already a step ahead of me. "We have not seen their scouts. Not yet. They must be out there, though." He rubbed his chin, as thickly bearded as any of ours, as his gray eyes moved from rock to tree to ridgeline, missing nothing that could be seen.

I felt it, too. Eoghain was not an emotional man—none of the Tuacha were, not really—but he was clearly disturbed. What we'd seen of the Peruni did not make them seem all that subtle, but they were also professional when it came to the practice of war. They wouldn't be sitting in terrain like this, so close to Cor Hefedd, without scouts out.

Unless Cor Hefedd had already fallen, and these were just reinforcements moving to join the Peruni garrison amid the ruins of the castle.

After all, we'd had no news from the Galel since we'd left, all those weeks before. King Uven had considered the inevitable war between the Galel and the Peruni Empire of Ar-Annator all but started after the sorcerous attack on Cor Legear, when murdered men had walked and tried to kill us and the king, while the Empire's envoys fled into the dark. If the war was already over, and the Galel had lost…

Well, then we'd have one hell of an E&E ahead of us. It would take many more miles and weeks of travel to get somewhere we could hire or steal a ship to get us back to the Isle of Riamog.

Something put my hackles up as I scanned the hills and the trees around us. There was something wrong here, some threat that I couldn't see, but I was suddenly starting to sense.

Eoghain was already pulling both of us back before I could even say anything. If *I* could pick up on it, it was pretty certain that the Tuacha already knew about it, whatever it was. We slid down the hill, gathering our horses, which were getting nervous, and faded back into the trees.

Just in time, too.

Shadowy figures appeared above the rock where we'd been set up only minutes before. These guys weren't Avurs. Keeping low to the ground, I might not have seen them at all if Diarmodh hadn't pointed. They wore no armor, unlike the Avurs, and in fact, with the exception of the lead man of the three, who wore a cape over one shoulder, all wore only dun trousers that might have been homespun, or maybe buckskin. Their long hair was braided or drawn into ponytails, and they wore no ornamentation. From where I sat, watching through my M110's scope, I could see spears, but that was about it.

The dangerous part was that we hadn't seen or heard these guys until they were almost right on top of us. But they'd certainly seen us. They were closing in on that boulder with a purpose, and they had cover from our previous position. If our spidey senses hadn't started tingling, they'd have been on us before we'd have seen anything.

I expanded my scan, since we had some standoff and cover. If we hadn't seen any sign of those spear-wielding scouts before, I wasn't entirely confident that we'd spotted all of them now.

There. Three more were crouched amid a crown of massive granite boulders higher up in the foothills, with good overwatch on the finger as well as the valley on the other side. None of them moved a muscle, and if not for the wind stirring a bit of hair, I might not have spotted them without conducting a few more slow, careful scans. Scans that I didn't think we necessarily had time for.

As it turned out, we really didn't have time.

Most of the platoon had moved up into the trees behind us by that time, and were spread out by teams, trying to keep the horses quiet. I saw a few rifles leveled, but nobody had taken a shot. I didn't think anyone would, not yet. The risks associated with hard compromise were too great, and we'd all been through too much to be cavalier about them.

Even the Galel, as peacock colorful as their tunics, breeches, cloaks, and shields were, had shrouded their armor and covered their shields, and were as far back in the trees and the shadows as possible, their hands on their horses' snouts to keep them silent.

However, as carefully as we were moving, they'd still seen *something* near that boulder.

The three scouts closed in on the boulder, creeping around the back of it, until they were right where we'd been. I watched through my scope as the man with the short cape cast around the ground, bent down and peering at the grass and the dirt, his spear held easily in one hand.

I drew a bead on him, carefully easing my rifle's selector to "Fire." Sure, a gunshot was definitely going to give the game away, but I knew a tracker when I saw one. We were already made.

My shot echoed off the mountainside. The man in the cape jerked and dropped limply to the dirt, while the other two vanished as thoroughly as if they'd sunk through the ground itself.

CHAPTER 3

IT said something about how we'd adjusted to this wild existence that nobody froze, nobody freaked out because I'd taken a shot without any coordination or prior planning. We just reacted.

The scouts up in the rocks above had also disappeared, but that was the most likely defensive position, so we started moving toward it almost immediately, bounding quickly through the trees and up the hill, even as Diarmodh and Eoghain held on the boulder where the two surviving scouts had disappeared.

A horn call went up from the valley. Whether or not the Peruni knew exactly what that *crack* had been, they knew they were not alone, and that something had just gone terribly wrong. That was assuming the scouts hadn't already signaled them.

Bounding was habit for us, though unless those shirtless scouts had bows, then we probably could just rush them. That had its own problems, though, including the potential to over-penetrate and get flanked. These guys were good at vanishing into open ground, which meant that they could potentially pop out of a fold of microterrain right where we weren't looking if we weren't careful.

Having rifles doesn't make you immune to spears.

With my Team One and Orava's Team Four having pushed up faster, that left Bailey's Team Two on rear security, holding most of the horses while Gurke's Team Three covered the flank. The Tuacha were floating between teams, as had become somewhat normal, while the Galel pushed up behind Orava, swords in hand, ready and eager to close with the enemy.

They might dress like peacocks, but those guys were *fighters.*

We stayed in the trees, Santos just behind me and on the flank, where he could quickly pivot and bring that Mk 48 to bear on the crest of the finger that we were currently working our way up, even though he might have had one belt left. Once that was gone, that sucker was going to become a very heavy club. Rodeffer was right in front of me, and Farrar was trying to get up front as fast as he could.

Aside from the horns on the other side of the finger, the wilderness had gone quiet, even as we worked our way up toward the top of the hill. The only sounds were the whisper of the wind in the treetops, the faint crunch of the soil under our boots, and our own breathing as we moved quickly uphill.

I signaled Rodeffer to slow down and take cover at the edge of the trees, about fifty yards from the boulders where we'd seen the overwatch element. I glanced over at Orava, but the Menninkai team leader was already cueing off us, shifting to the left and into the rougher ground and thicker brush leading up to that stand of boulders.

The Menninkai were generally shorter than most of us Americans, not to mention the Tuacha, who tended to be tall and built like Hercules. The Menninkai were stocky and hard as woodpecker lips, and had mostly adopted our clothing and equipment, though they wore plain green instead of the digital woodland camouflage we'd brought through the mists from The World. They had adapted to our way of war pretty quickly, too. Not as quickly as the Tuacha, mind you, but quickly enough.

We got down in the prone or on a knee behind tree trunks, including one big, twisted, fallen giant that provided cover for at least two of us, weapons trained on the boulders above, covering for the Menninkai as they maneuvered on the enemy.

I felt the need to move, to act, starting to claw at me. We were on the low ground relative to the scouts, and things weren't standing still waiting for us. I didn't think for a moment that those men who had disappeared into the grass were just lying there, hiding, and I was equally sure that the Peruni were already maneuvering up the slope. When either Diarmodh or Eoghain fired behind us, probably picking off one more of the first band of scouts, that urgency got even more intense.

But the thing about warfare is that it's a team sport. You either fill your role and cover your teammates' backs, or everything falls apart and people die.

That was a lesson that had been drummed into every one of us by the Marine Corps for years. The reality of this war-torn and monster-haunted world had only reinforced it tenfold.

So, I held my position and watched my sector, though I still had to pick my head up from time to time to check on my boys and the overall situation. We had to cover the Menninkai, but I was also a team leader, and that meant watching the bigger picture.

Movement caught my eye. I shifted my gaze, dragging my rifle muzzle with it.

For a moment, I saw nothing but grass, waving slightly in the wind. The hillside above me looked empty and abandoned.

I kept scanning, looking for whatever it had been that I'd seen. It took a moment, even as a crash of suppressed rifle fire echoed from the hilltop, but I finally spotted my guy.

He was flat on the ground, slithering carefully and slowly through the thicker grass, almost entirely obscured by a low bit of brush. He had to be pretty flexible to hide behind that small a bit of concealment.

Unfortunately for him, concealment is not cover.

Bracing my rifle against the tree trunk, I let my breath out slowly, my finger tightening on the trigger. It broke just as he started to move, the shot blowing through the brush and hitting him in the junction between shoulder and neck with a hissing *crack* that blended with the more intense gunfire coming from up higher. He spasmed with the hit, and I must have hit an artery, because blood painted the brush and the grass red as he tried to crawl away.

He didn't get far.

I resumed my scan, but the gunfire above had suddenly died away with one last shot that continued to echo off the mountains.

Then the thunder of hoofbeats sounded, and another horn call reverberated from over the hill.

"Move!" Gunny had figured it out a moment before any of the Peruni had showed themselves.

Santos opened fire with a ripping, stuttering roar, raking the first rank of cataphracts as they crested the rise, entirely too close on our flank and with the advantage of being uphill. Unfortunately for them, that advantage was somewhat nullified by a belt-fed machinegun.

Bullets tore through scale armor and flesh alike, and the first two cataphracts crashed to the ground, trapped under flailing, screaming horses. More rifle fire joined the machinegun fire, and nearly a dozen of the Peruni cataphracts went down in the first few seconds. The remainder quickly wheeled their horses and ducked beneath the crest of the ridge.

We put on more speed, no longer bounding but pushing hard for those boulders. That was the most defensible position around, and if we could get into the rocks, the Peruni would have the devil's own time getting at us.

Of course, there was the question of just how long we could hold out there with the food, water, and ammo we had left. Even if Cor Hefedd still stood, we were on the wrong side of the mountains, and without getting a rider through, it was unlikely that we could get word to the rest of the Galel that we were still alive, let alone in need of help.

Still, immediate survival came first. So, we pushed up the hill for the boulders.

Orava and his Menninkai team were already there ahead of us, set in and bringing fire down on the Peruni on the other side of the slope from us. Rodeffer beat me into the rocks by a good five paces, throwing himself into the prone behind a big rock on the other side of a twisted, windswept bit of scrub.

I got into the rocks just ahead of Farrar. Two of the enemy scouts were sprawled nearby, their blood still dripping into the dry soil between the boulders.

It took moments to get the rest of the platoon up into the rocks, the horses secured as close to the middle of the little crown of stone as possible. There was no guarantee they'd be under cover, but it was the best we could do.

Santos was panting as he threw himself into a position where he could shoot down along the finger we'd just climbed. "Down to half a belt."

We were all in the same boat. Unless a miracle occurred, we were about to go black on ammo within the next few minutes.

I wasn't convinced that no such thing as a miracle was possible. I'd seen stranger things happen since we'd come to this world.

Still, as we set in, we had to at least plan on no miracles. Tigharn offers such favors sparingly, and we don't get to choose the time or the place.

The cataphracts were still down there, but they'd learned quickly from the first volley of gunfire. They weren't pushing our position or even showing themselves much. Most sane men who see the effects of firearms for the first time learn really fast how to take cover. Or else they don't live long, and these men were warriors. Survivors.

Note I said, "sane" men. I didn't necessarily class the Dovos nal Uergal in the north as sane. They'd thrown themselves at our weapons with wild, screaming abandon and had died in droves. The Peruni of Ar-Annator and its empire were different.

After that initial burst of violence and mad scramble for position, things got quiet. We could hear them maneuvering, hear the horn calls directing the spearmen and the cataphracts, but like I said, they'd learned fast. They didn't show themselves.

The first arrows landed short.

I ducked at the faint whistle of the first shafts, but they slammed into the dirt about ten yards in front of me, their blackened heads burying themselves in the dirt. Their fletchings were blood red.

"Find me those archers." I really wished we still had the 60mm mortars that Orava's team had brought out, but we'd used the last of those rounds in Gremman, and we'd left the tubes behind during that frantic breakout past a full army led by Dullahans. Besides, without eyes on where the arrows were coming from, it would be difficult to get warheads on foreheads from up there.

The next flight went overhead, one of the arrows shattering against the big finger of rock near the middle of the hilltop, while most of the rest sailed past, disappearing into the brush and the grass farther down the back side of the hill.

They were ranging us, trying to bracket our position. It was the same thing we did with indirect fire, only with ammunition that cost a lot less.

This time, though, I'd seen movement, and I'd spotted at least several of the feathered shafts flying up from where the archers had taken cover. I didn't know where their spotter was, but I'd settle for discouraging any further flights of arrows.

I shifted my position, laid my crosshairs on the brush that provided the archers some of their cover, and fired.

Dust kicked up from the bush, and I might or might not have heard a faint scream. Santos had been watching, however, and he followed up with a quick burst of machinegun fire that shredded the bush and kicked up more dust.

The arrows stopped coming.

"Well, that seems to have done the trick, but I can't do that more than once or twice more." Santos sounded almost apologetic. "What happens when they figure out that we're black on ammo?"

"Well, then they pelt us with arrows until they can get the spearmen and the cataphracts in close." I kept looking for targets, but they were doing a good job of hiding. I wondered if the spotter wasn't one of the scouts, instead of an armored Peruni who might give his position away with a glint of sunlight on metal. "Then it comes down to blades and terrain."

Santos grunted. We'd been there before.

We set in to wait.

CHAPTER 4

THE hours that followed weren't silent, though they were quieter, as we avoided expending ammo on noises. We had to make every shot count. Not that we'd been especially wasteful of ammunition before that, but now, down to our last magazines, we had to be especially careful.

The day got hotter. There was no water up there amid those rocks, not after the dry days that had already preceded our arrival. There were some depressions where rainwater had probably gathered, but they were either bone dry or little more than slowly cracking mud. Fortunately, we'd filled our bladders and canteens every time we came across water, so we were set for a little while.

I could hope that the Peruni were going to get thirsty and fall back to find water, but I suspected that if they'd been there for any length of time—which it looked like they had—then they'd come prepared. They had enough people that they could send riders to replenish waterskins for everyone without breaking their encirclement, anyway.

The archers kept their distance and conserved their own ammunition, just like we were doing. I could still hear horses and men moving around down the hill, and the occasional horn call, but I couldn't see much. They'd figured out that they needed to maintain their distance and stay behind cover, so they were being careful.

My team was on the east side of the tight perimeter we'd set up within the rocks, with something of a view of the pass, though the shoulder of the mountain obscured the slot through the ridgeline itself. I kept my eye up there, but so far there was no movement.

I didn't know if the Peruni had sent for reinforcements once we'd clashed. It would make sense, but without actually seeing a rider, there was no way to know. I kept my eye out anyway. If they had reinforcements on the way, we'd be in a world of hurt.

Still, as the day wore on, nothing appeared up in the pass or on the plains below, at least where we could see. We waited, watched, ate, and slept a little when we weren't on security, and looked for targets of opportunity.

The Peruni and their Avur auxiliaries were canny, though. They didn't give us one. Not for hours.

It's hard, sitting there under the broiling sun, tasting dust and the salt of your own sweat on your lips, trying to stay alert as time stretches and the enemy that you know is out there stays hidden. After long enough, even though your imagination starts conjuring up all sorts of nasty possibilities about what they're doing out there, time, heat, and motionlessness start to take their own toll.

We'd been under siege before, in Vahava Paykhah, but this was different. At least there we'd had some secure rear area to fall back to.

Shortly after the sun passed its zenith, we suddenly got a wake-up call.

Something shadowy went overhead with a leathery sort of flapping sound. I quickly rolled to my side and scanned the sky above us. I didn't see anything at first, but then I spotted a flicker of movement. Something small and dark, moving almost like a bat, except that it seemed to fade when I looked straight at it.

I'd seen something like it before. As I turned back toward the slope below, moving quickly just in case that was intended as a distraction as well as the surveillance that I knew it was, I caught a glimpse of the look on Santos's face. He recognized the sound and the phenomenon, too.

We'd first encountered things like that in the north, on the first night in this strange world. None of us had ever gotten a good look at the little flying things summoned by various sorcerers, warlocks, and shamans to spy on us, but we'd seen and heard them from the Land of Ice and Monsters to the Corsair lands north of Lost Colcand. They were either summoned creatures or sorcerous constructs, and we could destroy them, either with a bullet or with the Tuacha's prayers, but that was about all we knew for sure.

It gave us an important bit of intel, though. We knew that while we hadn't seen a Dullahan, one of the headless abominations that had led the Peruni forces in their pursuit across the wastelands of the northern marches of the empire, the Peruni down there still had a wizard. Or maybe an Avur shaman. Either way, there was going to be weird stuff to deal with.

That made everybody a little more alert. There was a faint stir around the perimeter, even as the horses stamped and snorted, nervous at the nearness of preternatural weirdness. We had to be even more ready, now. I'd hoped that there wouldn't be any spellslingers down there, but that hope had apparently been in vain.

Still, that flapping phantom overhead was the only sign. No abomination from beyond rose out of the grass. Nothing else happened. Everything went even quieter than it had been.

That didn't make me relax any. If anything, it made matters worse.

As the sun dipped toward the ridgeline above us, I was getting antsy. Careful not to expose myself, I reached up to wipe the sweat away from my eyes. Something was coming. I could feel it. The air seemed to be getting thicker, hotter. The pressure felt like a thunderstorm was coming, but there wasn't a cloud in the sky anymore.

I really didn't want to fight sorcery while bottled up in that mess of rocks. But it was either that, or a forlorn hope charge against a prepared enemy that had far greater numbers.

Depending on what happened, that might actually be a better option, even with the limited amount of ammunition we had left, but that was ultimately Gunny's call, and he still had us hold our position.

Something about the rising pressure made me suddenly turn around, bringing my rifle with me. "Stay on the perimeter." Santos nodded, glancing over his shoulders at Farrar and Rodeffer, just to make sure they didn't succumb to the temptation to look at whatever was happening behind them. That's how security gets dropped and units get flanked.

Bearrac was at my side in an eyeblink, seeming to materialize out of the dust and the rocks. The big man could *smell* when something eerie was up.

While I didn't know exactly what I was looking for, I started toward the middle of our little perimeter, mostly on instinct. I slung my rifle as I went, drawing the Sword of Iudicael and the small buckler that I'd affixed to the outside of its scabbard. Something told me that the Sword was going to be more useful than the rifle here shortly, even leaving aside the need to avoid accidentally shooting one of us by opening fire from the inside of our redoubt, behind the guys on security.

Bearrac already had his blade in his massive fist. As usual, he was a couple steps ahead of me.

It took a few paces before I noticed the murmurs.

We'd almost gotten used to a constant, sibilant whisper on the air out on the grasslands. It wasn't natural, it wasn't always there, but the things that haunted the cursed lands that had once been the Commagan Empire never really shut up, even when they didn't present that much of a threat.

This wasn't a whisper, though. It was a low, sonorous murmur, different from the other sorts of sorcery we'd encountered but no less disturbing. I couldn't make out words, and I was kind of glad that I couldn't. I didn't think I wanted to know.

Even as we advanced toward where the horses were starting to shy toward the south, pulling at their pickets, I felt the vibration in the ground.

Bearrac put out a hand to stop me, actually grabbing my sleeve and dragging me backwards. I felt the ground heave under my boot even as he did so.

A mound rose out of the dirt, broken suddenly by a clawed hand. At first, I thought something was digging its way out, but after a moment I realized that the hand itself was formed out of the dirt. As was the arm that followed it.

The thing continued to coalesce out of the dirt even as it hauled itself up. It wasn't leaving a hole, which was weird, though not quite as weird as a long-armed, clawed gargoyle being sculpted out of the dirt with no other visible means of formation.

I call it a gargoyle, but it wasn't that detailed. It was a vague, amorphous, humanoid shape made of dirt, with the only defined parts of it being those claws. They looked like they could probably take my head off with one swipe.

As it hauled itself erect, the nearby horses screaming in terror, it opened its eyes. Unlike the rest of it, which was obviously still made of dirt, shedding dust and clods at every movement, they were black chips of obsidian, without iris or sclera, utterly featureless yet burning with hate.

It wasn't a human sort of hate, either. Whatever was at the heart of that thing, it wasn't natural. It wasn't as bad as the oily horrors from the Outer Dark brought across the veil by Dragon Mask in service of Vaelor, but it was awfully close.

There are times when it's a good idea to take stock and try to figure out what you're up against before taking action. This was not one of those times. Sure, I didn't know for sure what the Sword was going to do against something made of dirt, but when there's an eldritch abomination of any sort manifesting in the middle of your position while there are a whole lot of bad guys outside, immediate action is necessary.

So, with a wordless prayer that this would work, I attacked.

Bearrac, as usual, was slightly faster than me. He cut at that thing's head with his own sword, long and leaf-bladed, the blow lightning quick. The creature ducked, but I was on it a moment later, and when it ran out of room in the next second, it threw up a hand to try to stop my blade.

Whatever that thing was, it wasn't all that smart. It stared as its clawed hand and arm just disintegrated at the blessed blade's touch. Dust fell in a cascade to the dirt, and it looked up at me, those black eyes almost uncertain.

Just for a moment, though. Then it leaped straight up and back, landing on one of the bigger rocks above Gunny's position.

Mathghaman had been waiting for that.

Most of the time the Tuacha can kind of fool you into thinking that they're ordinary people. Oh, they have an aura of dignity and grace that is impossible to disguise, and if you pay attention, you can tell that they're something different, but the really impressive stuff they can do is usually kept hidden until moments like that.

I'd seen Mathghaman leap a ruined wall that still stood a good ten feet high, coming down into the middle of a mass of heavily armed enemies, and start reaping them like a scythe-wielding harvester in a field of wheat. This wasn't quite the same, but he was up on top of that rock in a heartbeat, grabbing that thing by the throat as his sword flashed in the sun.

The creature's neck crumbled under his grip, and something dark seemed to slip past him as the thing disintegrated, falling to dust and a shower of clods on top of the rock. The shadow almost looked like it dove into the ground at the base of the boulder.

Bearrac advanced on the spot, already starting to chant. More eyes were starting to turn inward, curious as to what was happening.

"Watch the enemy!" Mathghaman was still atop the rock, his gray eyes scanning our surroundings. "They advance while we are distracted."

I didn't dare turn back toward the perimeter, not while that thing was still somewhere on the inside. We each had our priorities. That's how a team's supposed to work.

Bearrac and I closed in on the spot where the shadow had disappeared into the dirt, our swords poised to strike. Unfortunately, since it was a spirit of some kind, it could manifest just about anywhere.

I don't know exactly how I knew to turn around. Maybe my mysterious guardian gave me a nudge. I pivoted as fast as I could, drawing the Sword of Iudicael back swiftly, ready to strike.

The demonic golem, its arm restored, was rising straight out of the dirt behind me, moving faster this time. It wasn't quite fast enough, though.

I was already bringing the blade down like the stroke of doom, all of my weight behind that swing, even as I tucked my elbow to keep it under control, a tight cut instead of a wild chop. The smoky gray, razor-sharp sword blade, that never seemed to get nicked, scratched, or stained, went through the earthen construct like a hot knife through butter.

For a brief moment, I looked into those black eyes, and despite their featurelessness, I could have sworn I saw fear and terror there. Just for a split second.

Then the blade cleaved right between those eyes and the thing fell apart again, only this time a faint wisp of smoke floated away with what might have been a faint, despairing scream.

The scream that sounded on the other side of the hill was a lot louder. I didn't know what had happened, but if I were to guess, I'd say that whatever the shaman or wizard had summoned to arrange this little end run wasn't happy about the way it had gone, and had gone after its summoner in retaliation.

Too bad. Don't mess with that stuff, and you don't have to worry so much about keeping such things happy.

Horns brayed. Hoofbeats thundered, a dull roar transmitted through the ground. Spearpoints flashed in the sun, suddenly far too close, and then the arrows came whistling down out of the sky, smacking off rocks and thudding into the dirt. Fortunately, we had good cover. We'd had some time to get into good positions. Unfortunately, that cover limited just how much we could engage the spearmen and cataphracts that were coming for us.

More arrows smashed themselves to splinters and flying bits of iron on the rocks. Another horn call sounded, and then the bare-chested auxiliaries rose out of the grass only a few yards in front of us and charged.

They didn't come in a screaming wave like the Dovos nal Uergal had. They ducked and wove, moving up across the strip of open ground between the trees that we'd used for concealment on the way up and the rocks. They were tough targets, that was for sure. Several gunshots rang out, and dust kicked up at their feet, but only one of them went down, and he might have just dropped to take cover.

Then the first of them, a man burnt bronze by the sun, his hair and beard so blond as to be white, his eyes dark flecks of hate, was right on us, ignoring the arrows pelting around his ears, a long knife in one hand and a short axe in the other, already taking a stab at me with the knife as he drew the axe back for a swing at my head.

I muzzle thumped him in the center of the chest and pulled the trigger at the same time I made contact.

My bullet tore through his sternum, blowing his heart and a chunk of his spine out through his back. He went over backward, a look of shock on his face, and landed hard in the dirt, blood dribbling out of a mouth gone slack.

More gunfire *crack*ed around the perimeter, as more of the half-naked auxiliaries tried to get their pound of flesh ahead of the cataphracts that were now surging up the hill from the north, their horses in tight formation, long lances held in two hands and leveled at us, reins held loosely in the forward gauntlet as they controlled their mounts with their knees.

"Hold what you've got!" Gunny's voice cracked out over the hilltop. "Make every shot count!"

I had thrown myself back into my position on the perimeter as soon as the arrows had started falling, and now I had a perfect shot on one of the lead cataphracts. I didn't know what they thought they were going to accomplish with a heavy cavalry charge on a prepared position, but I wasn't going to interrupt them while they were making a mistake.

Except to punish them for it.

My first round took the rider in the neck, just beneath where his scaled aventail nearly reached his hooked nose. He jerked, but the height of his saddle and the stiffness of his armor kept him from falling. Instead, he sort of sagged in his saddle, though the long spear fell from his suddenly limp fingers.

The others faltered a little. They had to know this was suicide. They had weight and armor and shock on their side—or they would, if they hadn't been slowed by the terrain, and weren't coming toward boulders where they couldn't maneuver except to sort of circle around and poke at us with their spears.

There was something off about this. The Peruni were too good at war to charge a mass of boulders with cavalry. This was Dovo-level tactics.

Until I looked to one side and saw the spearmen, now with swords drawn and shields up, moving up on the flank, coming through the same trees we'd moved through before.

So, that was the play. Distract us with the cavalry while the infantry flanked us. Those guys *could* get in the rocks and then we'd have one hell of a bad day.

"Santos! Right flank!" I was shifting my own aim down that way, even as Santos rolled to his right, dropped the Mk 48's bipods on a flat rock, leaned into the gun, and unleashed hell.

The last of his final belt went pretty fast, the suppressed machinegun chattering rapidly as he swept his cone of fire across the oncoming skirmish line of swordsmen. Bullets smashed through shields and armor alike, and men dropped, most of them falling onto their faces as they struggled up the hill, some thrashing around and screaming as the rounds punched through less vital parts of their anatomy, putting them out of action without killing them outright.

Then the belt-fed went empty, even as I leaned out around another rock and dropped three more with as many shots. They got lower and more cautious, but they kept coming another few paces while we picked off several more of them, then the horn brayed again, and they fell back into the trees, moving with a disciplined speed that got them out of our line of fire quickly without it turning into a rout.

More gunfire *crack*ed to the south. Another flanking maneuver. And as the sounds of fighting intensified, and Mathghaman, Fennean, and Conall raced in that direction, I could tell that the bad guys must have gotten a lot closer over there.

The cataphracts had backed off. They'd done their part, though men like that had to be chafing hard at leaving us to the footsloggers. Hell, *I* was chafing at holding here on the northeast side, now that we were staring at empty grassland and dead bodies, knowing that the fight behind us was getting rough. The gunfire was getting more sporadic, and I could hear the clash of hand weapons now. Maybe they'd just gotten that close that quick, or maybe Gurke's and Orava's teams had gone dry on ammo that much faster. It didn't matter yet. We still had to watch the flank, or the Peruni would come up and take our brothers in the back.

It was a good thing we hadn't gotten sucked into the immediate fight, too. Even as we stayed in the prone, seemingly staring at nothing, I saw movement in the grass. Barely thinking about it, I brought my rifle up and put a round into the grass, aiming low. That was something I'd learned in a tracking course, a long time ago and in a different world. The Rhodesians called it a "cover shoot." Aim low at likely cover when you see movement, because even if you don't hit him, you'll probably spit some frag into his face, making him react and giving you a better target.

That was precisely what happened. The man with the brown hair, braided and knotted on one side of his head, rolled away from where I'd hit, exposing himself as he clapped a hand to one eye, blood welling around his fingers.

I shot him through the temple.

His sudden death didn't deter the rest of his companions. A hail of stones and short, nasty throwing axes pelted our position a moment later, and Rodeffer let out a grunt. I didn't have time to check on him, but I hoped he was all right. He was still shooting, anyway.

We swept the grass with most of the rest of our ammunition. Shirtless warriors jerked and died, even as some of them leaped up to rush at us, only to drop and practically disappear into the grass almost before we could draw a bead on them.

Sometimes they weren't quite fast enough. I suspected they'd practiced evading arrows and sling stones, not 175-grain bullets moving at two thousand five hundred eighty feet per second. Several more miscalculated and died, their blood soaking the grass and the dust as they gasped out their last.

But they were getting closer, and we were running out of ammunition.

"Last mag!" I slapped the final twenty-five-round PMAG into the magazine well. The fight behind us was getting desperate, and Tuacha rifles barked off to my right, as the swordsmen began their flanking attack again.

Then, suddenly, a new horn call sounded. Higher, clearer somehow than the Peruni horns. Somewhere behind me, Cailtarni gave a great, whooping shout, taken up by the other Galel knights in a moment.

Something drew my eyes up toward the pass as the echoes of that horn call rolled across the mountainside, in time to see the last light of the sun glinting off tall helms and gleaming Galel spearpoints.

With the red, blue, and gold banner of King Uven himself fluttering from the foremost lance, the knights of Cor Legear charged down upon the Peruni's flank, even as we drew our swords and prepared to come to grips with the enemy.

CHAPTER 5

KING Uven reined in just outside the circle of rocks atop the hill, still looking up at us as he doffed his helmet. The sun had just gone down behind the ridge to the west, the pale sky steadily darkening, casting a blue shadow over the hillside. Some of that pale light that lingered in the west glinted off his helmet as his horse shifted under him, the massive warhorse clearly still wound up and looking for something to crush.

"You left us little enough of a fight." There was a wry note in his voice, speaking the Galel tongue that was so similar to the *Tenga Tuacha* that we didn't need the Tuacha's mind speech to understand it. Yet there was also a weariness, something that went clear down to his bones, a sense that he was being flippant because he had to in front of his men.

We hadn't left him much of a fight, it was true. Faced with our firepower on one side and the charge of a Galel battalion on the other, the Peruni and their auxiliaries had chosen the better part of valor and faded, a braying horn calling the retreat just before the shirtless bush fighters and the scale-armored swordsmen fell back, down the hill and back toward the grasslands beyond. They'd disappeared into the terrain only a few minutes before the king reached us.

"We didn't know if you were coming, so we didn't want any of it to go to waste." Gunny sounded even more tired than King Uven did, and a couple of the Galel knights stiffened at the flippant rejoinder, at least until Uven laughed. There wasn't a whole lot of humor in the sound, but he recognized the comment for what it was.

As the Galel surrounded the hilltop, we started to come out of the rocks. A few of us still held rifles ready, though all the machineguns were now slung, and more than half of us were down to blades or axes. It had been a near thing.

I joined Bailey, Gurke, Orava, Mathghaman, Cailtarni, and Gunny as we came down to meet the king. Even in the dying light, I could see that there was more to the weariness in his voice than just the lateness of the hour.

King Uven was a young man, as kings go. I'd guessed early twenties when we'd first met him, a couple of months before. Even in the twilight after sunset, though, I could tell that he'd aged, just in those two to three months.

His cheeks were slightly hollower under his beard, his eyes slightly more sunken. I didn't doubt, just judging by his body language, that there were deep crow's feet around his eyes now. He'd been ready to go to war with the Empire of Ar-Annator a week before we'd left his lands. I didn't know what had happened in the meantime, but it clearly hadn't been easy on him.

He scanned our numbers as more and more of us came out, and I could tell that he was counting, as well as looking for particular faces or liveries. He said nothing yet, but when his eyes turned to Gunny and Mathghaman, I could tell he knew exactly how many of us had gone out, and he had just compared it to how many had come back.

The two numbers were definitely not the same. And I was pretty sure he'd noticed exactly who was missing, too.

"Come." He turned his horse back toward the pass. "Let us make haste for Cor Hefedd." He turned and looked over his shoulder at us. "I know I need not tell you that these wildlands get more dangerous after dark." His eyes wandered toward the east and the grasslands below us. "Even without a wizard on the loose."

The Galel held their position as we saddled up and got moving. It didn't take long. We had fewer horses left, too.

With our rescuers forming a ring around us, we started up toward the pass and friendly territory.

After over two months and several hundred miles of riding, marching, and fighting, alone and unafraid in lands haunted by the remnants of curses unleashed centuries before, stalked by monsters from beyond, and hunted all the while by the Peruni and their allies, both savage and preternatural, we'd made it back. We had the Sword of Categyrn, and we had made it back.

Of course, it's never that easy.

* * *

The encampment seemed to cover every bit of cleared ground that the farmers who lived near Cor Hefedd could spare. Horses cropped grass in the higher meadows, and the farmers watched the knights and men-at-arms with a dualistic combination of resentment and relief.

There were more men and animals in that small valley than the land could support for long. That accounted for the resentment. If this small regiment stayed in place for too long, they'd eat the locals out of house and home, and fall wasn't far away.

On the other hand, the threat we'd fought on the other side of the pass accounted for the sense of relief, along with the fear that these men were going to move on before too long.

It's hard, living off the land in a war zone.

It had been too dark to see much when we'd ridden in the previous night. The moon was almost new, and the stars hadn't been bright enough to penetrate the shadows under the trees. A few fires had flickered in the growing chill of the night. We were far enough south of the Land of Ice and Monsters that winter itself was still a good way off, but summer was coming to an end, and starting to issue those little warnings.

Now it was morning, and from where I stood in the great hall halfway up the round tower that was the castle of Cor Hefedd, I could look down the valley and see the tents and the myriad ribbons of smoke from the morning cooking fires.

Bailey joined me with a yawn. We'd been put up in the castle, as guests of the king, even though there wasn't a whole lot of room. Most of us had slept there in the great hall, wrapped in our Ranger rolls, weapons still close at hand despite the fact that we were supposed to be secure.

After a while, the mind just doesn't accept that any place is secure anymore.

"Man, if the war waits too much longer, these people are going to be hurting." Bailey echoed my own thoughts. "Funny, isn't it? We got used to being able to fight in any weather at any time of the year. Hell, *we* still can, thanks to the *Coira Ansec* and some judicious hunting. But without internal combustion engines and year-round crops from all over the world..." He shook his head. "I can't say I ever thought about the logistics of the thing that much."

"*We* never really had to," I pointed out. "We went where they sent us and cashed our paychecks." I scratched my beard. We'd all gotten shaggy once it had become evident that we weren't going back to The World any time soon, if ever. Typical of Recon Marines, as soon as we could get away with ignoring Marine Corps grooming standards, we would.

That observation, though, raised some interesting questions. While we'd been responsible only for our immediate mission, some of us had become students of war, delving into subjects high above our pay grade. And now here we were, effectively free agents in a world that appeared to increasingly be at war, even if it wasn't as coordinated as a world war would be with radios, missiles, and jet engines.

What did that mean? We'd aligned ourselves with the Tuacha and their allies, but we were our own independent force in many ways, not auxiliaries or a part of whatever organized forces King Caedmon commanded. We had a certain freedom of action that none of us, as much as we might have fantasized about it over the years, had ever really experienced before.

Were we really ready for everything that freedom of action entailed?

We'd done pretty well so far, but that had been more a matter of agreeing to missions offered by our allies.

Before I could really go down that rabbit hole—and Bailey would definitely have gone down it with me—there was a stir near the stairs, as the king came down from the chambers that Lady Loncheta had handed over for his use, at least for the night.

If I'd thought he'd looked rough in the dark, he looked even older in the light of day. The crow's feet around his eyes belonged to a man in his forties, not his twenties. There might even have been a few streaks of gray already in his beard.

He wasn't making an entrance so much as he was trying to slip down into the great hall to see if Gunny and Mathghaman were awake. He didn't quite tiptoe, but he was moving quietly, avoiding getting too close to any of the men sleeping on the floor.

The two of us turned to face him, not *quite* standing at attention, but at least holding ourselves respectfully. We'd seen King Uven spattered with blood not his own, raging with grief at the murders of men he'd trained with and gone into battle with. We weren't monarchists, but this man deserved respect.

Gunny had been awake before me, and now looked up from where he was sharpening his axe. That was a bit of weapons maintenance that neither Bailey nor I needed to worry about, not with the Swords of Iudicael and Categyrn. Neither one of those blades ever took a scratch or a nick. Granted, I'd needed to sharpen my Bowie after half decapitating a man with it, but I'd done that before I'd fallen asleep.

Gunny looked over at us and inclined his head. We were already moving, Bailey diverting on his course slightly to kick Gurke awake. The loud snoring stopped, followed by a stream of profanity that was cut off when Gurke realized that King Uven was in the room with us.

Orava was awake, too, and joined us as we moved to follow Gunny, Mathghaman, Cailtarni, and the king up the stairs.

Lady Loncheta's quarters were only one floor up, though it was a bit of a longer climb to get above the great hall. She had cleared out completely, apparently going to one of the farms outside the castle while the king was there.

We'd been in that castle before, but even then, poor as it was, it was somewhat more ornate than King Uven seemed to prefer when he traveled on campaign, presuming that was what this was. If Lady Loncheta had taken some of her finery with her, the king hadn't bothered to try to replace it. His armor hung on a stand near the bed, which didn't look like it had been slept in. Unless I missed my guess, the king was sleeping on the floor, wrapped in his cloak, as long as his men were sleeping in tents outside.

He turned to face us. "It gladdens me to see you alive. We had all but given up hope." He turned to Cailtarni. "Galan?"

I glanced at Cailtarni. The older man had been right there beside us when it had happened.

"He sacrificed himself, my king." Cailtarni bowed his head. "He challenged the dragon that guarded the Sword of Categyrn and drew it down to the ground where it could be slain."

King Uven's eyes got distant. "He would have liked to die that way, I think. He was one of the bravest men I have ever known."

His gaze came back to the present. "The Sword of Categyrn? What of it? You said the dragon was guarding it."

Cailtarni might have stiffened a little. I could kind of understand why. We'd been asked to come along to assist the Galel knights on the quest. Yet the appointed leader of the expedition had been killed, and one of us now bore the Sword.

All of us turned to Bailey. He slowly and carefully drew the Sword, identical to the Sword of Iudicael at my side except that the accents set into its hilts were silver, instead of gold. Laying the blade across his forearm, he held it out for inspection. "It's here."

King Uven's eyes locked on the mythic sword for a moment before they rose to meet Bailey's. "You?" There was surprise in his voice, though not the outrage that might have come from a man who had expected to have one of his own take possession of such an artifact.

Bailey looked a little uncomfortable. "I didn't take it so much as it was kind of dropped in my lap." That was putting it mildly, and I noticed that he didn't immediately point out that he'd been the man who'd killed the dragon, driving Galan's spear into one of the holes he'd blasted in its scales with a .50 cal. Sean Bailey might have been the slightly more aggressive of the two of us, but he wasn't a braggart.

"This is the man who killed the dragon." Gunny wasn't above bragging on his boys, especially when it appeared that Cailtarni wasn't going to come out and say it. The older knight had been a good fighter and one of the team out there on the plains, but now that we were back amidst court politics, it seemed like he was wondering about what side he should come down on.

I didn't like that. I'd been a little wary of Cailtarni, as attractive as his daughter was, since I'd first met him. He'd seemed to be okay out there, but now my earlier misgivings were starting to come back.

He allayed some of those misgivings a moment later. "It seems that not just anyone may lay hands on the blade, my king. There was a mystic will about this, somehow."

"I do not doubt it." The king's eyes had moved back to the Sword in Bailey's hands, then to its sister weapon at my side. He was thinking deeply. Finally, he looked around at all of us. "Truly, Tigharn's ways are mysterious. It would seem that whatever His reasons for bringing you here, bearing the Swords was one of them." He reached out toward the blade in Bailey's hands for a moment, then withdrew his hand with a short bow. "Bear them well and justly."

Bailey still looked a little uncomfortable. I simply said, "We do what we can."

The king took a step back and addressed the lot of us. As tired as he looked, he stayed on his feet, probably because unless we sat on the floor, there was nowhere that all of us could sit. He was that kind of guy. "Well, my friends, you return to us in grave times." His shoulders slumped slightly. "I know not whether the Empire means to invade or simply to threaten it long enough that we strip our frontier provinces bare before winter while we position more of our forces to counter them. They have kept larger and larger armies lurking on our borders ever since just after you left."

He rubbed his forehead tiredly. "Not only that, but attacks by bandits and raiders deeper and deeper into the kingdom have only increased. Even messages between castles have become rare, as travel within the kingdom becomes more hazardous. We have not the forces to deal with both problems."

"That's probably why the raids have stepped up." Gunny was blunt. "Have you captured any of the bandits?"

"A few." The king laughed without humor. "I think you will be as unsurprised as I that we found Peruni gold in their pockets."

"They are not even trying to hide it, then," Mathghaman mused.

"No, they are not." King Uven sighed, and he seemed to sag a little. "Of course, I know what their envoys would say. They would point out that raiders can attack Peruni villages and caravans, as well."

"Plausible deniability." The king frowned at my statement, but after a moment, he nodded.

"Yes. That is a good way of putting it."

I wondered, then, if this was new, or if they just hadn't put a name to it. These people—and I counted pretty much everyone I'd met since crossing through the mists to this place—didn't put as high a priority on naming and categorizing everything as we did back in The World.

One thing I'd learned over the years, mostly in Syria, was that there really is nothing new under the sun when it comes to warfare. The toys get a little more expensive and advanced, but every time we think we've discovered a new tactic or strategy, it turns out someone has already done it before. Sometimes centuries before. This place was no different.

For a moment, it looked like King Uven hesitated, as if he wasn't sure whether or not he should say what he had in mind next. Finally, though, he took a deep breath and took the plunge.

"I cannot stay here at Cor Hefedd indefinitely. I have been touring the frontier castles and holdings for the last month. I am due to leave here tomorrow morning." He looked from me, to Bailey, to Gunny, to Mathghaman. "I know that I have no hold over you. I asked for your help and you more than gave it. Yet now, I would ask if you would accompany me south? I ride for Cor Chatha next." He got grimmer. "It is the lynchpin of the southern defense."

In the tone of his voice was all the information about why he was going there that anyone needed. While I didn't have the map of Cor Legear's kingdom memorized, I knew that the frontier with the Empire of Ar-Annator got a lot flatter and more open the farther south you went. If Cor Chatha was the lynchpin of that defense, then it was Important with a capital I.

We all looked at Gunny. We were exhausted, strung out, and almost completely without ammunition. How much we could contribute without a week or two to reset was a question.

It was a question Gunny was thinking about, too. “We would be honored, King Uven, but we are rather desperately in need of resupply and rearmament.”

The king nodded. “Of course. I ask not for an honor guard or a vanguard. I ask only for your company as we ride.” He smiled wanly. “My men must carry their own weight for a while.”

The look on Cailtarni’s face at that was not a happy one. But when the king turned to him and asked for a more detailed account of Galan’s fall, he relaxed. Perhaps he’d realized that the king was not casting any aspersion on his own honor, and in fact classed him with us, simply as one who had ridden on the quest for the Sword of Categyrn.

I hoped so. As aggravating as the older man could sometimes be, a bond had formed between us during those months in dangerous, haunted places. I’d hate to see that go away because of rivalries based around his kingdom’s politics.

Still, if the Empire of Ar-Annator was employing irregular warfare to weaken the Kingdom of Cor Legear from within, they would certainly turn to treason at some point.

It bore watching.

CHAPTER 6

IF we'd been concerned about resupply, it seemed someone was way ahead of us.

A wagon arrived from the west, the evening before we were supposed to depart. It had no escort, and was driven by a single man, though that man was clearly a Tuacha, and I could tell that from almost a mile away. Golden-headed and straight-backed, he radiated the sort of assured strength and grace that marked that people.

Mathghaman had seen him first, or maybe he'd sensed him coming. I can never tell; he's just always ahead of me, somehow. If it had been anyone else, I might come to resent it, but Mathghaman was the kind of man who does these things without an ounce of condescension or guile. He just did them.

At any rate, he was already halfway to the wagon by the time I got to the gate and headed down the road.

I caught up just before he reached the wagon, though not without a sneaking suspicion that he'd known I was coming and slowed down so that I could catch up. He didn't stop and wait, but he slowed his pace.

The man in the wagon reined in as we met him. His hair was short, spiky, and gold, his mustache outswept. He might have been Fennean's brother, except he was twice his size. This man was the biggest Tuacha I'd ever seen, and most of them are not small. Hell, *I'm* not small, and a bunch of them make me feel that way.

"Oncu!" Mathghaman looked up at the giant. "I've not seen you in nearly three years. What brings you here?"

The blond giant grinned behind his enormous mustache. "I had just turned into Aith an Rih, and your lady met me on the dock." He waved at the wagon behind him. "She courteously asked me to turn around and sail to the Kingdom of Cor Legear, bearing these gifts for you. She seemed quite insistent that you needed them."

With a faint frown, I grabbed hold of the edge of the wagon's bed and hauled myself up, Oncu watching me with a faint smile. I let out a low whistle when I saw what filled the bed.

While the *Coira Ansec* gave us weapons and ammunition in every way identical to what we might have drawn from the armory or the ammunition supply point back in The World, the packaging tended to be somewhat different. Still, it was always easy to tell what was what. And that wagon was loaded with plenty of loose and linked 7.62x51, some explosives, replacement mortars and ammunition for same, .50 caliber RAUFOSS, and what looked like pistol cases, with holsters, magazines, and ammunition. From what I could see, it looked like .45 caliber ammunition, too.

"How did she know we'd need all of this?" I knew I was asking a stupid question as soon as the words left my lips, and the faint smiles on the faces of both men only reinforced that knowledge.

"The Lady Nuala has insights that few others can boast of." Oncu didn't wait for Mathghaman to say it.

"She can see things others may not, and often she can see what will be before it happens."

"Well, she sure picked up on something." We had sent no messages back to the Isle of Riamog, and in fact I had no idea whether or not Nachdainn had taken the *Radala Farragah* back, or if he still waited at anchor off Lemmanonius. We'd been off comms, so to speak, for a long time. That Nuala had somehow known we'd need resupply was just one more example of how our Tuacha friends could be spooky, though in a good way.

"Come." Mathghaman turned toward the castle. "We still have some time to distribute this before we leave."

* * *

So, with our mags topped off, fresh batteries in NVGs and radios, and reloads carefully distributed on fresh pack-horses, we set out with King Uven's entourage, riding out of the valley and heading south. I gathered that this was a somewhat reduced force from the one he'd ridden out with, since the knights and their retainers who remained at Cor Hefedd as we rode out noticeably outnumbered the forces that had been stationed there when we'd first ridden through, heading into the ruins of the Commagan Empire after the Sword of Categyrn.

King Uven was obviously worried about the impending war, and even though Cor Hefedd was hardly the most auspicious place to attempt an invasion, there was good reason to reinforce it. As he looked over his shoulder though, just before we rode out, I could see the uncertainty in his eyes.

He saw me watching him, and met my gaze for a moment, then turned forward. He wouldn't comment on it. He couldn't. He was a king. The buck stopped with him, and he knew it, even though he was probably at least five years my junior.

Still, he was wondering if he was making the right call. Wondering if the men he was leaving at Cor Hefedd might turn out to be vital elsewhere. Wondering if maybe he was riding away from what could turn out to be the end run that shattered his kingdom, if the Dullahans led a horde of Peruni, Avurs, and other tribal auxiliaries—not to mention whatever monstrous or sorcerous abominations they could summon—through that narrow gap, counting on all eyes to be on the south.

Everyone who's ever had to make any kind of battlefield decision knows those doubts. They don't ever go away, either. Even if your choice worked out, it always comes with a cost, and you wonder whether you could have mitigated that a little bit more by making a different decision.

I knew that, just from my own experiences on a small team. I could only imagine how haunting it must be for a king.

With the King and his retainers at the head, and our platoon not far behind, we rode south for Cor Chatha.

* * *

The first four days went quietly. It seemed strange, riding without the need to hold security every step, without worrying about stealth and finding the most tactically advantageous route through the terrain. Following a road felt downright bizarre.

I didn't think that any of us had unwound much at all. I found myself searching the woods and the fields around us as we rode, my hand on my rifle's pistol grip, sniffing the wind, watching the flights of birds for indicators of enemy movement or presence. My ears were pricked for any sound that might indicate a threat.

When I glanced over my shoulder, I saw Rodeffer making the same scans, riding with the same coiled-spring tension. I definitely wasn't the only one.

Only the Tuacha looked somewhat relaxed, but even that was something of an illusion. Their eyes moved everywhere, and I was sure that their awareness went deeper than just where they looked. Again, they were spooky that way.

Very little of the time we'd spent in this world since crossing the mists hadn't been under threat. We'd just spent the majority of the last two to three months in combat on some level. After a while, the habits that go along with that state of constant alertness and preparedness for violence become hard-wired. They don't get turned off, because there simply is no "off" switch anymore.

Eventually, that switch might get rewired. Not anytime soon, though. And it turned out that our hardwired combat mindset would turn out to be a lifesaver.

* * *

Night was falling, and we were still almost ten miles from Cor Wudrun. The castle itself, with its main round keep and three smaller round towers at the corners of an outer wall, was clearly visible, silhouetted against the sky from the hilltop where we'd halted, but when you're limited to the pace of a fast horse—or, in this case, the slowest horse we had—ten miles at sunset is going to take too much of the night to cover. So, we circled up on the hill, the Galel setting guard as they had been for most of the trip.

We set our own watch, just like we'd done since we'd left Cor Hefedd. The king had given us a bit of a look the first time, as if he thought we didn't trust his men. The fact that Cailtarni and his own retainers had joined us might have somewhat defused his objection, though there seemed to be some friction there, nonetheless. I put some of that down to Cailtarni's personality. Even after all we'd been through, I could occasionally find the man a bit overbearing.

I had Santos put me down for the middle watch, then rolled up in my poncho and poncho liner and tried to get to sleep.

* * *

I awoke to the blare of a trumpet just before first light.

There was a faint glow in the east, over the ridge of the mountains that were already noticeably lower and more rounded than they had been near Cor Hefedd, but sunset was still probably a good half an hour away.

It took a second for the meaning of that trumpet call to penetrate the fog in my brain. Hardwired alert we might be, but fatigue still takes its toll, and we'd been in the saddle for a long time. Even so, while I tried to remember what that call was, I was already rolling out of my Ranger roll and grabbing for my weapons, which were right beside me, partially covered by the poncho. Noise meant threat. So, I was already ready to fight even while I was still waking up.

Weapons clashed in the dark, even as several of the Galel threw more wood on the fires, sending up great blazes to illuminate the hilltop.

"Contact, north!" Baldinus's voice rang out over the campsite. He'd been on watch with Pöllö, which told me that we really were right at the last watch.

An arrow whistled through the air overhead, landing in the dirt not far from where I'd bedded down. It didn't have a whole lot of energy left, but it was still a threat. Fortunately, I'd slept in my mail and cammies, so even if it had hit, I probably would have been fine. That wasn't calculated to make me relax, though.

I got to my feet, wishing I had a bigger shield than the buckler I carried with the Sword of Iudicael. Two more arrows came in, but it was already looking like they'd been loosed at random into the encampment, without really being aimed. That didn't make them any less of a threat—if anything, it made it harder to take effective cover.

The king was on his feet, already in his armor, bareheaded and with his naked sword in his hand. Six of his retainers surrounded him, and I got the sudden impression they were doing whatever they could to keep their sovereign from charging into the fight while the men on the perimeter could handle it.

And handle it, they did. Even as I got up to where I had a decent view of the fighting, close enough that I didn't even need to use my scope to get a better look, I saw that the raiders—all Galel but wearing little armor and bearing not much more in the way of weapons but spears, axes, and bows—were already being forced back, and as more of the king's men got on horseback and started to maneuver, they were going to be flanked and cut off in a moment.

I frowned. Something seemed off. A force that small, that poorly equipped, shouldn't have had the stones to attack the royal encampment, guarded not only by a whole lot of knightly skullcrushers, but also by Tuacha and the strangers from afar with the boom sticks. That was Dovo-level desperation. Or stupidity.

Unless it was a diversion.

I'd barely thought it when something made me turn around. Maybe my luminous guardian tapped me on the shoulder. Maybe I heard something. Whatever alerted me, I spun around, snapping my rifle to my shoulder as I did so, dropping the muzzle level once I'd cleared the king and his bodyguard.

The thing was scrabbling along the ground like a spider, moving fast. For a moment, its movement reminded me of a camel spider, one of the cousins to scorpions that you find in the Middle East, that will charge you, if only to get into the shade between your legs. The fact that it was shaped like a man made things that much worse.

Yes, I said it was shaped like a man. It even had been a man, once. It wasn't anymore.

It was hard to see in the dim light, even as the bonfires roared higher and spilled their flickering glow across the hilltop. I could see the milky film over its dead eyes, and the darkened, desiccated flesh that covered its bones. This thing had been dead for a long time, and it looked like pictures I'd seen back in The World of bog mummies. Whatever was in the driver's seat, it wasn't the man this thing had once been.

"Shot!" I was well back from the fighting, and about to open fire awfully close to friendlies. It was usually advisable under such circumstances to issue a warning first.

Unfortunately, the malignant spirit that was wearing the bog mummy like a skin suit could apparently hear, too.

It snapped those milky eyes toward me, then surged off the ground, even as I put a bullet through its throat.

About like I should have expected, the gunshot did absolutely nothing. It kept coming. Didn't even flinch.

It was on me in a heartbeat, faster than I could possibly drop the rifle on its sling and draw the Sword. I went over backwards as it came off the ground and slammed into me, clawlike fingers grasping for my throat.

If not for the fact that I'd yelled and fired, even though my rifle was suppressed, so the *crack* was slightly quieter than the *boom* it would have spat otherwise, I wouldn't have survived the next few heartbeats. I let go of my rifle and grabbed for its wrists even as it slammed me down on my back and knocked the wind out of me. That thing was *strong*, and even as I put everything I had into fighting to keep it off me, I felt my own hands forced inward. It was like trying to hold a hydraulic press open with your bare hands.

Then a spear transfixed the revenant through its side, plunging all the way between its ribs to slam into the ground. Then the man gripping the spear, one of King Uven's knights, planted his feet and heaved, trying to pry the dead thing off me.

It swatted him with a casual backhand that knocked him sprawling.

It turned back to me, leering at me, foul liquid dripping past its teeth, smelling like stagnant swamp water. Its hands inched closer and closer to my throat. I tried to throw a knee into its side, more out of defiant desperation than anything else, with a predictable lack of result.

Then half a dozen big men in armor, including Santos and Farrar, grabbed it and tried to drag it off me.

It was like trying to pull a car—or an ox—off somebody. They strained and pulled, but it was like the revenant weighed an actual ton. And once they finally got it to budge, after a moment's utter stillness, broken only by the grunts of effort, it started to pull me off the ground with it.

Then Bailey appeared over my shoulder and stabbed it with the Sword of Categyrn.

The undead creature had fought in utter silence up until then. With a sepulchral moan, it suddenly let go of me, throwing the men holding it to either side as it leaped backward, even farther than it had jumped to attack me in the first place. Smoke rose from the wound in its shoulder, barely visible in the firelight.

Strangely, that firelight never seemed to glint off those cataracted eyes.

It crouched in the grass, just for a moment, then it leaped over one of the sprawled knights—moving away from where Bailey was advancing on it with the Sword of Categyrn—and went for King Uven.

It moved even faster than before, or at least it looked that way. It smashed two of his bodyguards away, sending them tumbling to the ground like rag dolls, and lunged past the king's guard, batting his sword aside and seizing him by the throat.

Standing tall, somehow larger than it had been, it lifted him into the air, his feet kicking uselessly against it, his eyes rolling back in his head as his sword slipped from his fingers.

CHAPTER 7

I was still struggling to get some air back in my lungs, but I drew the Sword of Iudicael as I staggered forward, shoulder to shoulder with Bailey. More of the king's knights were closing in, along with the Tuacha, but I was pretty sure that the two of us had the weapons most likely to actually be able to hurt that thing.

Bailey attacked it first, even though it suddenly drew a rusty, pitted blade from its belt and parried his swing. To make matters worse, it didn't even look at him as it did so. His next two strikes were batted away almost contemptuously. As long as he couldn't touch the monster itself with the blade, it seemed it wasn't bothered.

Whatever this thing was, it was bad juju. This was something more than the shambling monstrosities we'd faced in the Land of Shadows and Crows, or in the haunted ruins of Barmanak. No minor spirit animating a dead body, this was something ancient and deeply evil, more like the revenant sorcerer I'd fought in the Barmanak ziggurat.

I remembered all too well how that had gone. I'd barely been able to touch that thing, and it had drawn me in and almost horribly murdered me. We hadn't killed it, either, but only buried it under the gateway of the citadel, using too much of our explosives in the process.

Still, we had no choice. We could either fight that thing, and hopefully at least force it to let go of the king and flee, or else lay down and die.

We hadn't come all this way to lie down and die. Not yet.

The knights had drawn back somewhat, unwilling to risk striking their king. Mathghaman was circling the creature, but while his long, leaf-bladed sword was a force to be reckoned with—almost as much as the man wielding it—it wasn't one of the Two Swords.

The smoky blade in my fist was.

Even as Bailey sparred with it, I did my best to dash around to its other side, the pain in my chest notwithstanding. I was starting to be able to breathe again, but that hit had slowed me down.

Still, the revenant only had two arms, and one of them was tied up with holding the king by the throat. It had to either drop him or leave itself open to me.

It knew the nature of the weapon in my hand. Probably better than I did, if the thing from the Outer Dark that was wearing that corpse like a suit was as potent and ancient as I thought it was.

Throwing the king to the ground, where he lay motionless, his eyes rolled back in his head, it leaped backward, trying to bring that rusted sword to bear against both of us. Bailey pressed his attack, though, lunging forward with a vicious series of cuts.

The revenant blocked every one of them, even while it kept its other hand extended toward me, ready to try to counter any move I made.

I was hurting, still, not nearly as agile as Bailey. When I lunged, it just kind of danced out of the way, but right at that moment, Bailey got mad.

I could have almost sworn that I caught a glimpse of a shining figure behind him, just as he took a brutal slash at the revenant, snapping that rusted sword off at the hilt before he stepped in, whipping the point around in a tight circle and lopping its arm off just below the elbow.

The Sword of Categyrn went through the revenant's withered flesh like a machete through a sapling. The arm fell lifeless to the ground, and black smoke bled from the stump.

Those milky, flat eyes turned on him, then, and the faint light around him seemed to fade, just a little. He faltered, almost dropping to one knee, as the revenant began to summon some eldritch sorcery to crush him.

But while it was focused on him, it wasn't focused on me.

My first cut took its other arm off, just below the shoulder. It snapped its head toward me, but my back cut had already begun.

Its head rolled free and fell to the ground with a faint *thump*, and then a wisp of black smoke raced out of the stump of its neck with an ear-splitting scream that felt like someone had just rammed a spike through my ear.

Down the hill, the raiders suddenly turned and fled.

* * *

We gathered around the king where he lay quivering on the ground. There was a dark discoloration around his throat, and it was creeping up his jaw like black tendrils of rot. His eyes were still rolled back in his head, and he was foaming at the mouth a little. He was alive, but he was badly hurt, and I don't think any of us expected that this was going to go well.

Mathghaman knelt beside him, even as the sun began to rise over the ridgeline. The desiccated corpse that had been the revenant was already crumbling to dust behind us.

Conall joined him a moment later, putting a hand on the king's forehead. He closed his eyes and murmured faintly, and it seemed like Uven relaxed, just a little.

I didn't know if that was a good thing or a bad thing.

"We must hold this position." Mathghaman stood, leaving the king in Conall's hands. The slender man had taken a lead role in much of the mystical warfare that we'd had to engage in lately, and I didn't doubt that there was more at work in the king's condition than just the physical injury he had to have sustained, being held off the ground by his neck. "We cannot move him now."

"What if the raiders return?" I didn't know the man who asked the question, but that was no great surprise. We hadn't had enough time in Cor Legear to get to know a fraction of the people there, and that had been before King Uven sent out the war arrow. From the looks of some of the Galel we'd been riding with over the last four days, there were some seriously senior dudes in this unit, possibly even the lords of castles themselves.

"The raiders were little more than a diversion for the revenant." Mathghaman's voice was cold, even, and clear. "They stood no chance against you otherwise, and they knew it, which is why they fled as soon as Conor cut it down. They will likely not return, and if they do, we shall deal with them. Keep on your guard. We must help the king before we can move him."

"Speaking of help." Cailtarni, wiping blood from his sword, stepped through the ring of armored men surrounding the king, though he didn't look down at his sovereign. Instead, he glared toward Cor Wudrun. "I cannot help but notice that none came from yonder castle."

"We are nearly two leagues away, Lord Cailtarni." That would be Lord Feth, older than even Cailtarni by nearly a decade, gray-haired, black-bearded, wiry, and mean as an old bear with a toothache. At least, that was what I'd seen over the last four days. The man snapped at everyone except the king, and even then, his respect seemed almost grudging. I didn't think it really was, since I'd been watching him the entire time, and there didn't seem to be any malice to his attitude. He was just a mean old man, who didn't have a soft part on him. "It takes the same amount of time for men you do not like to cover ground than those you do."

Cailtarni, for his part, ignored the barb. "With matters as tense as they are, they should have had patrols out. Unless they knew not to." His voice dropped as he finished speaking, the dire implication clear, even if he didn't say it out loud. While he hadn't spoken of it before, there was clearly some bad blood between Cailtarni and whoever was lord of Cor Wudrun, and there didn't seem to be much he figured that worthy wouldn't stoop to.

"You do not know that." The man who spoke was old enough to be Uven's father, and wore the same red and blue, though without the gold accents. Lord Vepogenus was, in fact, the king's uncle, and his right hand in the field. "The king would have words with you about the readiness of your tongue, Lord Cailtarni, were he awake."

"Were Buthud doing his duty, the king should have little reason to be unconscious," Cailtarni snapped. "Do not tell me that it has escaped everyone else's notice that we rode unmolested for four days and nights, and only now that we are here, on *his* doorstep, we are attacked. And by a creature that could only be summoned by the blackest sorcery, at that!" The old man was getting seriously worked up. He stabbed a finger in the direction of the castle, the walls tinged red even as the sun rose higher. Some kind of red sandstone, maybe. "It would not be the first time!"

"Your feud with Lord Buthud's brother is well known, Lord Cailtarni." Vepogenus kept his voice stern and even, undisturbed by Cailtarni's fury. "Yet he was judged and punished accordingly, and Lord Buthud condemned him beside me. It is over."

"The taint of sorcery oft lingers, even after the worst is over." We might not have had a dog in this fight, not really, but Orava had seen some seriously heavy stuff, and we had, after all, put the revenant down, so he probably figured we still had a place at the table. Gunny shot him a look, and he subsided, but it had been said.

Vepogenus, however, had taken charge with the king incapacitated, and he wasn't going to allow things to fall apart because Uven was down for the count. "We will hold here until the king can be moved. Then we will proceed to Cor Wudrun and find aid, or answers as to why it is refused." He glared around at the assembled knights. "Until then, set your watches and hold your ground."

I watched the lot of them as they dispersed to their areas of the encampment. Most seemed more concerned about the king than much else. Cailtarni harrumphed, but I'd come to expect that from him. A few cast darker looks toward Cor Wudrun.

Without knowing more of the history, I couldn't judge. It did seem a little ominous, though, the fact that not only had we been hit within line of sight of the castle, but that a revenant had come along for the ride. Either things were not at all well within the Kingdom of Cor Legear, or else the Peruni had infiltrated more than we'd feared.

We headed back to our positions, while Conall chanted over the king, praying for his deliverance from whatever curse or venom the revenant had borne with it.

* * *

Mathghaman came back to our section of the camp just after noon. "Conall thinks that we can move him soon. He is injured and poisoned, but he should recover in time. The sorcery was the worst part, and he still fights it."

Gunny nodded. "Team leaders, make sure everyone's ready to move in five minutes."

I just held up a thumbs up. We were already there. Nobody really wanted to hang around that hilltop for long, not after what had just happened. No sane man wants to linger where the dead have walked so recently.

Mathghaman spoke briefly to Bailey, then moved to join me. I was watching Cor Wudrun at the moment, and he stepped up next to me, his arms folded, following my gaze.

"What do you think?" I had to ask. "I've got to admit, the more I see, the more it looks like there are some good people among the Galel, but they're mostly a proud, fractious lot who would be at each other's throats constantly if not for the threat of the Deep Ones on one side and the Peruni and their tribal auxiliaries on the other."

"Tell me, Conor," Mathghaman said in reply, "have you ever known men to be any different?"

I had to think about it. Mathghaman had a way of forcing me to take a step back and look at things from a different angle. "You seem to be."

He laughed softly. "You yourself saw me cut down a man who had been closer to me than a brother." He shook his head. "Such things are perhaps somewhat rarer among us, as we are fewer and longer lived, but do not look for perfection among men, Conor, whether they be Tuacha, Menninkai, Galel, or any other. Our sojourn on this world is one of labor and war, both within and without. None of us who dwell in the flesh are exempt from it."

His gray eyes were still fixed on the distant castle, however. "That does not mean, however, that Lord Cailtarni is wrong. There *should* have been riders from Cor Wudrun here by now. That there are not does not bode well."

"So, we need to be ready for another fight as we get closer." It wasn't a question.

"Yes, indeed, Conor. Yes, indeed."

* * *

We ended up loading the king onto something like a travois, a triangular framework of poles cut from nearby saplings and tied to the back of a saddle. King Uven traveled light, with packhorses instead of wagons, and Oncu hadn't accompanied us, instead heading back to the coast and his ship after he'd dropped off our resupply. That took a few extra minutes to get set up, and then we were moving, riding slowly so as not to jostle the wounded king too much on the way.

He was still unconscious, murmuring in his delirium. It didn't look good.

"Guns, I'm taking the team on ahead." I'd pulled Allon up alongside Gunny Taylor's horse, a big bay named Eghan. It wasn't so much that the pace was so slow that was bothering me, but we didn't have much in the way of scouts out, and the continued silence of Cor Wudrun was a potential problem. If we ran into an ambush with the king as a casualty…

"Do it. But take one or more of the Galel with you." He turned in his saddle, then grimaced, lowering his voice. "I'd say take Cailtarni, but he's got a grudge. Too bad Galan didn't make it."

"I think I can get Morbrec." The young man, barely out of his teens, hadn't come with us on the expedition to the east. He was one of Lord Feth's retainers. Yet he'd been tagging along with us as much as he could on the way south from Cor Hefedd, plying all of us with questions about our weapons, where we came from, how we fought, and what we had seen in the north. He was also aggressive as hell when the fighting broke out. He'd do, if I could pry him away from Lord Feth. The old man was as liable to deny him out of sheer cussedness as he was to let him go.

"Give it a shot." Gunny turned his eyes back on the fields below us. We hadn't gone far, and we were still in the wilds, so to speak, but we still should have seen *someone* nearby, if only gathering firewood in the stands of trees in the lower ground. Something was clearly wrong, and Gunny wanted scouts out as badly as I did.

I didn't have far to go to find Morbrec. He was riding alongside Chambers, asking more questions. "Lord Morbrec." Even the young knights were addressed that way, and it didn't hurt to follow the Galel's cultural mores. They were a sight better in my eyes than some of what we'd had to deal with in Syria. "I'm taking my team to ride ahead. I wondered if you'd like to ride with us?"

Morbrec was a lean, black-haired young man with sweeping mustaches that he probably grew as long as he did to make up for a patchy beard elsewhere. He was currently riding bareheaded, his helm tied to his saddle horn. Now his eyes lit up and he nodded. "Of course." He bowed slightly to Chambers, who gave him a bit of a two-fingered salute—none of us had ever quite figured out just how to respond to some of the bows and other greetings in this world, which were a lot stranger to us than we might have thought before we'd come through the mists—and spurred his horse to join me.

Linking back up with the rest of the team, we started down the valley at a trot. After about half a mile, we spread out, getting off the road and using the smaller paths between fields. Under different circumstances, I might have just crossed the fields, but it was still the middle of harvest time, and if these *weren't* bad guys, then trampling their crops might be a problem.

We started to see people, but they were cautious, if not furtive. A few reached up to tug at caps or forelocks, but they kept their distance. I traded a glance with Santos. He noticed it, too. It wasn't *quite* the sort of furtive evasiveness that you saw just before the intersection in the middle of town blew up, but it wasn't exactly a warm welcome, either, even with an obvious Galel knight riding in the middle of our formation.

The woods thickened after about two miles, as we neared a creek—the stream was too narrow to really call it a river—running along the east side of the farms, and we had to angle back toward the road.

As we rode out onto the packed dirt and stones, our horses' hooves clopping a little more loudly, we finally saw a reception committee.

Six horsemen rode toward us, clearly coming from the castle. Only four were in armor; the other two looked like older farmers, wearing padded jerkins over their tunics and carrying spears and what looked a lot like hunting knives. The man in front was almost as big as Oncu had been, and his horse was nearly the size of a draft horse to bear his weight. In full armor, he had to weigh three hundred fifty pounds. His livery was green and gold, and a bristling gray mustache obscured his mouth above his coif.

He reined in, his spear in one mailed fist, and watched us with cold, narrowed eyes. He clearly didn't know what to make of the men in green and brown, wearing mail but otherwise dressed strangely, carrying odd weapons in addition to our swords and axes. His eyes lit on Morbrec, but without recognition.

"You do not appear to be of the raiders who have ravaged our outer farms of late." His voice was a booming foghorn, echoing across the nearby fields and trees. "But I have not seen your like before. Declare yourselves, or stand and fight."

Morbrec rode forward, lifting a hand in greeting. "I am Lord Morbrec. I ride for Lord Feth, in the service of King Uven, who comes behind us, sore wounded."

The older man didn't seem overjoyed by the prospect. Nor did he panic. His face clouded and might have gone a little pale.

"Truly?" He glanced over our shoulders toward the way we'd come. "The king himself?"

"The king himself." Morbrec didn't seem intimidated by the other man's apparent seniority, but that might have just come with being one of Feth's retainers. I didn't expect a lot would seem intimidating after working for that bitter old man.

The big man sighed deeply. "While I fear how this may be taken, we can offer you no shelter in Cor Wudrun."

Morbrec's face stiffened. "First we receive no aid when attacked by raiders and a sorcerous, undead monstrosity on your own lands, then you would turn the king himself aside? What treason festers in Cor Wudrun?"

The older man's eyes turned hard, even as hands all around reached for weapons. I had my eye on the big man himself, my thumb resting on my rifle's selector. If this went hot in the next moment, he was going to die first.

"You should take care, throwing that word around, whelp," the big man growled. "In fact, under different circumstances, I would call you out to defend your words with steel here and now." His glower got darker as he looked around at the rest of us. "If you did not bear the royal badge on your shoulder, I would strike you dead for that even without a challenge."

Morbrec's frown deepened still further. "Then what possible justification can you have to turn aside your king, even as he lies sore hurt?"

With another sigh, the big man's face seemed to go a little gray. "A plague, Lord Morbrec. A pestilence that sprang up like a foul wind, only two days hence, and has laid low Lord Buthud and all his household, as well as half the farmers in the lands around." He leaned on his saddle, even as the vanguard of the king's cavalcade came into sight on the road behind us. "I doubt indeed that you would wish to bring King Uven, wounded and weakened, into such a place."

* * *

"I was out to supervise my harvest when it struck. There was no warning. I myself was turned away before I could reach the gates." Lord Canaul, the massive mountain of a man who had challenged us, stood before Lord Vepogenus, Lord Feth, Mathghaman, and Gunny. The rest of us waited at some distance, but I could hear well enough. "None know from whence it came, but it is dire. A dark cloud passed through the castle in the night, and all but four in the castle fell into a deep sleep. Those four can barely stand." He twisted his huge hands together. "Nearly a dozen of the farms around the keep were struck down, as well."

Vepogenus watched him, his own brow furrowed. "The timing could not be a coincidence." He looked to Mathghaman, who seemed to be the kingliest man there. To be fair, Mathghaman, who was only the Tuacha da Riamog's King's Champion, was probably kinglier than any other man alive who wasn't a Tuacha himself.

"It would not be. This was an ambush, carefully planned." True to his way, Mathghaman didn't offer any particular solutions. That was not his place, and he would not overstep himself, even if every man there wished that he would.

"I do not pretend to know how to lift the curse, whatever it is," Canaul said. "But the king must not go near Cor Wudrun."

"Cor Legear."

The king's voice was a hoarse rasp, and all eyes turned toward his travois. He hadn't stirred since the attack, but now he was sitting up, though he was clearly still in a lot of pain, and he looked like he was about to pass out again at any moment. "I… cannot… go all the way… to Cor Chatha. Take me… to Cor Legear."

He slumped down again, exhausted. At least he'd woken up. I knew that a few of his knights had feared he was a dead man, even though he was still breathing and his heart was still beating.

"I will ride with you." Canaul's voice brooked no argument. "Lord Buthud may not offer the king his hospitality, so I will place my body and my blade between him and further harm." He looked toward the rest of the men who had ridden out with him to meet us. "Lord Usconbitus will defend this place in my stead."

"I will stay." Conall came out of the press and faced Mathghaman. "One of us should, if only to try to lift the curse and help these people."

Mathghaman eyed him as all others turned toward him. Then he simply inclined his head, acknowledging Conall's offer and accepting it at the same time.

It worried me a little. Conall was the closest we had to an out-and-out mystic, in a place where such people were worth their weight in gold. If there really was Peruni sorcery at work here, trying to tear the guts out of the Kingdom of Cor Legear before a full-scale war broke out, we'd probably find we missed Conall sorely.

"Cor Legear it is, then," Vepogenus said.

CHAPTER 8

IT was still a long ride to Cor Legear, and we weren't going to make it in less than a week. That meant stopping for shelter in more than one place. Aullun was the strongest hold between Cor Wudrun and Cor Legear, and while it would take us a few days to reach it, we'd probably need to stop for a couple of days there.

Provided it wasn't held against us. From some of the murmurings around the campfires, the king's welcome at Aullun was a little uncertain.

Canaul didn't say a word about any of it, but from what I gathered, there was another feud between Buthud and the castellan of Aullun, Lord Urgant.

Seemed like everywhere you turned, there was a feud of some sort here. It sort of reminded me of places in Syria, even among the Kurds. Kurdish clans can hate each other *almost* as much as they hate Turks or Arabs.

Except, I still liked the Galel a lot better than anyone I'd ever run across in Syria.

The king was doing a little better, though he was still weak, and still couldn't walk or ride. He would occasionally sit up on his travois to talk, though he tired quickly.

It turned out that the revenant's claws had punctured his neck, and the wounds were festering. He often lapsed into fever, and while the black tendrils along his neck and jaw hadn't spread any more, they hadn't gone away, either. I wondered whether it was just a matter of poisoning, or if there was truly a curse of some sort involved.

Vepogenus had hoped to reach Aullun in three days. We didn't make nearly that kind of time, but just after noon on the fourth day, we came over a rise in the rolling, open country and rode toward the spire of Aullun.

The castle was taller than even Cor Legear, if on a smaller footprint. The single round tower that formed its heart was slender and tapered toward the sky, flaring out ever so slightly before its peaked roof. Thatched roofs clustered about its base, inside a double wall with earthworks. Overall, it had the look of having been built later upon much older fortifications.

Unlike at Cor Wudrun, we were met by a full honor guard while we were still some distance away from the castle. The band of nearly a company strong was led by a man in gold-chased orange. From the look of studied, stony indifference on Canaul's face, I figured this had to be Urgant.

Just going by first impressions, I had to agree with Canaul's opinion of the man.

Urgant's armor and surcoat were gaudier by far than even the king's. His weapons were inlaid with gold, and his helmet was almost entirely gilded. He carried that helm in the crook of his arm as he rode, allowing a man in considerably less of a panoply carry his lance and its banner behind him. The look on his face was one I could only call *smarmy.*

"Why, Lord Canaul." Urgant's voice matched his expression. "I hardly expected to see you on my lands."

"I am here to escort the king, Lord Urgant. Nothing more, nothing less." It sounded like Canaul would prefer to be slowly eviscerated before being polite to Urgant.

Urgant arched an eyebrow. "The king?" he said, as if disbelieving that the king would deign to be escorted by the likes of Canaul. He looked past Canaul at the rest of us, strung out in a column four deep and almost a mile long behind Canaul and two more of the king's retainers.

I didn't know for sure that there was another feud between Cor Wudrun and Aullun, but if there wasn't, it looked a lot like there easily could be. If I'd hailed from Cor Wudrun, there probably would have been right then and there.

Lord Vepogenus rode forward then, his red and blue surcoat looking muted next to Urgant's finery, his expression all but blank. The nose-in-the-air aura of superiority didn't entirely leave Urgant's face, but there was a flicker in his expression, just for a moment.

I watched him carefully. There was something going on behind the mask, there, but I couldn't tell what it was. And it *was* a mask. This man might naturally be that arrogant, but just for a second, I thought maybe I'd seen a bit of nervousness.

A glance at Vepogenus showed me that the old man had seen it, too. And he wondered.

Urgant bowed his head slightly, but only slightly. Lord Vepogenus might be the king's right hand, but he was not the king. The castellan of Aullun looked over the older man's shoulder. "So, the king is truly here?"

"He is." For a moment, I thought that Vepogenus wasn't going to elaborate beyond that, and Urgant's eyes widened slightly in question, as if he was thinking the same thing. "We were ambushed just north of Cor Wudrun, and the king was sore wounded. We call upon your hospitality for a day or two, Lord Urgant."

Once again, there was that odd flicker in Urgant's expression. I was starting to seriously think that we needed to pull off now, push through the night, no matter how hard it taxed the king, and fort up somewhere as far from Aullun as we could get. Something was up in the Kingdom of Cor Legear, and from watching Urgant, I was starting to suspect that it wasn't all just because of the Peruni.

It wasn't my call, however, and Vepogenus apparently didn't think that we dared take the king much farther through open country without at least a day or two to rest. He motioned to Urgant to lead the way, even though the castellan hadn't said anything in invitation. Urgant bowed stiffly, drew his horse around, and started toward the castle as we fell in behind him.

While he could be somewhat overbearing, I thought that Cailtarni might be able to shed some light, so I fell back next to him. "I take it Urgant isn't exactly that well-liked?"

The older knight laughed softly. "He is hardly thought about. His father was a great hero and a greater knight. When the pirates of the south took the daughter of his friend Gurthinmoch, even though he was not obligated to do so, Broichan set out to rescue her, and even though all of his companions were slain, he held his ground, the girl behind him, against thirty men." Cailtarni looked up toward the front of the formation, where Urgant rode at the head of his own retinue, hardly looking back at the men behind him. "The son of Broichan has distinguished himself by no such deeds, yet he will remind all and sundry of his patrimony. The fact that Broichan became fabulously rich in the course of his adventures has only aided his son's dissolute ways." He sighed. "He is not alone in his generation. It has been many years since the last war with the Empire, and the bandits and raiders they send seem like pinpricks to those like Urgant who live far from the frontiers. He still thinks he should be more important in the kingdom than he really is."

"Is that why he wears all that gold?" It seemed not only gaudy, but ultimately impractical to me. Of course, I came from a somewhat different school of warfare, where camouflage is important—no matter how much some people back in The World treated it more like a fashion statement—but all the same, I remembered Galan telling me about how the knights of Cor Legear had to learn all aspects of warfare.

Cailtarni nodded with some dark amusement. "Indeed."

"Great." Cailtarni laughed softly at the tone of my voice and clapped me on the shoulder, but he had little comfort to add.

I watched Urgant as we rode toward the castle. It was entirely possible that some of my suspicions were darker than they needed to be. Maybe the discomfort I sensed wasn't treason, but instead just a jumped-up kid who thought he should be in charge of more than he was.

That wasn't call to relax, though. Pride has driven men to do some pretty terrible things.

We'd definitely set a watch that night.

CHAPTER 9

SOMETHING woke me up in the middle of the night. I knew it wasn't my watch, since there was no one nudging my boot or standing over me to let me know. The room high in the tower of Aullun was quiet and dark.

None of us were snoring. That was kind of a warning sign in and of itself. Some of us snored like sawmills—when we were somewhere secure. Some subconscious influence in this world had consistently silenced those snores when we were under threat.

I reached for the Sword of Iudicael where it sat next to my rifle, even as I scanned the room. Everything was still. *Something* had awoken me, though, and I didn't think it was just that time of night.

I glanced down with a frown. I'd reached for the Sword first, not for my rifle, or the .45 that I'd added to my increasingly heavy collection of weaponry. Granted, I left the pistol in my ruck more often than not, but right then, it was probably a better choice for this kind of close quarters than my rifle.

Still, I'd reached for the Sword first.

Rolling quietly to my feet, I drew the blade, and it glinted faintly in the dimness. No one else was up, which gave me pause, just for a moment. *Had* I just woken up at random? Maybe from a nightmare that I didn't remember?

That would actually be a welcome switch. I'd had some hair-raising dreams since coming here.

Hell, I'd had hair-raising dreams since Syria.

A moment later, though, the wail that echoed from the stairwell just off the room where we'd bedded down banished that hope.

Bailey came awake in a moment, snatching for the Sword of Categyrn. That was interesting. The only reason I could see it was Bailey was the moonlight coming in the tall, narrow window behind me, but the fact that he'd been the one to wake up, and that he'd grabbed the Sword, just like I had, was interesting. From the look he gave me as we linked up at the door to the stairwell, he was thinking the same thing.

We weren't the *only* ones up, fortunately. Franks and Gurke were on watch in the stairwell itself, with their rifles. Franks was currently trying to cover both up and down the stairs while Gurke looked for the source of the wail.

"I think it came from above us." Gurke's voice was a hoarse whisper that still echoed in the stairwell. He practically winced at the loudness of the sound. Recon Marines don't like to be loud; it's why we usually subvocalized in hide sites instead of whispering. Whispers travel farther.

Dropping his voice, he moved to join the two of us, careful not to get too close to the Swords. Not that he was worried about us or the touch of the blessed weapons. Gurke could be a pain sometimes, but he was obnoxious, not evil. Still, it's inadvisable to get careless around three feet of razor-sharp steel in the dark.

"That noise just started a minute ago, but I can't figure out where it's coming from." That bothered Gurke. Even after all this time, the eerie stuff still bugged him. "I could swear that it's coming from above us, but that's impossible unless it was already here when we got here."

"Maybe it was." I peered up the spiral staircase, but saw nothing but the moonlight on the stones. "Maybe it came in afterward anyway."

"We would have seen it." Gurke was being deliberately obtuse, I was pretty sure, and I was too groggy to put up with it.

"Not if it can fly through windows." I didn't know at that point whether I was being serious or just giving Gurke a hard time. Maybe both. We didn't always get along all that well, he and I.

He turned to look at me. "Thank you for that, Conor. Thank you so *very* much."

"You guys stay here." Bailey was usually more of the one for banter, but right then another shriek came echoing down the stairs. Gurke was right. It was *definitely* coming from somewhere overhead.

With a nod, the two of us started up. Bailey hadn't been quite as unnerved by the spooky stuff as Gurke, but he still hadn't embraced it, at least not until he'd killed a dragon and been, in so doing, anointed as the Bearer of the Sword of Categyrn. He still wasn't entirely *comfortable* with any of it. That was only because he was sane. I wasn't comfortable with the spooks and monsters that haunted seemingly every corner of this world, either. Only a madman would be.

Still, being the Sword Bearers, we were probably the best equipped to deal with anything weird, aside from one of the Tuacha.

The stair spiraled up to the right, which seemed arbitrary until you understood that the vast majority of men are right-handed, which means that they would have to fight with their weapons at a poor angle, while the men fighting down, defending the tower, would have room to swing. It was a detail that you wouldn't think about until you had to fight through it.

Both of us, almost simultaneously and without saying a word, switched the Swords to our left hands and kept moving. Adapt, improvise, and overcome.

The wail came again. Actually, it had never gone away, but rose and fell enough that it almost seemed like it. Whatever was going on up there, it didn't sound good.

The thing was, I had no idea who was up there. I was fairly certain that Urgant's quarters and those of most of his family and retainers were below. We might be "guests" in Aullun, but we hadn't exactly been given the grand tour.

Judging by the noises drifting down the stairwell, there might well be a reason for that.

The stairs spiraled upward, seemingly endlessly. We passed where the next floor's door should have been, but there was only a stone wall. That was weird, but right then, it wasn't an immediate threat.

It was the middle of the night and there was screaming. Press the immediate threat.

Coming around the next curve, we got a hell of a shock.

There was no door to the topmost chamber. The stairs just went up to the floor and stopped. The entire top of the tower was one big open room, and anyone entering it would simply walk up the stairs and onto the floor.

That wasn't the shock, though. The luminous, transparent figure, swathed in tattered rags to the point that it was impossible to tell if it was male, female, or even human, swept down through the opening in the floor, screaming like the damned, and charged us, long arms reaching out, tipped with claw-like hands.

Both Swords were already in the guard position that Mathghaman had taught us, but the phantom didn't even seem to notice. It swept toward us with a shriek that physically hurt.

We both struck at the same time, even as those clawed hands snatched at us. Both blades went through thin air as if nothing was there, and those talons disappeared into us. For a moment, the stairwell turned deathly cold, then the phantom just kept going down the stairs, wailing and shrieking, loud enough to wake the dead. Still, no one seemed to wake up or come to investigate. There was something deeply wrong going on here.

Of course, the phantom was wrong enough. But I didn't think, after it had swept past us like that, that it was the biggest threat. Otherwise, everyone would have been on their feet, weapons in hand, looking for monsters to kill.

The two of us shared a glance, then shrugged and kept going. The phantom hadn't hurt either of us, and it looked as if it couldn't.

Not that such things were powerless. Bearrac had warned me about creatures like that in the north, dark spirits that fed off pain and suffering, drawn to scenes of violence and death. They might not be able to hurt a man physically, but they could get into his head, destroy him from the inside out. That was why Bearrac had urged us not to even think about them too hard.

This seemed like something else altogether. If not for the sudden temperature drop, I would have thought it was just an illusion. Some sort of mystic projection or something. Which was a problem all on its own, though my next thought as Bailey and I moved up the last few steps before the landing and whatever awaited us in that room at the top made it even worse.

I had just remembered what that thing had reminded me of. The same illusory phantoms that had attacked Derelei and me on the battlements of Cor Legear, just before the real attack, in the shape of the possessed corpses of several of King Uven's guards, came after us.

That boded all kinds of trouble.

Now, stairs are a nightmare in close quarters combat, even without the right-hand twist and the realities of sword fighting. You've got multiple angles to worry about, and when you reach the top, you're going to be exposed to more angles than you can cover. Especially if the top is just a hole in the floor, which this appeared to be.

So, Bailey and I, our Swords leveled, crept our way up to the lip of the landing above, crouched down so as to stay out of sight until the last minute, and set up with Bailey facing back the way we'd come and me facing the top of the steps.

We really should have at least brought our pistols.

Facing opposite directions, we'd positioned ourselves so that we could just see each other in our peripheral vision. I gave a nod, Bailey returned it, and we stood straight up, rising straight into the room at the top of the tower.

It was dark, empty, and still. A round table stood in the center, with several benches and small shelves set around the outside, alternating either facing the table or the tall, arched windows around the exterior wall. Several elaborate candelabras stood on the table, along with a massive, ancient book in an ornate bookstand, illuminated starkly by the moonlight coming through one of those tall windows, but the candles were dark and unlit.

I moved up into the room, my sword in a forward guard, my buckler held over the hilts to protect my hand. Less than useful against spooks and phantoms, perhaps, but it was still a good idea to stay ready. We'd seen things pop out of the ground and try to eat our faces off before.

Bailey swept the other half of the room with his eyes, then turned to follow me, turning sharply at the top of the steps to cover my back as I moved toward the table.

Another scream echoed through the tower. I resisted the urge to head back downstairs immediately and try to deal with it. The first manifestations had come from up here, and so we needed to clear this room first.

The book lay open, the pages stirring slightly even though there was no breeze. Goosebumps prickled my arms at the sight. There was something deeply wrong here.

Reluctant to take my eyes off the book, I scanned the rest of the room. The shadows under the windows might have been a little darker than they should have been, but nothing moved except those restlessly rustling pages. No lambent, evil eyes glittered in the darkness. No new phantoms materialized. There was just that eerie, unnatural movement in the pages of the book.

Something warned me that touching that book with my bare hands wouldn't be a good idea. It wasn't anything I could necessarily put into words, but I reached out with the Sword of Iudicael and pressed one of the fluttering pages down with the point.

The book caught fire.

I stepped back almost involuntarily, bringing the Sword up to where I held the hilt next to my ear, the point still aimed at the book which was now fully involved, bright yellow flames eating away at pages and cover alike. An acrid smoke rose from the conflagration before drifting off through a window.

"That ain't good." Bailey hadn't turned to face the fire, though he was now positioned so that he could watch the rest of the room while still keeping it in sight out of the corner of his eye. "I think something's rotten in Aullun."

"Sure looks like it." The flames were dying down. The book had been reduced to ashes faster than it probably should have. I still didn't take my eyes off it, not yet. There were all sorts of creepy things that could come crawling out of that pile of ash, which had filtered down through the bookstand onto the tabletop. The bookstand itself appeared to be untouched. "I think we know why Urgant seemed so off."

"We need to get Uven out of here, then." Bailey was well ahead of me. I was mostly worried about what kind of sorcerous abominations might come out of the shadows at any minute, and he was thinking big picture. "If Urgant's already been playing around with sorcery, then this is a trap."

Another scream echoed through the tower, long, drawn out, and finally fading into a distant wail that seemed to die away somewhere outside. The smoke had drifted away, and all that was left of the book was ash.

I tore my eyes away from the pile of cooling cinders and turned toward the stairs. The quiet that had just settled over the castle seemed somehow even more eerie than the screams and wails. "Let's finish the clear."

* * *

The quiet didn't last long as we descended the steps, and soon the entire castle was in an uproar. The noise got louder as we cleared our way down, finding the rest of the platoon up and with weapons in hand when we reached our sleeping quarters. Mathghaman was already heading down toward the great hall, the rest of the Tuacha behind him. We fell in with our teams, sheathing the Swords and accepting our pistols from our ATLs. Whatever was going on, we weren't the sole investigators anymore.

We came out into the great hall at the base of the tower. It was dimly lit by a couple of candles and the moonlight coming in the windows high up in the walls, since the fire had been allowed to die down as night rolled on. Now, that just meant it was dim enough that I could barely make out the two sides who were shouting at each other.

Urgant, wearing little more than an unbelted tunic, his previously immaculately groomed hair and beard now in disarray, was pointing at Vepogenus and bellowing. Vepogenus, who was much more dressed, in tunic, breeches, and boots, his sword by his side, was watching the castellan with his jaw set and his eyes hard.

"*You* brought this here!" Spittle flew from Urgant's mouth. "Never have such haunts crossed my threshold, until *you* came!" He stepped forward, one of his knights trying to hold him back, as Vepogenus and several of the king's retainers took an aggressive half step forward in reply. I'd been in enough brawls as a Marine to recognize the signs that things were about to get out of control. "What did you do, Vepogenus? Did the Peruni buy you, or did they simply find a crack in that façade of honor you wear with such pride?"

He turned to look at us as our motley little warband came down the steps and into the hall, finding ourselves just about in the middle of the standoff. That pointing finger swiveled toward us. "Or was it them? You bring foreigners into my house, and sorcerous phantoms come screaming through my halls!"

"You mean the phantoms let loose by the book one of *your* people left open in the upper room of this tower?" Bailey's voice cracked across the room. "A book that just so happened to burst into flame when the Sword of Iudicael touched it?"

There was a moment's silence at that, then the shouting started again, this time too loud and too confused to make much out.

Cailtarni's voice rose above the clamor. "You harbor sorcerers and witches, and accuse the Bearers of the Two Swords, not to mention your own king?" He shoved his way to the front of the press and drew his sword, pointing it at Urgant. "I name you traitor and maleficarus, Urgant. Defend yourself and your castle, or submit and burn!"

* * *

The courtyard underneath the shadow of the tower looked like it had been used as everything from parade ground to amphitheater to dueling ground. It was now laid out as the latter, with a ring set up with willow poles topped by small red flags. Benches had been set up around it, just beneath the massive double doors that led into the receiving hall just below the great hall.

Those benches weren't going to be all that full, from the looks of things. This wasn't a duel for the majority of the farmers and husbandmen who supported the castle. This would be witnessed only by those who had already been in the great hall when Cailtarni had issued his challenge.

Cailtarni and Urgant stood at opposite sides of the ring, with Vepogenus standing in the center. Regardless of Urgant's accusations, the king's right hand would oversee this. He stood in full armor, the scales of his breastplate trimmed in gold, though even that was scarred up. His helmet was under his arm, but his well-used sword hung at his side, and I got the distinct impression from the way he looked at Urgant that he wouldn't mind using it, whoever won.

Cailtarni was pulling on his gauntlets, already clad in the battered, patinaed armor he'd worn across the plains and mountains of the Empire's northern marches. His gaze was fixed on Urgant, unblinking and baleful.

I'd had my issues with Cailtarni. He was loud, often overbearing, and seemed to have decided unilaterally that I was going to be his son-in-law. Yet he'd never backed down from a fight, and it was definitely to his credit that he'd been the first to issue the challenge to Urgant.

In a way, I felt bad about that. If anyone should probably have issued that challenge, it should have been one of us. He'd called *us* servants of the Outer Dark, after all.

I stepped up next to him, and he spared me a glance. "Stand aside, Conor. I know what you would say, but I'll not have it. *I* challenged, and *I* shall fight him."

I didn't really have an answer to that. I glanced over at Urgant in his gold-chased armor, pulling his gilded helmet on. "He's younger than you. Probably faster." As much as he seemed soft to me, I didn't doubt that Urgant was a fighter. You didn't get appointed castellan in this society otherwise.

Cailtarni smiled tightly and without humor as he pulled his helmet onto his head. "Younger, yes, though I would say rather, 'Less experienced.'"

"I hope you're right." My eye caught a young man standing behind Urgant, glaring daggers at us. "Who's the kid?"

Cailtarni looked up as he flexed his fingers around the grip of his shield. "Vist. Urgant's son, and worth less than the father, if you can believe it." His eyes narrowed. "He has been gallivanting around the kingdom for the last several years with several of his dissolute friends. I wonder what brings him back at just this time?"

If he had any theories, he didn't feel like sharing them, because he then drew his sword and stepped into the arena.

Urgant watched him, pulling on his own gauntlets without hurry, then finally took his shield from Vist—who was still glaring at all of us, almost without blinking—and then drew his sword and stepped out to meet Cailtarni.

Vepogenus raised his voice as the two lords approached the center of the ring. "A challenge of honor has been issued and accepted. Let Tigharn decide who is in the right."

Apparently, there wasn't a lot of ceremony around duels of honor among the Galel. With those words, Vepogenus simply stepped back and ducked out of the ring.

Without further fanfare, the two Galel knights bowed slightly to one another, then began to circle, shields held up and swords held in high guard.

They came together suddenly, blades clashing briefly before parting and continuing to circle. I'd gotten to know enough about swordsmanship to know that they were testing each other, probing each other's responses.

The next exchange of blows was fiercer, though Urgant hadn't quite seemed to be ready for it. Cailtarni came in fast, aiming a brutal cut at his opponent's head. Urgant got his shield up in time, but Cailtarni had already pulled the stroke and dipped his point toward the other man's leg.

Only a fast parry and a leap backwards saved Urgant from a serious injury. He was off balance now, though, and while Cailtarni had tried to play off the age difference, it appeared that he was going to try to end this quickly. He stayed on Urgant, hammering at him with a flurry of blows, driving him back toward the edge of the ring, battering at his shield even while Cailtarni kept closing the distance and keeping his own shield inside of the other knight's sword.

Even as I watched Urgant desperately try to open some space to maneuver and strike back, however, I could see that Cailtarni couldn't keep this up indefinitely. He *was* considerably older than Urgant, and while it was subtle, he was already starting to slow, barely minutes into the duel. Eventually, he was going to run out of steam, unless he got a good hit in.

Just as I thought it, he got his hit. It wasn't a game-ender, but the blow to Urgant's gilded helmet tore some of the gold plating off it and knocked his opponent sprawling.

Urgant adjusted fast, rolling off his shield and coming up onto a knee with the targe held out in front of him to cover his head. He was clearly rattled, though. There was not only a bright scar on his helmet, but it was partially dented where Cailtarni had hit him. That blow had rung his bell, no two ways about it. The fact that he was ready when Cailtarni waded in to finish the job said a lot.

I saw it before Cailtarni did. He'd rung Urgant's bell, rattled his brain, but the man was still ready for him as he moved in, sword raised high to deliver the killing blow.

Urgant struck low, lifting his shield to protect his head and swinging beneath it.

Cailtarni saw the stroke coming and danced backward, but he was ever so slightly too slow. I couldn't help but flinch a little as I saw the cut go deep into his leg.

If that wound was as high and as deep as it looked, Derelei's father was in deep trouble.

For a brief moment, there was a pause in the fight. Urgant was still down on one knee, his shield up, probably hurting from that blow to the head, despite the fact that his helm had saved his life. He wasn't in a good position to maneuver. Cailtarni had taken a single step back, but he was hurt badly, and he seemed to falter, just for a moment.

Then he lunged, even as Urgant started to get up.

Cailtarni came down on Urgant's shield with all his weight, his own sword going high even as he crushed the other man to the dirt. The sword flashed in the sun, just for a moment, and the two of them went still again, locked in a clinch.

Then Urgant went limp and fell to the ground as Cailtarni drew his sword blade out of the junction where the castellan's shoulder met his neck. Red blood glistened in the morning light.

Then a rush of crimson poured out down his leg, and Cailtarni fell to the ground beside his opponent.

CHAPTER 10

VIST screamed. It wasn't a sound of grief, not really. It was pure, unadulterated rage and hate. It was the sort of sound I almost expected more from one of the things of the Outer Dark than any man, let alone a Galel.

"Kill them!" He pointed a quivering finger at us, where we stood across the ring from his father's retainers. "That dog killed my father on the ground! Their lives are forfeit!"

"Listen to yourself, boy!" Vepogenus roared. "You would declare war on the king's guests?"

"The king lies wounded, and who is to say that you did not put him there?" Vist was quivering, his fists clenched at his side.

"Watch yourself, boy." Vepogenus stepped into the ring, not far from the bodies of the two combatants. Cailtarni was still twitching, but even if he was still conscious, he didn't have long. Several of us were starting to move forward, in the hopes that if we could get a tourniquet on him, we might still save his life, but the standoff wouldn't allow for it. Arrows were nocked to bowstrings and raised threateningly as soon as anyone on our side of the ring took a step. "Such accusations can lead only one place."

Canaul, however, wasn't having it. The massive, barrel-chested knight, though out of his armor, strode into the ring. "Let him defend his words if he will!" He stood above the two dead men, his feet apart and his hand on the blade at his waist. "Come down here and fight, boy, if you would dispute the results of a legal duel!"

Instead, Vist snatched the bow from a man behind him and shot Canaul in the chest.

Or, at least, he tried to. His aim wasn't that good, and the arrow lodged in Canaul's shoulder, slowed but not stopped by his padded jerkin. He jerked at the impact, gritting his teeth, but despite the blood that immediately started to soak his sleeve, he simply reached up, snapped off the arrow, and threw it on the ground at his feet.

That must have been just a little too much for Vist. He turned and fled inside the castle, several of his younger companions running inside after him, yelling and screaming.

There was some hesitation at first. I don't think the men-at-arms of Aullun knew exactly what to do. The duel had perhaps appeared to be inconclusive, but Urgant was dead and Vist was screaming bloody murder that the foreigners and the men who had brought the wounded king to their doorstep were trying to kill everyone inside.

It was confused and chaotic, and apparently someone decided to play it safe, because even as we started forward, the big double doors of the tower swung shut with a *boom.*

We were outside, while King Uven and a few of his retainers were shut inside, outnumbered and effectively unarmed.

This had just gotten a lot more interesting than we'd hoped.

* * *

The standoff solidified over the next hour. Vist had disappeared inside, and the doors were barred. Some of the men-at-arms up on the walls seemed to think they should keep us covered, and so long as the king was inside and we were outside, our status was a little iffy. Most of the men on the ground, however, who had seen the duel, and were then confronted by an increasingly irate Vepogenus, either laid down their weapons or joined us, especially after one of Vist's cronies, who hadn't made it inside in the initial rush, beat on the doors and called for someone to let him in, only to be met with silence.

"Bring it in." Gunny's voice was relatively quiet, but it carried to the team leaders, at least, who had been drawn up near him and Mathghaman. We joined him quietly, forming a discreet but solid perimeter, hands on weapons, just in case.

"What should we do?" Generally speaking, the platoon leadership had fallen to Gunny and Mathghaman. The King's Champion had declined to *lead* the platoon, recognizing that Gunny had filled that role since well before Captain Sorenson's disappearance. He was the best advisor we could have had, though, and Gunny often deferred to his judgment, regardless.

Mathghaman didn't respond right away. From the look on Bearrac's face, he was all for beating down the door and making Vist explain himself. That was Bearrac, though. Mathghaman was the wisest, and a great warrior in his own right, but Bearrac was the bull of the group, and would happily fight his way through most things.

Mathghaman studied the men around us and the castle looming overhead without comment or change of expression. "There is some dark power at work here. I doubt now that Urgant, arrogant as he might have been, knew anything about it. Why else would he have made the wild accusations that he did, and then accepted a duel?"

"You're thinking the kid?" Gunny had pitched his voice even lower, so that his words didn't travel far. None of the Galel knights around us seemed to notice.

"Possibly." Mathghaman's eyes were fixed on the windows above the great main doors leading into the tower. "Cailtarni did say that he had been traveling with 'dissolute' friends."

"So, again, what do we do?" Gunny sounded more than a little pensive, and I could imagine why. We'd agreed to accompany the king, but we weren't his people. What obligation did we really have, especially if this was turning into a civil war?

Of course, if it was a civil war, I expected that there was probably plenty of outside influence involved. That was the way every other such conflict I'd been involved in or adjacent to over the course of my Marine Corps career had gone. And if there was sorcery involved, then the Peruni and their headless Dullahan generals probably had more than a little to do with it.

There *were* other forces that wielded sorcery in this world, of course. I just hadn't seen any Fohorimans or corsairs this far south, and the Empire of Ar-Annator was right there across the border, had a history of sorcery, and had been gearing up for war for months.

That didn't solve our problem. We were essentially free agents, so which way we went was kind of up to Gunny's and Mathghaman's decision.

"Vist!" It looked like the battle lines had essentially settled out, with those outside who were still loyal to Vist—which didn't seem like a large number—having surrendered and been sequestered without their weapons. Vepogenus stood in the middle of the battleground, looking up at the windows above the doors. Several of us shifted to cover those windows with our rifles, just in case. Neither Gunny nor Mathghaman had declared for Vepogenus as such, but we were still awfully close, well within arrowshot. We were still inside the inner wall, and there wasn't anywhere in that courtyard that was out of range of an archer up in the tower. It was as much a defensive killing zone as it was a ceremonial auditorium. "Open the doors! If you let us in, all will be forgiven!"

That was questionable, and probably up to the king, not to Vepogenus, but I could give him some props as a negotiator. Most of the Galel we'd met so far were more likely to fight than talk. Not that I could fault them for that.

"If you keep these doors shut, however, I must assume that you are holding the king hostage, and declare you rebel and traitor, your life and all your holdings forfeit." Any congeniality in that grim old man's voice was gone, and his tone was as icy cold as winter in the Land of Ice and Monsters.

From the looks I could see among the knights nearby, though, there was a question of just what he could do.

Laying siege to the castle could be a long and costly process, especially at the spur of the moment and with fall coming on. This force wasn't ready for it, and the walls were between us and about seventy-five percent of the king's regiment.

He was met, however, with neither defiance nor surrender. Instead, only silence and stillness replied to the old man's ultimatum. If Vist had heard, he wasn't responding.

Vepogenus waited for a few more minutes, but still got no answer. Finally, he turned around, his face stony and his mouth tight, and strode back toward us.

He halted before Mathghaman, and for a moment, it looked like he was considering whether to demand or to ask. Finally, he bowed his head. "Lord Mathghaman. The word of your fellowship's prowess has traveled far, as have tales of your own exploits. Would you help us?"

Mathghaman turned to Gunny. "I do not make the final decisions for this brotherhood."

Gunny looked up at the tower. "Do you want to take the tower or rescue the king?"

Vepogenus seemed to think that over for a moment. I was sure that ultimately, he wanted to do both, but given the situation, he had to prioritize. "The king's life is most important. We cannot storm the tower while he lies inside." He looked over our exotic weapons and equipment. "Can you get inside and rescue him?"

"That depends." Gunny ran a thumb along his jaw. "Can you find us a way in that doesn't involve taking a battering ram to that door?"

* * *

The standoff continued throughout the day, and we needed just about every minute of it.

While we'd done a fair bit of close quarters work since coming through the mists, our last shooting package had been over a year before for us. Tactics can be practiced easily enough, but precision pistol shooting, which is vital to a hostage rescue mission, is a perishable skill.

With the rest of the castle outside the tower now secured, Gurke set up a pistol range outside where we could rotate guys through for a refresher as well as sort out who was going to be on an entry team and who was going to be on the cordon with a rifle. We could *not* afford to have a .45 caliber flyer hit a hostage or miss a bad guy just before a knife went into the king.

Team leaders went first. Bailey, predictably, did better than I did. I was a touch slower, and my group was about an inch wider, but I was still hitting in the A zone, so we were good.

Once that was taken care of, even as the *pop*s of pistol shots continued on the other side of the wall where a crowd of Galel had gathered around to watch, curious about these strange foreigners with their strange weapons, Gunny, the Tuacha, and the team leaders got down to planning.

Now, most of the raids we'd done in Syria hadn't come with the advantage of thorough advance intel on the layout of the target house. Of course, most of those compounds had been relatively simple compared to the tower we had to clear now, so kicking in the door and clearing the whole building had been pretty quick without a whole lot of detailed planning.

This was a whole different can of worms.

The tower was a good ten stories tall, and while the great hall and the upper room each took up about two stories, that still made for eight levels of rooms we had to clear. The defensive architecture of the stairs presented its own problems, too. Fighting up those steps, even with pistols against swords and axes, was going to be a bear. Better to find a way up to the top and clear down, but it wasn't as if we had helicopters here. Ladders would be good, but good luck finding a ten-story ladder that could get us up to the top of the tower.

So, we needed a pretty sound plan, a good distraction, and as extensive a picture of the inside of the tower as we could get.

This wasn't the world we'd come from, so there were no blueprints. The tower had been built over the course of a generation, and all the information we could get was by word of mouth. We were building sand table models of each floor, while we tried to work out a plan of attack and simultaneously tried to figure out, with Vepogenus's help, where Vist might be keeping the king.

I glanced up at the tower, even as Gunny put the finishing touches on the dirt map of the second floor up. The sun was high, and there were no clouds in the sky, but somehow that tower looked like it was in shadow. Not a good sign.

We had six hours until dark, and we were going to need every bit of it.

* * *

Sounds started to drift out of the tower about an hour before sunset. They were hard to make out at first. In fact, they were hardly noticeable at all.

Over time, though, we picked up on the droning, until it became a constant background buzz, with a strong overtone of fingernails on a chalkboard. It rose and fell, rather than being a consistent tone, but it never quite went away. I couldn't make out whether it was a chant or background noise to something weirder than that, and I wasn't sure I wanted to.

"We need to step up the timeline." Gunny was watching the tower, his eyes narrowed, the crow's feet around them deeper than usual. "I don't think we've got until nightfall."

As much as I didn't want to try to storm that place in broad daylight, I had to agree. Something was going on in there.

"Lord Vepogenus!" Gunny headed down toward where the king's second-in-command was directing some more of the royal forces inside the walls. He turned to shout over his shoulder. "Assault teams, start getting into position."

I looked around at Rodeffer, Farrar, and Santos. "That's our cue, gents."

We were lightly loaded, though we were still in mail, helmets, and chest rigs. We had our blades in addition to pistols—which were going to make the next phase slightly awkward—but the rifles had been left behind.

It felt strange, at first, heading up toward the top of the inner wall without weapons in hand. We needed to move quickly, though, and timing was going to be vital. The next few minutes would make or break this op.

We waited in the guard tower just about twenty paces from the main tower keep itself, joined by the rest of the platoon, even as the Galel outside the castle piled green wood and leaves onto the bonfires lit in the fields outside. Great, white plumes of smoke began to billow across the fields, over the walls, and toward the tower.

It had taken some serious guesswork, argument, and agonizing repetition of contingencies to figure out where those fires would be placed. It had still been a coin toss as to whether or not the wind would cooperate.

Or maybe it hadn't been. Fennean and Diarmodh had been down there a lot, come to think of it. Neither seemed to have the same direct line to powers above that Conall did, but they were still Tuacha.

Even as the smoke began to pour over the inner walls and obscure the tower, the *boom* of a ram hitting the main doors started to echo through the courtyard. That was our go signal.

If Vist had archers inside, this could go badly in the next few seconds, but that was largely what the smoke was for.

There'd been a time when I might have let one of the others take lead. That's the way it's supposed to work, after all, even in the regular grunt fireteams. The team leader is supposed to coordinate, not get stuck in first.

But there's a time and a place, and we were past the point where I really *needed* to coordinate these guys. We were all professionals and warriors. That was the only way we'd survived here. There's no room in a place like this for someone who needs to have his hand held for every move he makes. Besides, we'd all trained and fought together for so long that we were now a finely tuned machine, each man already knowing what the others were going to do even before they did it.

So, I burst out of the tower at a sprint, pulling a ladder with me, bent half double to make myself a smaller target, just in case Vist did have archers watching the walls, and led the way toward the tower.

CHAPTER 11

The door had been shut, but not barred. That might have been an oversight. It might have been someone inside who'd realized that he was on the wrong side of things, leaving a route open. Either way, it meant we didn't have to climb to the window above it, so we left the ladder against the battlements, drew our pistols, and headed inside.

We were in a guard chamber just above the great hall. The inner door was shut, and there was no one inside, though we had split on the way through the door, weapons up, clearing every corner just to make sure. Then Santos was moving to the door, his pistol pointed at the opening, while Farrar moved up behind him, reaching for the handle.

I suppressed a cough as the smoke got thicker. We were on the far side of the tower from the fires, but that didn't make much difference when our screen was beginning to blanket the entire castle.

Farrar eased the door open. The guard room was getting crowded, as the rest of the platoon quietly made entry, stacking up behind us. We were staying soft, since it didn't sound like anyone in the tower knew we were there yet, but we still needed to move fast.

The door creaked a little as it opened, but then Santos was going through, his .45 leveled, gripped in two hands, punching the gun out as he cleared the threshold and entered what had once been Urgant's quarters. Farrar went in right behind him, pivoting to cover his back as he made entry, and I was right behind Farrar. We spread out to cover the entire room, the four-poster bed in the center along with the chests against the walls creating some dead space that we needed to clear.

"Moving." Santos kept his pistol pointed as he swung around the bed, confirming that there was no one hiding behind it or underneath. All the while, that droning continued, uninterrupted by the steady, rhythmic *boom* of the ram hitting the doors downstairs.

"One and Tuacha up, everyone else, down." We did know that there were several floors excavated underneath the tower, extending about three stories into the hilltop. It had to have taken some serious work to dig them out, but it was also possible that much of the stone the castle had been built from had actually been quarried from the hill itself, which would make some sense. We hadn't asked, though. We just needed to know where we needed to go and what we needed to clear.

Mathghaman and Bearrac beat us to the door and the staircase. They hadn't trained as long as we had, but the Tuacha being the Tuacha, they flowed out into the stairwell like they'd been doing it for decades. They made the JSOC guys look like amateurs.

Much like their rifles, the Tuacha's pistols were different from ours. The best way I can describe them is a cross between a LeMat and a Mauser C96. They still handled them as if they'd been born with them in their hands, and the one time I'd picked one up, it had fit my hand better than even the 1911 MEU(SOC) pistol that I was now carrying.

Fennean, Diarmodh, and Eoghain followed Mathghaman up the steps while Bearrac held security on the flights leading down. Then it was our turn, and Santos took the lower level while I led the way after Bearrac.

There were a lot of us on those stairs at the moment, but there were at least three levels to clear between us and the top. Mathghaman hardly paused at the door to the next room up, which had been just below our quarters only a day before. He simply flowed in, the rest following, as we pushed up to continue past, covering up the stairs as the Tuacha vacated them.

They'd have that room cleared in an eyeblink, and we'd probably slow them down, but they were team players, anyway.

I found myself out front, my pistol pointed up at the curve in the staircase, and kept moving.

The stairs were tough going. My legs were already starting to burn, regardless of the miles we'd covered on foot. My heart was hammering in my chest and my breath was getting a little intense. It wasn't just the stairs, either. Close quarters combat tends to do that.

We worked our way up toward our former sleeping quarters. The stairway hadn't changed at all since the night before, though it was currently slightly better lit than it had been, since the sun was still up.

It also hadn't changed in one other important way. The noise that throbbed through the tower was getting louder as we moved up. Whatever was happening, it sounded like it was centered on that upper room. Again.

Still, we had to clear each and every room in the tower, at least until one of us found the king. We couldn't take the chance that we'd bypass where he was only to get him killed while we ran toward the noise.

I paused at our former door just long enough to get a squeeze from Rodeffer, then we were both going through, tucking our weapons just long enough to clear the threshold before punching them out as we each pivoted toward the inside of the room. There aren't really any corners in a round tower, but old habits die hard.

The place was untouched since we'd left it. Our rucks were even still there—we'd grabbed weapons and gear when the challenge had been issued, but had left the packs behind, somewhat to our chagrin when those doors had closed. From the looks of things, no one had even set foot in the room since we'd left it. We quickly consolidated and started out into the stairwell again, as that creepy droning got louder, falling in behind the Tuacha as they flowed upward, effortless and silent.

They paused sooner than I'd expected. Bearrac stepped out toward the outer wall as Mathghaman turned inward, right about where I would have thought there would be a door, but there hadn't been when Bailey and I had gone up those stairs after the phantoms. Suddenly, there was a door there.

I felt a chill. Had it been there all along, but disguised? Why hide a door that high in a tower? And how had it been hidden? Some clever trick of stonework? Or something more sinister?

Either way, it was there, and Mathghaman went in, Fennean on his heels.

Gunfire erupted from inside, and there was a sudden hitch in the droning chant.

The rest of the Tuacha flowed into the hidden room as the gunfight got more intense. I was right behind Farrar, and I urged him up the steps as a strangled shout that sounded like Vist echoed down the stairs. That had definitely come from that upper room where Bailey and I had found the grimoire.

We raced up the last flight of stairs and burst out into the upper room. The table was still there, but now King Uven was lying on it, phantoms circling above him, their faces skeletal, their bodies mere rag-draped torsos with grasping hands reaching for the king. Vist drew a wicked-looking knife as he stepped away from a hooded and cloaked figure bent over what looked an awful lot like the book that had burned to ash when I'd touched it with the Sword of Iudicael.

The hooded figure looked up as Vist raised that knife, his eyes glittering in the pale glow cast by the circling phantoms. I caught a glimpse of eyes that gleamed deep beneath the hood as a hand reached out and a strangled cry was cut off by the thunder of gunfire.

Farrar and I had both identified the most immediate threat, which was Vist. He was about to plunge that dagger through King Uven's heart. Both of us shot him through the skull from ten feet away, the heavy .45 caliber bullets smashing through bone and brain matter, spattering the sorcerer with gore.

That one didn't seem to notice, but pointed a finger at Farrar and said something in a language that sounded an awful lot like something I'd hear from Dragon Mask. The sound of it immediately gave me a headache, and

Farrar staggered as if he'd been hit, dropping to a knee, which unfortunately put the king between him and the sorcerer.

I kept moving, sidestepping out of the fatal funnel of the stairwell and around the table. The sorcerer turned to me, then, that pointing finger tracking toward my face.

I shot him twice in the chest, once in the skull, putting out that glittering light in his eyes permanently.

The phantoms went nuts.

Shrieking and screaming, they started to spin around the room like something out of a haunted house cartoon. The temperature dropped precipitously, until my breath was coming out of my mouth and nose in a cloud.

The rest of the team was in the room by then, guns up and searching for targets, but there were none. We couldn't exactly shoot things that weren't remotely physical, and the two living men who had been targets were both very thoroughly dead.

Even as we spread out and closed in on the table where the king lay, his tunic off, apparently unconscious and sweating despite the icy cold that gripped the room, I thought I saw a darker shadow near the ceiling, and what might have been glowing eyes, faintly purple, glaring down at us.

For a moment, we just stood there, weapons still pointed at either the phantoms or the dead bodies on the floor, fingers hovering near triggers, not sure what to do. I'd hoped that killing the sorcerer might have interrupted whatever he'd set in motion, but it looked as if whatever it was, it was a little too far along.

Holstering my pistol, I drew the Sword of Iudicael. It had stopped this weirdness once. Maybe it could do it again.

Those vague purple pinpricks of eyes, that seemed to disappear when I looked directly at them, seemed to narrow. The phantoms, already agitated, swooped in at me with screams and howls, but none of them quite wanted to get within reach of that smoky, blessed blade.

"Vince, get the king off that table." Whatever was going on here, King Uven was at the center of it. If we removed him, maybe we could end this. Regardless, he was our package, anyway.

Santos holstered his own pistol and stepped toward the table as Farrar, who seemed mostly recovered from whatever the sorcerer had tried to do to him, and Rodeffer shifted to cover the room and the stairs. The gunfire down below seemed to have stopped for the moment.

I pointed the Sword at that shadow near the ceiling. It seemed like the thing to do. Once again, I got that impression of a pained squint, and then the shadow disappeared. In a split second, so did the howling phantoms. The silence that followed was almost deafening.

I keyed my radio. "Gunny, this is One. Package secured."

CHAPTER 12

"THAT doesn't look like a Galel."

Since the weirdness had finally dispersed after the shadow near the ceiling had disappeared, we had held our position instead of trying to move the king. He was still unconscious, and we didn't know exactly what had been done to him. It could be dangerous to move him under those circumstances. Of course, I also thought it was probably dangerous to keep him there, where sorcery had already torn aside the veil and started to let something through, but it was a balancing act, and Mathghaman seemed to think that holding what we had had been the right call.

"No, it is not." Mathghaman and I were standing over the bloodied corpse of the sorcerer. His face was a little misshapen from the bullet hole I'd put through the bridge of his nose, but we could still see enough of his features to recognize that he didn't belong there.

"He's not a Peruni either." I tilted my head to get a better look. The man was shorter than any of the Peruni we'd faced, though the closest I'd been to any of the ruling tribe of the Empire of Ar-Annator had been the delegation in Cor Legear, the same delegation that had murdered several of King Uven's guards to use as meat puppets in a sorcerous attack on us and the king before they'd fled over the border. They'd been tall, pale, and dark-haired, with spare, hawk-like features. This man was different, flat-faced and faintly squint-eyed. He was also shaved bald under the hood, with a neatly trimmed strip of beard on his chin. "Or an Avur."

Mathghaman shook his head. "No. He is of the Sontamnos. They are a tribe far to the southeast, beyond the lands of the Peruni." His eyes narrowed. "They are not subjects to Ar-Annator, though there have been tales of alliances between them. They are a secretive people, rarely venturing out of their mountain fastnesses. Even the Peruni fear their sorceries."

I may as well ask the obvious question. "So, what's he doing here?"

"That is the question." Mathghaman turned to Vepogenus, flanked by the two Galel guards who were watching as Conall and one of Urgant's physicians tended to King Uven. "Once the king has been taken downstairs, this body should be taken outside the walls and burned to ash."

Even with a gaping hole through his skull, the sorcerer's corpse still managed to exude a palpable air of menace.

Vepogenus, who looked older than he had only a day before, nodded. "What of Vist?"

Mathghaman looked down at the young man, who seemed shrunken and pathetic in death. "Bury him. He is beyond help or harm. A fool, lost now through his own foolishness." He seemed genuinely saddened, even though I didn't think he had ever met Vist before the day prior. That was Mathghaman. He could be grim and implacable when the situation called for it, but I didn't think there was a malicious bone in that man's body.

Vepogenus nodded, and called down the steps, even as Diarmodh, the physician, and two of Vepogenus's own men-at-arms carefully lifted the king onto a litter. Two more guards came up, wearing the badges of Aullun, and Vepogenus pointed them toward the sorcerer's corpse. They hesitated. They must have heard about who this man had been, and they were understandably reluctant to get too close.

A sharp word from the king's right-hand man, they moved quickly, though they still lifted the body gingerly. For a brief moment, I thought I saw the dead man's eyes flicker and move, but it might have just been my imagination, piggybacking on the Galel guards' own fears.

Or maybe it wasn't. I'd seen the eyes in the severed head of a sea serpent come alive again after we'd shot them out. Sorcery is wild and unpredictable, and that's one of the things that makes it dangerous.

The death of your own soul is, of course, one of the other things.

Even as the dead sorcerer was dragged down the steps and they got the king on the litter, Uven's eyes fluttered, and he lifted his head. A murmur escaped his lips, but I couldn't make it out before he slumped again. Still, he was moving, and that had to be a good sign.

Vepogenus stayed where he was as they carried the king down the stairs, moving with great care not to jostle their warrior sovereign. I watched them go, wondering how Uven would react when he woke up. From the first day we'd met him, months before, I'd always gotten the impression of a young man who would far rather be out in the fields and mountains, fighting back the enemies of his people, than holding court. To be carried around like an invalid, not to mention being taken hostage and nearly sacrificed to some creature of the Outer Dark, would be agonizing to him. I felt sorry for him, even though I knew that he'd probably hate that just as much as I would in his place.

Since Vepogenus hadn't moved to follow, I assumed he wanted to talk, and apparently Gunny and Mathghaman agreed, so we all just sort of stayed where we were as the guards moved down the stairs and out of the room.

That hard old man turned to us then and bowed his head. "You and your companions, Conor McCall, have done great service to the Kingdom of Cor Legear once again." Because I'd picked up the Sword of Iudicael off the battlefield in the north, I had become the Galel's go-to man to address, as the Sword Bearer. Bailey was one now, too, and was beginning to command as much deference. It always made me somewhat uncomfortable, since I wasn't in charge of anyone but Team One, which was Santos, Rodeffer, Farrar, and myself. Gunny and Mathghaman were running this rodeo. That didn't stop the Galel, though. "We owe you a great debt."

Vepogenus, for all his hard-nosed stoicism, however, looked old, tired, and downright uncomfortable. I thought I could see why, but I held my peace.

Bailey, however, didn't. "But this ain't over, is it?" He looked around the room. "Once might be an accident, but between Lemmanonius, the attack in Cor Legear, an ambush outside Cor Wudrun, and now this, I'm starting to think there's something rotten in the Kingdom of Cor Legear."

Gunny shot him a look, but if Vepogenus took offense, he didn't show it. He only nodded grimly. "We are a proud people, and that pride can leave openings for darker forces. I fear that our enemies are even now taking advantage."

"It certainly looks that way." Gunny was being somewhat more diplomatic than Bailey, who subsided with a glance down at the floor. The Galel might look up to us as Sword Bearers, but Gunny was still the man, and we had to respect that. "You're worried about more than just Aullun."

Vepogenus nodded, glancing off to the north and west, where Cor Legear lay. "There are those who believe they have a stronger claim to the throne than Uven. As odious a man as he was, I would not have counted Urgant among them." His frown deepened. "I fear we have greater challenges ahead."

"You think that some of those pretenders might have struck a bargain with the Peruni?" Gunny nodded toward the stairs where the guards had disappeared with the body. "Or with those… Sontamnos?"

"Or with the creatures they serve." Vepogenus nodded. "We have had no word from Cor Legear in some time, but I fear that news of the king's wound may have already traveled there. There are those who would quickly move to take advantage, with or without the urging of the things of the Outer Dark." He looked even more dour. "And yet, I must needs leave some of the king's bodyguard here, because we cannot leave Aullun ungoverned and unguarded."

We'd been there before. As far as I had heard, Fortrenn was still holding down the fort at Lemmanonius, where he had taken over after Achivir had been revealed as the pawn of a merrow. If we were riding into outright rebellion and civil war, I understood why Vepogenus might begrudge losing a single sword on the way.

Mathghaman and Gunny shared a look. While I make no pretentions about being the best at reading a room, I could tell what was going on.

Vepogenus felt the walls closing in. He could probably handle this himself, *if* he had a clear mandate from the king. Without it, King Uven being incapacitated, this could easily spiral out of control, particularly if any rebel lords were Machiavellian enough to accuse him of doing exactly what they were doing.

As the Sword Bearers, Bailey and I carried some weight with us. As just Recon Marines, obvious foreigners, we might be accused of, again, doing just what the Peruni were definitely doing, taking a hand in local politics. Even though those politics seemed to have some serious metaphysical repercussions attached. But as the Sword Bearers, at least in the Galel imagination, we were somehow above all that.

Vepogenus *wanted* to ask for our help. He wasn't sure whether he could or should, however. There was that Galel pride at work, but there was also a degree of uncertainty. Sure, we'd trekked across the northern marches of the Empire with Galel knights, but Galan had been the one tasked with retrieving the Sword of Categyrn, and he was dead while Bailey was carrying the Sword. Now, while some of the junior knights were still with us, folded into the king's bodyguard, Cailtarni was dead, too. He had some of the same faith in the Sword Bearers as the others, brought on by generations of stories of the hallowed weapons, but he still didn't *know* for sure where we stood.

There'd been a time when that would have been a question. When we wouldn't have known, ourselves, where we stood.

Now, however, that had changed, I think without most of us even realizing it.

Severed from the world we'd known, and Big Marine Corps with it, we had become essentially free agents. Our bond with Mathghaman and his Tuacha companions was one of mutual respect, shared hardship, and mutual assistance. We were brothers. It was simple as that. Mathghaman, and those who followed him, were bound in fealty to King Caedmon, but I'd gotten the impression that the King of the Isle of Riamog didn't mind his Champion being something of a free agent, himself.

There had been three ways that free agency could have gone. We could have struck out on our own and tried to conquer our own little corner of the world. Become warlords. Our first fight with the Dovos nal Uergal had demonstrated how ill-advised that would have been right off, and we'd learned a lot more in the year and a half since.

Likewise, we could have joined the first strong faction we'd encountered. Captain Sorenson had opted for that course of action, and it had ended with his heart being cut out to open the way to Vaelor's Throne.

We'd taken the third option, which left us still as free agents of a sort, but had essentially committed us to taking a side. Wherever and whenever the Outer Dark reached its claws into this world…

We were agin it.

The Marine Corps talks a lot about honor and integrity. Unfortunately, with a few notable exceptions, that's turned into corporate boilerplate. Here, it had to be genuine. The predators of the Outer Dark would eat you alive otherwise.

Gunny was apparently thinking the same thing. "There's sorcery at work here. I think that makes it our bailiwick." He glanced at Mathghaman and got a solemn nod. The King's Champion thought it was a good choice. That mattered to all of us.

Vepogenus was too old and too stoic to openly show his relief, but there was a flicker of it in his eyes. "I thank you, on King Uven's behalf." He took a deep breath. "We will ride out in the morning, once we have a wagon for the king to ride in.

"I hope and pray that we do not face worse than this in Cor Legear."

CHAPTER 13

IT took most of another six days to reach Cor Legear.

We stayed alert the entire way. We'd already been hit twice since reentering the kingdom. There was no room to relax. We rode with weapons at hand and heads up, watching the fields, the roads, and the trees around us, and we set watches at night. The Galel did the same. Everyone had taken the lesson of the last couple of weeks to heart.

Still, we rode up toward the massive, blocky structure of the citadel of Cor Legear unmolested. Whoever was pulling the strings on this infiltration and rebellion, they either weren't ready for us to move so quickly, or they had something worse in mind.

I tended to expect the latter, and I wasn't alone.

Banners flew from the battlements and the towers around the citadel, and I found myself frowning as I looked at them. Something was off. When I glanced at Vepogenus, who was riding with us, just behind the king's wagon, I saw the same scowl on his face.

Something was very off.

"Those aren't King Uven's banners." Gunny was the first one to put it into words.

"No, they are not." The tone of his voice promised violent death to *somebody*. "And only the king's banners may fly from the keep, and then only when the king is in residence."

Sure enough, there was a flag flying from the highest point of the huge, square keep. There was red on it, but it wasn't Uven's red, blue, and gold.

"The pretenders you were afraid of?" I didn't think any of us really needed to ask.

Vepogenus nodded. "Perhaps rumors have reached the city. The king has, after all, been struck down twice." He spurred his horse forward. "Let us find out."

Gunny glanced over at us, and then reined in, falling back to meet me first. "I'd say we should stay back, but you and Sean have some status with those holy pig-stickers of yours, Conor. You ride up there with him." He nodded to Santos, who returned it. "Vince and Roy can handle anything that comes along down here."

I nodded, and spurred Allon after Vepogenus. Bailey would catch up.

Vepogenus glanced over his shoulder as I pulled my horse alongside, and he nodded slightly. Together, even as Bailey pounded up the road on Ualtar, the big black that had become his primary saddle horse, we moved forward.

We got some looks as we rode into the city at the base of the hill. Some held open relief. Others were concerned. Others looked downright scared. Nobody stepped out to stop us or even inquire about our business as we rode toward the citadel, though. Somehow, I didn't think that was a good sign. It reminded me of some of the villages we'd rolled into in Syria, usually right before we got hit, either by ISIS or the Iranians.

The guards at the gate didn't seem to have changed much since the night that we'd tried unsuccessfully to intercept Brule and his Peruni friends as they'd fled the aftermath of their attack. They stepped forward, their spears held ready, but stopped as they recognized Vepogenus. The older man bowed his head and touched a hand to the rim of his helmet. "Lord Vepogenus. We did not know you were coming." There was a nervousness in his voice and manner that was somewhat telling. All was not well in Cor Legear, and these guys were wondering just how the king's uncle, a known warrior and skullsplitter, was going to react.

As for Vepogenus, he simply leaned on his saddle. "I'm sure you didn't. After all, we were supposed to be at Cor Chatha right about now." He glanced meaningfully up at the banners fluttering above. I still couldn't make out the heraldry, but that they weren't carrying the royal crest was even more obvious now.

The guards glanced at each other. The older man cleared his throat. "Ehm, Lord Vepogenus… We heard the news. It was thought… Well…"

"What was thought?" Vepogenus's voice cracked across the gateway.

The older guard glanced at Bailey, then at me. We were still odd-looking to those Galel who hadn't gotten used to our digital camouflage, our rifles, and the chest rigs we still wore everywhere. The silver-chased hilts of the Sword of Categyrn, however, and the gold-chased Sword of Iudicael, drew the eye more than the rest of our gear. Old boy's eyes widened slightly, as he gulped.

"We heard about the king's death, my lord." He looked up uncertainly, then past Vepogenus's shoulder at the wagon still trundling its way up the road. "We had assumed it would take a few more days to arrange to bring the body back to the tombs of his forefathers."

"The king's death, hm?" Vepogenus glanced at me, then at Bailey. "Who brought this news, my lad?"

"I do not know, my lord. Lord Tharain announced it only a few days ago. He said that raiders given gold by the lord of Cor Wudrun, who has sold his loyalty to the Empire, ambushed the king while hunting and slew him." The man looked steadily more nervous as he continued to talk, Vepogenus's unblinking stare boring into him. Vepogenus could give Gunny a challenge in the "basilisk stare" department.

"Did he, indeed?" His eyes narrowed, and he changed tacks. "Tell me, Aniel, what did you think when you heard this?" He was feeling the guard out. I could sort of understand why. We had a considerable fighting force with us, even without Bargoit and his fifty riders and men-at-arms whom Vepogenus had left back at Aullun. But we were at the doorstep of the strongest fortress in the kingdom. If this turned hostile now, we were not in a good place to prosecute a siege.

Aniel seemed to understand that he was being tested. He stood a little straighter. "I wished that I could have been there to defend him, my lord." His eyes flickered ever so slightly, as if he wanted to glance over his shoulder. Something about this was making him even more nervous. He looked for a moment like he wanted to say something more, but he bit back the words.

Vepogenus glanced at the younger man, who was wisely staying back and keeping his mouth shut. Then his eyes moved back to Aniel, who had taken half a step forward, as if to assert his seniority and shield the younger guard. Decent of him.

"If Tharain believes the king dead, what has he done in our absence?" Vepogenus's tone was almost friendly now, but if anything, that only seemed to make the guards even more nervous. I could imagine why.

"He has taken up the regency, since the prince is still a babe in arms," was the reply. "He is even now meeting with some lords of the south to prepare a response to Cor Wudrun's treachery."

"Is he now?" Vepogenus wasn't going to lay things out for these guys in the gateway, but from the look on his face, he was considering his options.

It was a tricky situation. If this Tharain had acted in good faith, it would do a lot of damage to just go charging in. Likewise, if he *hadn't* acted in good faith, charging into a relatively unknown situation in close quarters could be disastrous. We needed to be subtle.

Not usually a Marine strength, subtlety. But we could learn. We had been learning ever since we'd passed through the mists. Surviving that trek with Dragon Mask had taken some careful maneuvering.

"Well, send word to Lord Tharain that I am here to see him, if he isn't too busy." A threatening sarcasm dripped from Vepogenus's voice, and both guards picked up on it immediately. The younger man quickly turned on his heel and ran up the hill toward the inner gate, even before Aniel could turn to him to give him the order.

More and more of the king's knights were riding up to join us now. Canaul had held his peace even as he'd ridden up right behind the three of us, and had been sitting his horse listening as Aniel had described Tharain's accusation of Cor Wudrun. Given how angry the giant of a man had been at Urgant's insinuations of the same, I couldn't help but be impressed. He was more of a strategist than he'd appeared.

Aniel was watching the cavalcade moving up in front of and behind the wagon. I glanced at Vepogenus and then Bailey, wondering about that wagon. What would happen if Vepogenus simply announced, quietly enough, that the king was still alive? But again, probably not the time or place. We still needed to feel the atmospherics out, and the feeling down in the city hadn't been promising.

Finally, an honor guard of men-at-arms, in a combination of the royal red and gold and the red and white of the banners overhead, came down toward the outer gate. The younger guardsman wasn't in the lead; he was two paces behind the tall knight in green and silver who was striding down the slope faster than any of the men-at-arms. I could tell he was a knight more by the quality of his gear than anything else. Well, that and the way he carried himself. This was a man to be reckoned with. Lean, broad shouldered, with a fine featured, aquiline face and a massive, sweeping handlebar mustache, he radiated competence and confidence.

He also radiated a certain grim urgency as he got closer. He beat the guards to us by half a dozen paces and put his hand on Vepogenus's stirrup. "Lord Vepogenus. You have returned." He swallowed, and there might have been tears in his eyes. "The news… Is it true?"

Vepogenus studied him for a long moment, appraisingly. Finally, his voice low and words measured, he said, "Lord Argentocoxus. It is not. The king lives." He looked up toward the keep appraisingly. "Perhaps, however, it would be best not to say so too loudly, just yet."

It said a great deal about both the situation at hand, and Argentocoxus's character, that he followed Vepogenus's gaze and nodded. "Indeed." He glanced behind us. "How many survived?"

"Most of the band we set out with. I had to leave Lord Bargoit and fifty riders at Aullun." At the younger knight's raised eyebrow, he shook his head. "A tale for another time. How many riders does Tharain have here within the citadel?"

"Nearly two hundreds, and another seven hundreds plus two thousand men-at-arms camped on the outskirts of the city, with more coming every day." Both knights had spoken in low tones, and now changed their demeanors again as the rest of the guards caught up. "Lord Tharain means to quash this rebellion before the Peruni can take advantage."

That statement, of course, left the question of *what* rebellion rather open.

A rather pudgy, officious-looking man in red and white harrumphed as he caught up, shooting what might have been a glare at Argentocoxus if he'd had the guts, which he didn't appear to. "Lord Vepogenus." He bowed. "Lord Tharain is overjoyed that you have returned in this trying time. Please, come with me. I will take you to him."

Vepogenus looked at Bailey, Canaul, and me, nodded, then swung off his horse. The three of us followed suit, and the pudgy guy started to protest. "Lord Vepogenus, only..."

A raised hand and a steely glare silenced him. "The Sword Bearers come with me. Even Lord Tharain, in these trying times, would not refuse them."

The man blinked, then bowed again, turned stiffly, and headed back up the hill.

Without a backward glance, Vepogenus started after him, Argentocoxus at his heels. We fell in behind them.

"Dude." Bailey's voice was low, and he spoke English. "What the hell are *we* supposed to do?"

I shrugged, keeping my own reply as quiet as his question. "We're the Sword Bearers. Look intimidating and back Vepogenus's play."

Bailey returned the shrug with a lift of his eyebrows, and we headed up toward the keep with Vepogenus and Argentocoxus.

If I'd thought things were tense outside, it was nothing compared to the atmosphere inside.

The guardhouse at the top of the steps was downright crowded, with men in both the royal red of the king's guard and the red and white of what I was presuming was Tharain's people. They were also noticeably divided up into those two colors, with the king's men on one side and Tharain's on the other. It seemed that not everyone was thrilled with the would-be new management.

When we passed through the short hallway into the reception hall, it got worse.

Tharain stood on the dais, next to the throne. Judging by the red and white surcoat he wore, it had to be him. Slightly older than King Uven, he looked faintly softer, though none of the Galel knights could be called exactly *soft*. His hair fell to his shoulders in auburn waves, and his mustache was waxed and upturned.

It was the look on his face that made me instantly dislike him. He looked simultaneously self-satisfied and as unctuous as Urgant had been.

He was also surrounded by more men-at-arms in full armor, and though they didn't have their spears, they wore swords. Several more knights, notable by the finery of their clothing, the fact that they each wore their own colors, and that they wore swords but no armor, were also gathered near the dais.

The majority of the occupants of the hall stood along the walls to either side, and few of them looked happy. It almost looked like those armored men-at-arms were there to keep them away from Tharain.

Vepogenus strode up to the base of the dais and stood, offering no bow nor genuflection. "Lord Tharain."

Tharain turned his head slowly from where he was talking to a red-haired knight in yellow and green, looking down at Vepogenus with not quite contempt. "Lord Vepogenus. It is customary to render some homage to the Lord Regent."

Vepogenus didn't move a muscle, and didn't even acknowledge Tharain's words. "Tell me, Lord Tharain, where did the news of the king's death come from? I certainly sent no such missive."

Tharain was smooth, I'll grant him that. He didn't even blink. "A messenger arrived from Aullun only days hence." He looked around at the assembly in the reception hall. "As I was the highest lord here, and faced with such dire circumstances, the king's son being yet a babe, I acted as swiftly as I could, out of sheer necessity. We have yet to begin the formal mourning for our lamented sovereign, but the urgency of this rebellion, while the

Empire masses its forces on our border, meant there was no time to waste."

It was a practiced speech. I wondered how often he'd given it over the last couple of days. I wasn't the only one, either.

"Fine words, Lord Tharain," Vepogenus said, making no effort to disguise his disgust. "I'm sure that many of your peers have thought so. However, while your aims *might* be commendable, your haste is not. As I said, I sent no such message. Nor do I know of anyone in Aullun who should have, considering the king was still very much alive when we arrived there, even before we discovered Lord Vist's own treason."

Tharain's composure *almost* slipped, then. He was good, though, and I might have only imagined it. "You said he *was* alive? Does he live still?"

"He lives still. He lies wounded, but he lives. He is in the wagon we brought from Aullun, just outside the gate." Vepogenus stared Tharain down. "There is, therefore, no need for a Lord Regent."

"If the king lies wounded, to the point he requires a wagon, then I would say there very much is such a need." Tharain looked around at the assembled knights. "With rebellion in our own heartland and war on our borders, someone must take the reins while our king recovers."

If he recovers went unsaid, but was pretty loud, anyway.

"If anyone were to do so, it would be Lord Vepogenus, not you, Lord Tharain."

King Uven's voice was a hoarse rasp, but even as weakened as he was, he still made his words echo off the stone walls. All eyes turned toward the door.

Lord Canaul and Lord Deototreic flanked the king, who leaned on their shoulders, though he still walked under his own power, if barely. He was still in tunic and breeches, too weak to don his armor or his weapons, his hair hanging lank on either side of his face, his beard untrimmed, his face hollow-cheeked and pale, dark circles under his sunken eyes. He looked like death warmed over, but he was very much alive.

For a brief moment, everyone in the hall seemed to freeze, Tharain and his cronies included. Then, with a rustle of movement, the crowd at the sides of the hall bent the knee, genuflecting before the king.

Tharain and the group at the dais, however, seemed to still be frozen in shock. Tharain not the least.

"It is customary to render some homage to your king, Lord Tharain." Vepogenus's voice cracked across the hall.

The pause seemed to stretch, the silence as the echoes of Vepogenus's words growing downright oppressive. For a long, long moment, Tharain just stared at King Uven, his face still impassive.

My hand was on my rifle's pistol grip, ready to snatch the weapon up and open fire in a heartbeat. Out of the corner of my eye, I saw Bailey shift position, moving to where he could engage with a clear field of fire and not have to worry about accidentally shooting one of the loyal men along the wall.

Then Tharain's face twisted with fury, and he pointed a finger at the king. For a brief moment, it almost looked like that finger was crooked and clawed, but it passed quickly.

"It isn't bad enough that your lowborn family seized the throne and continues to cling to it! No, even an invalid child who would throw the crown into battle like a common man-at-arms *still* weighs down the throne when it must needs have a true leader sitting upon it! Well, I will stand by and bow to this folly no longer!"

His expression had been warped and twisted already, but when he threw his head back and pronounced a single name at the top of his lungs, I could swear that his face turned slightly gray, and his eyes might have flashed red. Just like his finger had appeared to be a twisted talon for a moment, the illusion passed quickly.

Or maybe it just became less noticeable as the windows high above suddenly went dark, as if night had fallen.

The candles hadn't been lit, and neither had the fires. It was broad daylight and late summer. There was plenty of light, and it was still plenty warm. So, when the sunlight coming in the windows was blocked, the entire hall was plunged into stygian darkness.

Bailey and I reacted almost immediately. We didn't have our NVGs mounted at the moment, since it was the middle of the day. That might have been an oversight on our part.

We had weapon lights, though, and both blazed to life in a moment, lighting the dais with an actinic white glare.

Just in time to see the knight in yellow and green go up on his tiptoes, his face turned to the ceiling, his arms slack at his sides. Something like black tar seemed to bubble from his mouth and nose, and his back arched with a sickening *crack*.

The man might have been innocent, though under the circumstances I doubted it. Bailey and I reacted to the threat immediately, anyway, even as his skin started to warp and ripple, darkening to the purple of a deep bruise. Both of us shot him through the head a split second after we'd registered what was happening. We were barely twenty feet away, which is spitball range for an M110. He'd also risen high enough off the dais in that short period between the lights coming on and when we fired that we didn't need to worry about accidentally hitting anyone behind him.

The two 175-grain bullets passed right through the knight's skull, smashing through bone and brain, scattering gore and black, tar-like *stuff* across the dais and the thrones. The stuff hissed and smoked where it hit, almost like it was some kind of acid.

We may as well have spat at him. The knight continued to levitate, warping and changing, smoke pouring from his eye sockets for a moment before they lit with a baleful purple fire.

Tharain and the rest of his cronies were falling back, banking on the sudden possession to hold the king's men at bay. For a moment, it looked like it was going to work, too, because one of the guards in red tried to move, only to have a swollen, bruise-purple arm smash him off his feet. His head snapped back with an audible *crunch,* and he fell with a limp finality to the floor.

The creature that had once been a knight of Cor Legear dropped to the floor then, landing in a predatory crouch.

The knight's hair had twisted and hardened into a mass of spines standing straight out from his head. One eye had swollen to the size of a softball, while the other was now as small as a pinprick. Both burned with that evil purple fire, smoke rising from each socket. His jaw dropped onto his chest, now full of so many teeth that even if his mouth hadn't turned into a cavern, he never could have gotten his lips around them. Every proportion of the rest of him had become warped and swollen, his shoulders and misshapen arms, which now had too many joints, having burst his surcoat.

A deep, subsonic growl vibrated through the entire hall, just before a swarm of screeching, flapping monstrosities burst through the darkened windows above and swooped into the hall in a cloud of wings, teeth, claws, and burning eyes.

CHAPTER 14

"PROTECT the king!" Vepogenus fell back, sword in hand, as the monster on the dais started to stalk down the steps and the flying things up near the ceiling swirled and swooped, screaming shrilly. The creature possessing the body of the knight in yellow and green probably figured that nothing could touch it, especially since we'd shot it without effect. It had reason to think that, as it smashed another man off his feet with a casual backhand, turning the man-at-arms' face into hamburger with a wave of its clawed hand.

Bailey and I were Sword Bearers, but we were at a distinct disadvantage right then. We couldn't keep our lights on that thing and draw and fight with the Swords at the same time.

"Cover me." I let my rifle hang and drew the Sword of Iudicael. This was a long shot, and I knew it, but shooting that thing hadn't done squat, and there was no way we were going to get everyone out of that hall before it started turning the crowd into blood pudding.

The Sword almost seemed to glimmer in the darkness as I drew it, pulling my buckler off the scabbard in the same movement, my rifle on my back already. For a moment, just a brief second, I thought I saw a luminous figure nearby, just out of the corner of my eye.

I was developing a theory on that figure's identity, but right then wasn't the time or the place.

Keeping the Sword in front of me, the blade pointed at the monster, I advanced in a slight crouch. It turned those burning purple eyes to me, and another deep, subterranean snarl came from its gaping maw.

I'd faced monsters that would have taunted me, tried to make me despair or turn tail and run. Even the dragon had spoken to us. This thing, however, seemed almost feral, more like the horrors Dragon Mask had summoned from the Outer Dark. It roared and leaped for me.

That thing was *fast*. I knew that if it hit me, I was a dead man. Yet there were a lot more men behind me who were going to be just as dead if I didn't put it down, so I charged it, dodging left at the last moment as I cut at that massive, taloned paw that had once been a hand, even as it blurred toward my face.

That cut probably saved my life. The possessed knight saw it coming and snatched its hand back, pivoting on its other hand and turning toward me as I kept moving, arresting my forward rush and starting to circle it. Bailey had barely moved, but he was still watching my back. I both heard and felt the *crack* as he took a shot over my head, and one of the screeching flying monsters let out a scream of rage and pain and flapped to the floor behind me, curling up into a ball of agony around the bullet that Bailey had put through its X-ring.

The monster in front of me was warier, now. Savage though it obviously was, it wasn't completely mindless, and it knew what I had in my fist. Unfortunately, as cautious as it had suddenly gotten, it was still a lot faster and a lot stronger than I was.

I found myself forced backward by a flurry of blows, just barely keeping ahead of the sweep of those massive, purple arms and the black talons that had sprouted at the ends of the knight's fingers. Those talons scored divots in the stone floor, smashed the corner of the throne's back to splinters, and whistled through the air right next to my ear.

I got a cut on the back of its hand on that one, and there was a faint flash and the smell of charred flesh as the thing dodged away again.

Bailey was still shooting, and more of the screaming winged monkeys, or harpies, or whatever they were, dropped. The hall was utter pandemonium as the Galel tried to fight off the winged monsters in the dark without cutting each other to pieces in the process.

After a few moments, Bailey's light was joined by more white weapon lights and flickering red torches, as the platoon pushed up with Gunny and Mathghaman in the lead, with more of Vepogenus's knights and men-at-arms right beside them. In all the dark and the chaos, it was entirely possible that some people were going to get shot or stabbed who didn't need to be, but right at the moment, I was too focused on staying alive and trying to kill the warped monstrosity in front of me to worry about it.

For a moment, it held back, shifting from side to side, those mismatched, glowing eyes still fixed on me. Then it sprang forward, lashing out with its slightly longer left arm, aiming for my head again.

I cut at the arm with the Sword, realizing almost too late that it was a feint. It skipped to the side as I extended my sword arm, and then bull-rushed me with a roar, its toothy maw snapping for my face.

Even as I spotted the bait and switch and tried to dive out of the way, I knew I was dead. That thing was just too fast, and I was out of position and slightly off balance.

Bailey saved my hide.

With more of our shooters flooding into the hall with weapon lights, backed up by Galel skullsplitters carrying torches, he had slung his rifle to his back and drawn the Sword of Categyrn. The only reason he'd been shooting was because I'd gotten the Sword of Iudicael out first, and I needed the light. Now he waded in, teeth gritted and the shining, silver-chased blessed sword in his fist.

He stabbed that thing in the side just before it hit me, and in a move that defied physics, it suddenly stopped dead, reversed course, and leaped away from both of us, going over the throne and skidding to a halt behind the dais, turning to face us.

Neither one of us had to say much. We split, going around the dais to come at the thing from both flanks, the Swords held ready, bucklers in place, more because we'd practiced that way than because we thought they'd defend against those talons worth a damn. Together, we advanced on the monster where it snarled and slavered, not attacking but not retreating, either. Behind it, Tharain still stood, in shadow but now slightly visible in the flickering glow of weapon lights and torches, staring with slightly too-bright eyes at the chaos he'd unleashed.

We didn't just charge in. We'd both gotten a bit too cautious for that. We'd seen where that led. Even if that thing was apparently on the defensive, it might just be a trap. In fact, it probably was.

Even so, there was something strange going on. While chaos reigned around us, the harpies swooping down on the Galel, who had formed tight knots of defensive formations near the walls, bristling with drawn blades, some of those same flying creatures getting shot out of the air by Marine, Menninkai, or Tuacha rifle fire, none of them came near us. It was almost as if we each had a bubble around us.

Or maybe the bubble was around the Swords.

We closed in on the hulking, possessed knight, the Swords held ready. I held the Sword of Iudicael over my shoulder, my buckler held out in front of my face, ready for a swing. Bailey had adopted more of a front guard, the Sword of Categyrn held point forward, the blade just over the rim of his own shield.

Things got stranger as we closed the distance. The creature still wasn't retreating, but its eyes were narrowed, squinting, as if it was staring into an intense glare. Neither of us had a light on, and the Swords didn't glow, so there was no *physical* light that could be blinding it. But it flinched as the squint got worse, and it ducked its head a little.

For just a split second, I thought I felt a presence behind me. Only for a moment. But I knew that whoever or whatever my mysterious guardian was, he was there.

As encouraging as that might be, I'd also been through enough not to think that his presence lent me any immortality. This thing could still rip my head off, whether my guardian was there or not.

Bailey went in first, stabbing at the thing's outstretched hand, and I moved quickly to take advantage, swinging for its head as it shifted to counter Bailey's attack.

It ducked under my swing, but it wasn't able to completely avoid Bailey's thrust. The point of the Sword of Categyrn went a hand's breadth into its palm, and it snatched that limb back, even as flame erupted from the wound and the taloned hand began to shrivel.

That almost seemed to give both of us a second wind, and we waded in.

Tharain was shouting something in a language that definitely wasn't the Galel's offshoot of the *Tenga Tuacha*. Whatever it was, it was keeping this thing in place to protect him, and that was its downfall.

I feinted forward, then ducked as it took another swipe at me. This time, though, I was ready for it.

The Sword of Iudicael cleaved through unnaturally warped flesh and bone. The creature tried to snatch its hand back, almost moving faster than the eye could follow, but it still wasn't *quite* fast enough. Its talons flew through the air, shriveling into acrid smoke as they fell away from its maimed hand.

Bailey and I spread out, circling around to opposite sides of the thing, which was trapped between us now, having to turn from one to the other. We weren't being courteous enough to come at it one at a time, either. Bailey stabbed it as it snatched its hand back from my stroke, and then, as it jerked away and pivoted toward him, I brought the Sword of Iudicael crashing down on its shoulder.

That time, the blade bit deep. Its entire arm came off with a spout of black, steaming tar stuff, the arm shriveling and smoking as it fell to the floor. The thing came back around and swung at me, fast as a striking snake, but that opened it up to Bailey.

With a leap that I wouldn't have advised under any other circumstances, he jumped up and split the creature's skull.

Blue-white flames erupted around the blade, and thick, choking black smoke poured from the wound. The scream that came out of that gaping throat nearly drove me to my knees with its volume and pitch. My hearing felt deadened when it finally stopped, as the creature shrank and writhed, more smoke and tar pouring off it until only the charred skeleton of a man missing one arm remained.

The harpies had ascended toward the ceiling with shrieks of dismay as the creature fell. Tharain stared in shock for a moment as Bailey and I turned to confront him, then he called out again.

Something hit the wall high above. Something big. The entire keep shuddered under the impact, and plaster dust cascaded down from the wall.

Whatever it was hit again. And again. A deafening *crack* sounded from the wall, and then a massive shadow smashed through one of the upper windows, sending exploding masonry showering down onto the floor. Men ducked out of the way, but at least a couple were struck to the floor. They lay where they fell and didn't move.

The creature was vaguely man-shaped, except for the crown of smoking horns that sprouted from its head and the huge wings that spread from its shoulders. It seemed made of smoke and burning tar, and its eyes were pits of flame. It cast its glance over the hall and men quailed, even as the harpies fled through the windows. Even those things were unwilling to get too close to that.

It glared around at the rest of the room, even as Gunny and Mathghaman opened fire on it. The bullets had about the same effect on that thing that mine and Bailey's had had on the possessed knight.

It dipped toward Tharain, seized him by the shoulders, and flapped upward, clearing the smashed hole in the wall in an eyeblink and disappearing into the sky, surrounded by the screeching cloud of harpies that had survived bullets and blades.

CHAPTER 15

THE darkness had dispersed as soon as the flying horror had vanished through the hole it had smashed through the wall. Canaul and Deototreic had helped the king to the smashed and splintered throne, and he sat himself on it despite the fact that he looked like death warmed over. He might fall over at any moment, but he held himself upright as he glared around the hall.

"Is this what we have sunk to?" His voice was still a rasp, and I could tell that Vepogenus would have preferred that he retire to rest, but Uven would not be deterred. "We allow a sorcerer to nearly seize the throne, on a *rumor?!*"

"My lord king…" The older man who started to speak, in a tunic of green and white, faltered as several pairs of steely eyes pinned him. "We… we had no way to know…"

"You had no way to know." King Uven might be wounded and weakened, but the acid in his voice would eat through steel. "You certainly didn't wait long to put Tharain on the throne! On his word that I was dead, without seeking to know for sure!" He glared with burning eyes around the hall. "He was right that there seems to be rebellion brewing in the kingdom of Cor Legear. Servants of the Outer Dark and the Empire of Ar-Annator are eagerly aided and abetted by my own lords."

A man in green and blue, somewhat younger than the older man who had stepped back, his eyes on the floor before his king's wrath, stepped out of the crowd. There was blood on his tunic and some still dripped from a cut on his forehead. He knelt before the throne. "My lord king. Some of us doubted, but Tharain insisted that the war was too imminent to wait. Indeed, there have been more attacks on the coast, and a Peruni army even now nears Cor Chatha, led by no fewer than three Dullahans, by last report." He looked up at Uven. "Had I known how deep Tharain's treason lay, I would have struck him dead where he stood. Please, believe me." I wasn't the only one who noticed that he didn't include the title "lord" when he spoke of Tharain any longer.

Uven watched the man for a moment, his face unreadable, his eyes bright. Maybe with rage, maybe with fever, it was hard to tell. He had already begun to slump in the throne, even with Canaul, Vepogenus, and Deototreic standing close by.

Finally, he sighed. "I cannot condemn all my lords, particularly not those who fought here in this hall as the denizens of the Outer Dark came in." His glare hadn't lost its force, though. "I can perhaps fault you for not crushing this uprising as soon as it began, but fear of the coming war has weighed heavily on our people for the last months. Perhaps it was inevitable."

He was looking awfully pale. "Still, were it not for the Sword Bearers, who have sworn no oaths to us and owe us no fealty, this kingdom would be now in the grasp of a terrible darkness." He turned to Bailey and me and bowed his head. "We owe them a great debt, one I doubt we shall ever be able to repay." There was pain in his voice then, that had nothing to do with his wounds.

I didn't dare look around at Gunny or Mathghaman, though, but only bowed my head. I thought I understood the king's agony. A moment later, I got my confirmation.

"We are but a bruised reed attempting to stand against the gale." His breathing was getting labored, and try as he might, he was slumping a little more in the throne. His voice was quieter now. "Honor demands that I ask no more of you, but the needs of my people demand that I request your aid once more."

I really wanted to look over at Gunny. He was the man in charge, as far as we were concerned. Yet the king was asking *me*, and as the Sword Bearer—one of them—it was solely on me to answer.

Fortunately or unfortunately, I knew what Gunny would say. The king wasn't asking for the platoon's aid. He was asking for *mine*. Mine and Bailey's. And under the circumstances, especially after all we'd been through, Gunny wasn't going to take that choice away from either of us, whether he thought he should or not. We'd become something more than just members of the platoon by taking up the Swords. Exactly what, we were both still trying to figure out, but Gunny and Mathghaman had both agreed that there was much more at work here than met the eye.

We had to feel this out as much as we needed to feel out any particular tactical situation.

"What would you ask of the Sword Bearers, King Uven?" That was maybe a little formal for me, but I'd been learning, hanging out with Mathghaman.

"Only that you accompany my knights to seek out Tharain and his traitors. Bring the Swords to combat whatever foul sorceries they have summoned into our kingdom." I got the distinct sense that Uven wasn't using the royal "our" there, but speaking of his people, the Galel. "I can only ask, not command. Yet I *must* ask, as king."

I traded a short glance with Bailey, at which point I felt a heavy hand on my shoulder. Mathghaman stood beside me, saying nothing except with that hand. Whatever call I made, he'd back me. Gunny sent the same wordless message as he stepped up beside Bailey.

"We will lend what help we can, King Uven." Bailey stood tall and looked the king in the face. "We seem to be somewhat between missions at the moment, and as far as I'm concerned, anybody who's friends with things like that…" He motioned toward the charred skeleton of the man who had been possessed by whatever had turned him into a warped, hulked-out monster. "Well, I think I'd just as rather see them dead."

Gunny gave a curt, tight-lipped nod. We were all on the same page. I was sure Gurke would probably find something to complain about, but while he always had to bitch about something, at least he wasn't the sort of contrarian Zimmerman had been. Gurke would complain, but he'd stick.

"Where would Tharain have gone?" With that out of the way, it was time to get down to planning, especially if this really was all part of an operation intended to soften the Galel up for an invasion by the Empire of Ar-Annator. I was just as happy to get past the political aspect and get down to brass tacks.

I'm no diplomat. I'm a Recon Marine, and that means that I'd much rather be out in the field, on the hunt.

King Uven, however, was nearly at the end of his strength. He slumped even lower in the throne, even as the queen, standing straight and tall but with the look of a woman who had only recently been let out of her chambers, trailed by several of her women, came sweeping into the hall, barely sparing a glance at the carnage and debris, going straight for her husband.

She looked at Bailey and me, bowed her head slightly, and then turned her eye on Vepogenus. "I assume you can handle this from here, Lord Vepogenus. My husband needs care."

"Indeed he does, my Queen." Vepogenus wasn't arguing, and he was hardly the sort of man who would be cowed, as formidable as the queen might be. He looked around at the assembled Galel lords and men-at-arms. "Get someone up here to help the king!"

There was a surge of movement. A lot of men were suddenly more than eager to prove that they were behind their sovereign. No great surprise there.

I just hoped that Vepogenus and the queen kept a close eye on all of them.

King Uven protested, but Queen Nectudad was having none of it. "It is time to let your loyal men handle things, dearest. Lest you overtax yourself and be useless when the real battle comes."

She knew what she was about. Uven grimaced but nodded his assent, and half a dozen younger knights shouldered aside the men-at-arms to lift the king from the throne and help him toward the stairs and his chambers. He fought some of them off, refusing to be carried, and finally rose to his feet, though not without assistance. He turned as he started to limp away, his arms around two burly knights' shoulders, but Vepogenus lifted a hand. "We shall see to it, my king. I will keep you informed."

Uven nodded as he was half-carried away to recuperate from his wounds.

Vepogenus waited until he was out of sight, then turned to the rest of us. "I suggest we retire to a different place, my lords." He glanced around at the detritus of the battle for a moment. "Somewhere less defiled by the arts of the enemy."

* * *

The other place turned out to be a barracks for those knights who might have come from far away. There were already swarms of young men and boys clearing out as much of the debris from the reception hall as they could, overseen by elders in brown robes. I didn't know what order those brown robes belonged to, but it seemed to be akin to the brothers who kept the temple above Aith an Rih. They were chanting constantly, and while they weren't as good at it as the Tuacha—no normal man ever would be—they were making up for it with volume and enthusiasm. We could hear them in the barracks. I expected they were doing what they could to try to chase any lingering darkness out, by sheer noise if nothing else.

"Where are Tharain's lands?" That was the first thing. Find out where the target's usual stomping grounds are, then narrow things down from there. If he didn't want to be found, though, I expected that we had a lot of recon ahead of us.

"He has many, but he is of the new breed." Vepogenus's disgust seemed to go deeper than simply Tharain's treason and embrace of sorcery. "He has built his wealth through closeness to the throne. He has no castle, no great number of kin to call upon. His chief dwelling is an estate in the hills just beyond the city." He pointed toward the northwest. "It is hardly defensible; he would come to the citadel in a time of war." The old man's lip curled. "He has hardly ever been the kind who would hasten to ride to the frontier."

"So, this little attempted coup of his wasn't all that surprising?" Gunny asked.

"Not to me." Vepogenus scowled. "Perhaps to others. He has always been a sly one. Smooth in speech and vague in intent." He suddenly sighed, and in that moment he looked even older. "Though I must admit that even I would not have suspected him of having sunk so low."

He wouldn't be the first. As little as I'd thought of Captain Sorenson, I'd never have expected him to turn to blood sacrifice and sorcery. Zimmerman even less so. Yet they had. No one is immune to the temptations of power, and preternatural power can carry a dangerous fascination, worse than wealth or command.

Sometimes, it's the ones who scoff at it the most who need to be most closely watched.

"You say it's not particularly defensible." Bailey wanted to get back on track. "Do we have a map?"

Vepogenus must have been expecting that, because he brought out a rolled parchment that looked like it had been sitting in an archive for at least a decade. When he unrolled it, I was surprised to see that it wasn't the somewhat vague sketch that we'd gotten used to using for maps in this world. It was a pretty precise drawing. It didn't have quite the elevation detail you'd get from a topographical map back in The World, but it was detailed enough that we could see roughly what we were up against.

Vepogenus pointed out the estate with the tip of his dagger. It was big, though not nearly as big as most of the castles we'd seen. A house stood at the top of a wide lawn which stretched partway down the hill above the river, on the other side from Cor Legear itself. Woods stretched for about half a mile in a crescent around the western side, presumably to provide the lord of the estate with hunting grounds. A road led from the bridge downstream up to the house, going through the woods for a short distance.

It didn't look like there was a lot of cover or concealment on the way in. While the woods might back the house, if the map was accurate—and it looked like a great deal of care had gone into drawing it to scale—then the house stood a good twenty yards from the tree line.

That was, of course, assuming that all we had to worry about was the threat of men with spears, swords, and bows.

We had a limited amount of time. If Tharain was desperate enough, he might fly the coop before we could corner him. We had to move.

Fortunately, we knew a thing or two about short-fuse planning for time-sensitive targets. We got to work.

CHAPTER 16

THE fields around Tharain's manor were quiet. Deathly quiet. There weren't any birds singing, or even moving. It was almost as if there was something lurking in there that even the animals didn't want to mess with.

We were already moving cautiously, having left the horses at the bridge over the river, slipping through the strips of woods standing between the fields on foot. Bailey and I had gone head-to-head in Rock-Paper-Scissors to determine which Sword Bearer team would take the close-in reconnaissance. I'd won, even when Bailey had insisted on best two out of three.

As I moved up through the trees behind Rodeffer, my rifle in my hands, hearing every footstep in the creepy, dead quiet, I wondered a little if I'd really *won*.

Rodeffer was getting jumpy. I couldn't necessarily blame him, not after what we'd fought in the reception hall of Cor Legear. It was pretty obvious that Tharain was into some heavy, sorcerous stuff, and we'd all seen enough of that sort of thing that we'd have to be nuts not to be a little jumpy. Power can be tempting and seductive, but the destruction it wreaks is damned scary.

And I'm not just talking about the physical destruction.

The carpet of leaves under the trees had mostly decomposed over the winter, spring, and summer, but the trees were now just starting to drop the first leaves of fall, and even though they weren't fully dried out yet, they still seemed to crunch deafeningly under our boots. I saw Rodeffer flinch a little bit with every step, and I almost told him to hold up and get a grip on himself, but just then he stopped, looking down at the ground with a silent, mouthed, *What the fuck?*

I moved up to join him, looking down at the base of the tree. It wasn't hard to see what had him rattled.

The ground around the tree roots was littered with dead animals. I counted three dead birds and two dead squirrels. Like most of the animals in this world, they were subtly different from what we were used to, but at least here in the south, they were still more recognizable than some of the twisted, mutant forms we'd seen in the Land of Ice and Monsters, or even up in the Corsair Lands.

There was no immediate sign of what had killed them, but when Rodeffer prodded one of the dead squirrels with his boot, it seemed to crumble, and a mass of maggots and worms squirmed out of the stiffened hide. Rodeffer gulped hard and turned away.

None of us were what you might call squeamish. Even before coming to a place where we might well have to go hands on just because we were out of ammunition, we'd all done our time up to our elbows in blood and guts. Even those who hadn't seen combat before that night we'd come through the mists had had to do some live-tissue first aid training—carefully executed someplace where the animal rights activists couldn't find it—so we'd all become a little desensitized.

Something about the sight of those rotting, maggot-ridden squirrels and birds, though, was just disturbing. Especially as I started looking a little more widely, expanding my scan of the ground around us.

It looked like every animal within a certain radius of the low stone manor house at the top of the hill had just dropped dead before rapidly decomposing.

Bad, bad sign.

I gripped Rodeffer's upper arm for a moment, just until he swallowed and nodded. He was good. It was pretty obvious that we were in a very, very dangerous position, however. Moving with even more exaggerated care, he continued toward the trees closest to the manor.

The leaves were starting to fall more thickly as we kept patrolling up through the thin strip of forest, almost as if the death that had struck the animals—except for the carrion eaters, anyway—had also affected the trees themselves. Whatever Tharain had done here, it was shaping up to be as bad as Dragon Mask's summoning that had turned Sgt Nelson-Hyde into black mist.

The woods led us higher up the hill, flanking the fan of fields, mostly fallow now, that lay on the gentle slope from the manor house down toward the river. We got just about even with the house itself and I called a halt to watch and listen for a few minutes.

We circled up under a huge, gnarled old oak, our knees crunching in the carpet of leaves, and stayed as still as possible, watching our surroundings and listening carefully. Most of us were careful *not* to kneel on any of the small, putrid carcasses that littered the ground amid the leaves.

There wasn't a breath of wind anywhere around that manor. Even outside, it felt stuffy, dead. I was really starting to dread what we'd find inside. The continued silence made me suspect that we were far too late to intercept Tharain himself, but we had to go in there and check, anyway.

After a few minutes, during which nothing stirred except one or the other of us shifting position ever so slightly, I decided we couldn't put this off any longer. I keyed my radio. "Five, this is One. No sign of activity. We're moving on the house now. Be advised, it appears that everything within a three-hundred-yard radius of the target building is dead. Birds, mice, squirrels, you name it."

I didn't have to elaborate on that. Gunny would get the message. So would Mathghaman.

I tapped Rodeffer on the shoulder. He grimaced a little, obviously reluctant, but got to his feet. In another life, on another world, I might have gotten on him later for that reaction. Santos definitely would have, if he'd seen it. Here, though, surrounded by so much unnatural death, I couldn't blame him. While the silence was in marked contrast to the pandemonium we'd seen in the hall, in many ways it was far, far worse.

We had to leave the shelter of the trees—not that they had provided any shelter for the wildlife—and advance across about twenty yards of open ground toward the manor house. The house itself had been built as an open square, only one story tall, the stones nearly as weathered as those of Cor Legear. The roof was thatched, unlike many of the buildings nearby, which were tiled. I frowned a little as I looked at it. The thatch was turning gray, almost as if it was rotting. It had to have something to do with the death and decay that surrounded the house. I didn't see someone like Tharain ever allowing his own property to fall into such disrepair that the roof started to rot.

As much as the situation called for caution, even with most of the platoon on overwatch from the other side of the river, Bailey on my M107 .50 cal and Applegate, Chambers, and Huuhka on their Mk 48s, we did *not* want to be out in the open for any longer than absolutely necessary. We crossed to the main doors fast, guns up and scanning for targets. Santos waited at the tree line with our team Mk 48, covering the three of us until we reached the door and stacked up, at which point he dashed to join us, turning to cover the six o'clock as he did so.

Rodeffer held on the door, his rifle pointed at the opening, where it was slightly ajar. I reached around him, my weapon held muzzle-high, and shoved the door open. It swung inward easily, and Rodeffer paused just a moment, taking a deep breath, redolent of mold and smoke, and then went through, his weapon leveled. I was right on his heels, my suppressor dropping level over his shoulder as we moved into the foyer.

The interior was dark and silent. Dust stirred on the floor at our feet. It was almost as if this place had been utterly abandoned for a long time, but I knew from our Galel allies that Tharain had been here just last week at least. Certainly not enough time for this kind of dust and decay to build up.

Cobwebs covered the benches and the chests that stood against the walls, and draped from the candelabra hanging from the low ceiling. My eyes narrowed as I triggered my weapon light, playing the cone of bright white illumination around the room, joined by Rodeffer's and Farrar's. Santos had ducked in, made sure that he had no monsters to light up immediately, then turned to cover the doorway. A Mk 48 wasn't an ideal room-clearing weapon, and if we hadn't just fought a warped, hulked-out monstrosity that had only gone down to the Two Swords, I'd have had him leave it behind and bring his pistol instead. As it was, however, we wanted the extra firepower.

The foyer was clear, so I quietly called, "On me," and headed for the door leading to the next room. We'd clear through counterclockwise. That had been decided in planning, so I didn't need to say it now that we were on the ground.

That door was open, though the room beyond was dark. It looked like all the shutters on all the windows were closed. I went across the threshold first, flashing my light like a strobe to avoid giving anyone or anything too much of a target to shoot at or throw something at.

We were in the kitchens. Two massive, wood-fired ovens dominated the room, with several trestle tables set around them for preparation. Pots and utensils were stacked on several shelves, though it looked like something had hit the shelves, as everything was in disarray and half the stuff was on the floor.

There wasn't a lot of food out, but what there was had rotted and was crawling with insects and worms.

We cleared it quickly. There was only one door, so we circled back around and returned to the foyer, pushing out into the courtyard at the center of the building to continue our counterclockwise clear.

The courtyard had once upon a time been a nice, relaxing place, with grass growing around a central fruit tree that looked a lot like an apple tree, and stone benches set around that. Now it was weed-choked and dying, the fruit on the tree's branches rotting where it hung. We quickly cleared the courtyard, just in case. There was only the dying vegetation. All of the interior doors were shut.

The next room had been a storeroom. If things had been decaying in the kitchen, that place was worse. We couldn't even take a step inside; the stench was so bad. Flies swarmed out of the open door, so thick that we almost couldn't see anything. We had to settle for clearing the room from the doorway, as the interior was a mass of putrefaction spilling off the shelves.

It was still with a certain amount of trepidation that we turned our backs on that mess and kept moving. Something about it made it feel like some monster would form out of the rot and come after us.

The next two rooms were bedrooms, covered in cobwebs and with the furniture cracked and crumbling. Then we came to the hall or dining room, and things got really bad.

The first thing that struck me, even before I crossed the threshold, was the smell. It was different from the stench of rot and decay elsewhere in the manor. This was sharper, more metallic. It reminded me more of the stink of the Outer Dark. It was the smell of sorcery.

There was light in the hall. It wasn't strong, but there were candles still burning, somehow. They were in a circle around the central trestle table, their wax black, their flames flickering between the ordinary yellow of fire and something almost greenish, poisonous and noisome.

There was a body on the table. Or, rather, what was left of one.

We'd seen men sacrificed to the Outer Dark before. Most notably, we'd found Captain Sorenson's corpse on an altar to Vaelor, far in the north, his heart ripped out and placed in the idol's hand above it. This was almost worse than that.

This man had been flayed, his skin pinned down with nails to the tabletop, eldritch symbols painted on the inside of his hide with some sort of black ink. His entrails had been drawn out and arranged in a strange and disturbing pattern over the table and down onto the floor—more disturbing than just the fact that his guts were out and all over the place. There was something about the pattern that made my eyes ache and something at the back of my mind itch.

The carnage on the table spread out across the room. The entire hall had been daubed with more weird, nauseating symbols, painted in blood. That blood was now crawling with flies. Their buzz was a constant background hum, and if I paid too much attention to it, it sounded almost like voices.

Maybe it was. *Something* had been invoked by this bloodbath, and I didn't trust that it had entirely disappeared, whatever it was. We'd seen that before. Sometimes the things from the Outer Dark, if they didn't get what they wanted out of a deal, turned back on the sorcerer who had summoned them.

"We need to get out of here." I was suddenly dead certain that Tharain wasn't there anymore. I still hadn't heard a sound that we hadn't made since before we'd entered the manor, except for the droning of the flies. This place was deserted, except for whatever otherworldly wickedness this vile act had summoned.

I didn't particularly want to wait around for whatever it was to stick its head out of the shadows, and as we started toward the door, I could tell I wasn't alone.

Even as we stepped through the door and back into the courtyard, still taking steps to clear it instead of just running through, I thought I heard a growl behind me. I pivoted as soon as I'd cleared my sector of the courtyard and checked the doorway again.

The candles had gone out. Almost as if they had only been lit for us. Still, at the moment, I almost thought that I could see two points of faint, purplish light. Almost like the fire that had burned in the misshapen eyes of the warped and twisted monster that had once been a knight of Cor Legear.

We needed to get the hell out of there. I might have been able to fight that thing in physical form, but this was now its turf, and I'd learned my lesson fighting that revenant in the ziggurat in Barmanak. Something like that needed a lot more preparation than I'd gone through before we'd left Cor Legear.

That didn't mean I wouldn't burn this place to the ground on the way out.

"Move." Keeping weapons high and eyes out, we headed across the courtyard toward the foyer.

I was expecting the attack to come from the hall we'd just vacated. Instead, it came from that rotting fruit tree.

There'd been something disquieting about that tree ever since I'd first laid eyes on it. It wasn't nearly as bad as the eldritch abomination in the center of Lost Colcand, which had manifested as a massive, ancient tree covered in eyes, but it still almost felt like it was watching us.

Now, it suddenly creaked toward us, its darkened, twisted branches, denuded of leaves but still bearing that blackened, rotten fruit, lashing out as we moved by.

One branch caught Rodeffer in the throat, knocking him sprawling, choking and gasping at the impact. He was still in the fight, and he shot the tree from two feet away, but he may as well have spat at it. Bullets don't do much against wood.

I ducked under another swinging branch. This thing hadn't sprouted any eyes, and it seemed to me less like it was a monster in its own right than it was a natural tree being puppeteered by whatever was lurking in the darkness back in the hall, but I still had to fight back *somehow.*

Letting my rifle hang, still in front of me because there just wasn't time to move it around to my back, I drew the Sword and took a swing at a gnarled branch as it came plunging down to hammer Rodeffer into the dirt.

The branch hit so hard that I almost lost my grip on the Sword. Still, the blade bit deep, and I stopped the blow, giving Farrar a moment to duck in next to me, grab Rodeffer by his chest rig, and drag him out from under the tree. As soon as they were clear, I backed away, keeping the Sword pointed at the tree, just in case, though once I was out of reach of those flailing branches, I still spared a glance around us, to make sure nothing else was creeping up on us from behind while we were focused on a tree that was moving like no tree ever should, even in a storm.

The rest of the courtyard was quiet, though that oppressive sense of malevolent watchfulness from the hall had only intensified.

"Rod, you okay?" He was on his feet, but I needed to be sure.

"I'm good." His voice was hoarse, but that was to be expected after just getting trachea-chopped by a tree.

"Back to the foyer. We'll clear it, then we pull off of this place." I already had a plan. Most of the walls were stone, but the roof was thatch, and the stone walls were all set within timber frames. And I had a thermate grenade in my chest rig.

Farrar moved quickly to the door to the foyer, and I joined him as Santos covered the courtyard, pulling Rodeffer with him. It took me two steps and then I was right at Farrar's shoulder. "With you."

We went through the door fast, even as Santos let rip with a thunderous burst aimed at either something in the courtyard, or maybe into the hall behind us. We swiftly cleared the cobweb-choked foyer. Nothing had changed since we'd made entry the first time.

Rodeffer and Santos swept in to join us, Santos once again quickly pivoting to cover our six. With hardly a pause, Farrar and I kept moving, heading for the main entry doors.

Those were still standing open, thankfully. We moved out quickly, clearing the immediate grounds around the outside of the manor house, then I pulled off to one side. "Get to the tree line. I'll be right behind you."

Santos didn't ask questions, though Farrar looked like he was going to try to stay back. "Move it, Mike." This was not the time for one of my guys to get heroically disobedient.

He still looked like he wanted to argue, even as I sheathed the Sword and pulled the thermate out, but I gave him the look that he'd learned not to argue with even before the mists, and he turned and jogged after Rodeffer and Santos. They didn't go far before Santos got down on a knee, bracing the Mk 48 against a tree.

I glanced back through the foyer. Everything was as still as it had been when we'd first approached. The tree seemed to have stopped moving. That oppressive sense of being watched was still there, though.

I pulled the pin on the grenade and lobbed it up into the thatch over the door. The rot might have moistened the reeds, but a thermate incendiary burns at just over four thousand degrees Fahrenheit. I don't care how sorcerously decayed your thatch is. That stuff will burn it down.

The entire roof erupted in flames as I ran for the tree line. There might have been a distant roar of rage, but I couldn't be sure over the crackle of the fire.

Tharain's house was a dry hole for our purposes. I just hoped that burning it down would at least contain whatever he'd summoned long enough for the brothers to come and exorcise the place.

We had other trails to track down.

CHAPTER 17

WE gathered in the citadel of Cor Legear again, to report to the king before we did anything else. He was upstairs, in his quarters, sitting up in bed and looking better than he had since he'd been wounded. We'd gone up the back way, since the brothers still had the reception hall blocked off, making good and sure that Tharain's sorcery hadn't left any unpleasant surprises behind.

He looked up as I came through the door with my team, Gunny, and Mathghaman. Vepogenus and Canaul were already there, along with a bunch of other knights, most of them showing some gray hairs and a lot of scars, as well as Nectudad and several of her younger ladies-in-waiting. The queen stood at her husband's shoulder, clearly concerned and somewhat unwilling to let him talk to us just yet. That I could understand; he'd nearly died more than once since Cor Wudrun. Yet King Uven was an aggressive go-getter, and being an invalid was probably eating at him.

"What did you find?" His voice was still weak, but getting stronger. He still looked pale and wan, but the old fire in his eyes was definitely there. Of course, this was a man who'd staggered into the hall to face Tharain when he could barely walk, so I didn't think that fire had ever really gone away.

The others deferred to me. I was not only one of the Sword Bearers, but I'd been the team leader on the ground, so that left it up to me. I started in my slightly stiff, still somewhat halting *Tenga Tuacha*. I could understand the language a lot better than I could speak it, even then.

"Tharain's definitely been invoking the Outer Dark, and probably for some time. That place is a nightmare." I briefly described what we'd found, without going into too much detail, mainly because Nectudad was present, along with the other ladies. I could see in both the king's and the queen's eyes that they knew I was leaving such things out. The king was filling in the blanks. So was Queen Nectudad, though she was equally obviously relieved for the sake of her younger ladies that I wasn't being too graphic. "He's long gone, though. I think either the thing that possessed Lord Artbranan went back to rip his head off, or he set things up so that if his little coup went south, that thing would be waiting for us to do just what we did."

"I see you burned the place." The plume of smoke was still visible through the window to the northwest.

"It seemed like the thing to do." I was slightly defensive about it. Gunny hadn't said a word, nor had Mathghaman, but Gurke had openly wondered why I'd done it without consulting higher. *What if that had just made the thing stronger?*

I'd seen fire work to keep some of the darker things at bay in the north. I wasn't going to apologize.

King Uven wanted no apology, however. He nodded, then winced. He was still pretty beat up. "I would have done the same. I pray that the fire banished the thing."

"Brother Erop is already on his way with several of the Brethren to cleanse the place, my king," Vepogenus rumbled. Uven nodded.

"So, then." He'd apparently dismissed the fire and the abomination right on his citadel's doorstep to get to the next problem. It wasn't that King Uven didn't recognize the threat. He just accepted that the best men to deal with it were on it, and now he had another problem to address. "Now that I have had some time to rest, I have been thinking. This is more than just a squabble over the throne. That lies at its root, certainly. Tharain has always believed his claim stronger than mine. Were he a nobler man, I might even agree with him." He took a deep breath and sagged back slightly against the cushions. He was fighting to get back on his feet, but that revenant had taken a lot out of him.

That was worrying. Was this just a wound, or a curse? Or both?

"This is more than another of our many feuds, though. The use of sorcery… such has been anathema among our people for untold generations. This is far, far worse than the contest over who wears the crown. Tharain has not only sold his people to the Peruni, but he has sold his soul to the Outer Dark."

"Along with many others," Vepogenus said dourly. "He is hardly alone. We believe that fully a maniple of knights and their men-at-arms went with him."

"And yet the question remains." The king's voice had gotten hoarse again. "Where did they go? Tharain has no great hold to take refuge in. We must find him and end this rebellion before the Peruni sweep across the border."

Gunny, Mathghaman, and I shared a look. Gunny nodded, then stepped forward. "King Uven, it just so happens that locating the enemy is something that my boys and I are very adept at."

The expression that flitted across the king's face was a mixture of relief, determination, and a certain degree of chagrin. On some level, despite the fact that he and his men had initially requested the Sword Bearers' aid, it had to sting, asking outsiders to help solve an internal matter. Even with the Peruni and their patrons of the Outer Dark involved, this had to, in some way, feel like something that *he*, King Uven, had to deal with. It was his throne being challenged, his people being sacrificed to the insatiable predators beyond the veil.

I knew that not all of us were all that comfortable, as Americans, with what amounted to fighting to prop up a monarchy. Even though the United States of America was as distant now to us in time as it was in space, we all had that mindset ingrained in us that kings are antithetical to everything we stood for.

And yet…

I'd fought to defend far worse people in Syria. I knew men who had worked personal security detachments for politicians who were out-and-out criminals, corrupt as hell, who made the man who sat on the throne of Cor Legear look like a saint by comparison.

Captain Sorenson had embraced that "hearts and minds" doctrine in the north, to our detriment and the loss of not only those Marines who were killed as we trekked across the frozen Land of Ice and Monsters toward Taramas's citadel, but also those whom we'd later had to kill to keep Vaelor from being freed from his prison beneath the Teeth of Winter. Here, we had to do something somewhat similar, if aligned to an actual moral compass, unlike Captain Sorenson's courtship of the Dovos nal Uergal and Dragon Mask's Vaelor-worshipping renegades.

King Uven was a king, but not the caricature of a king that we'd grown up with. He was no arrogant despot, lording over a captive population because of his birthright. He was a leader, a warrior who appeared to genuinely care about defending his people and his country, rather than the power inherent in his position. It was entirely possible that another king might not be as good as Uven, but not only was he a good king, going by everything I'd seen, but his people believed in kingship. It wasn't our place to worry about their form of government, not when it was functioning justly. That was something our superiors back in The World might have taken more seriously into account.

Furthermore, those of us who were left were the sworn enemies of the Outer Dark, even more so since Bailey and I were Sword Bearers. It honestly wouldn't matter if King Uven was an arrogant jackass; as long as he still held the line and his enemies wielded sorcery against him, we'd probably still feel obligated to go after them.

I was suddenly reminded of the old Vietnam vets who went to Africa after the fall of Saigon, looking to keep up the fight against the Communists. In some ways, we were no different.

"I cannot repay you as you deserve." The king sagged back against his cushions once more, his strength still nowhere near what it had been. He looked around at us.

"Tharain is a wily one, and there are many places where he might have hidden himself." He let out a long sigh. "I fear that even with the threat of the Deep Ones on one side and the Empire on the other, there are still too many who would tear this kingdom asunder, either out of jealousy or because of old slights clung to throughout the years."

Gunny rubbed his hands together, less out of eagerness and more out of a need to get to work. "Well, let's get a map and start planning, shall we?"

* * *

The plan mostly in place, we were heading down the stairs when Queen Nectudad called my name down the steps.

I paused and turned to look, along with everyone else. Nectudad wasn't a great beauty, but she had a matronly warmth about her that extended not only to the king and her family, but seemingly to everyone in her vicinity.

She was beckoning to me, and when I glanced at Gunny, he nodded and started ushering the others down the steps to give us some privacy.

"Yes, Queen Nectudad?" The formality seemed appropriate, though I wouldn't call her "my queen," since she wasn't.

"I thought I should let you know, since you and Derelei, Cailtarni's daughter, seemed to be getting close when last you were here." Her voice and her eyes were sad, and I thought I could tell where this was going. She sighed. "She went with Lord Emcat, one of Tharain's loyal men. And she went willingly."

It had been months since I'd seen the girl, and while there had been some attraction there, aided by the fact that I'd fought off shambling, possessed corpses to save her, I was still somewhat surprised by how much of a pang that news suddenly gave me. Her flirting had been at least partially driven by ambition, that I knew, but she'd been attractive, warm, and engaging. Her father, dead now after challenging Urgant, had held designs of marrying the two of us, more because I bore the Sword of Iudicael than anything else, but he hadn't been a bad man. I hadn't seen her as the kind of ambitious that would run off with a rebel lord at the drop of a hat.

"She believed you and her father lost, and feared that if Uven fell, she would be reduced to a lower status in the aftermath. So, she attached herself to what she saw as the rising power." Nectudad put her hand on my arm. "I am sorry, Conor. I wish I could have warned you before she latched onto you in our hall, all those months ago."

I nodded. "I understand." Derelei wouldn't be the first woman I'd been disappointed over. Probably wouldn't be the last, either. "Thank you, Queen Nectudad. I appreciate your telling me."

She patted my arm. "You are a strong one, Conor, and a stronger watches over you. You will be all right. I just wished to let you know, before you found out more… abruptly."

I bowed my thanks and headed down the steps.

We had a lot of work to do. That was probably a good thing, after that news.

CHAPTER 18

WITH the number of target sets and their widely dispersed locations, we wouldn't be able to do this as a platoon. We had to split up into teams.

The Tuacha, somewhat to my surprise, didn't take a target to themselves, but split up to accompany our teams. There were only five of them, and four teams, including the Menninkai, so it ended up a little lopsided. Fennean went with Orava's team, Diarmodh with Gurke and Gunny, while Eoghain went with Bailey and Mathghaman and Bearrac came with us. I'd known we'd miss Conall, but he was still back at Cor Wudrun, trying to help the people there against the sorcerous plague.

We rode out from Cor Legear in the early hours of the morning, before the sun was up. Fortunately, it was getting late enough in the year that we didn't need to sacrifice *too* much sleep, though as Recon Marines, that almost seemed wrong. Lack of sleep was almost a vital part of who and what we were.

Bailey, Gunny, and I shook hands in farewell. "Make sure you get comms checks at least once a day." Gunny wasn't going to micromanage over the radio—that wasn't his way—but it was an old truism of Recon that if you can't get comms, you're useless and you may as well extract. We had to be able to coordinate and get word back if this was going to be anything but a long ride. And if we *did* find Tharain, then the faster we could get word back and get the full force of the Galel armies moving, the better.

Gurke had heard and nodded and waved. He wasn't being a jerk, avoiding our little circle. He was just having trouble with his horse. The buckskin with a dark mane didn't seem to like him very much, and didn't want to stay in one place. He'd swapped out his old mount, which had been going partially lame by the time we returned to Cor Legear, but his new one wasn't much of an improvement.

After short farewells, we turned our horses' noses toward our targets and rode out into the predawn dimness.

* * *

As settled and civilized as it was, the kingdom of Cor Legear still had plenty of relatively wild parts, and we had to ride carefully through them, weapons at the ready and eyes out. Especially since the kingdom was now effectively in a state of civil war. The bandits who had been ravaging the land at the behest of the Empire of Ar-Annator were now the least of our worries, but they could cause a whole lot of trouble nevertheless, especially if we let our guard down.

So, we mostly rode in the dark or the woods, avoiding the roads and farms as we went. Not everyone was in open rebellion, but it paid not to take chances.

Unfortunately, in keeping with Recon's bailiwick of going into the hardest, nastiest terrain where no one else in their right mind wants to go, we added an extra two days to our movement toward our objective. We passed most of it in silence, concentrating on security and most of us mulling over our own thoughts on this whole situation.

Mathghaman and Bearrac weren't uncomfortable with the silence. They were the sort who could talk for days or remain silent for a year. The Tuacha were different. If there was something to talk about, they'd talk. Well, to a certain extent. I'd never found Mathghaman to get too revealing about much of anything. Bearrac wasn't either, but he was slightly less mysterious about it. It all amounted to the same thing, but Bearrac, being the bearish sort of man he was, just seemed like he'd rather be fighting or hunting than answering deep and age-old questions.

As for the rest of us, we watched and we thought. I found my thoughts straying to Derelei far more than they had on the way through the northern marches of the Empire of Ar-Annator. Having hardly just met her, while I'd somewhat appreciated her interest, there simply hadn't been time for anything else to develop, whether she had wanted it to or not. Now it looked like her interest had been purely a matter of ambition, and that bugged me more than anything.

The longer I stewed on it, though, the more I became convinced that most of my annoyance had nothing to do with Derelei or her choices, as bad as they might be. No, I was more pissed at myself because I'd started to fall for the act. It didn't help that, as aggravating as I'd occasionally found him, I'd come to consider Cailtarni a friend and a teammate, up until he had fallen dead next to Urgant in the courtyard at Aullun.

Finally, we neared our objective, and I was able to push the constant background roar of introspection aside and concentrate entirely on the mission.

The trees had gotten steadily thicker and the weather worse as we worked our way north and west, toward the coast near the northern tip of the kingdom. The terrain got rockier, and the farms smaller and farther apart. This was bandit and pirate country, and we rode with fingers near triggers, heads up and scanning every shadow, every notch in the terrain. Still, we'd picked our route carefully enough that we saw no one, and nothing except for a few deer, boar, and wolves, all of which steered clear of us.

When we'd made camp about a day out from where we were really going to start doing our Sneaky Pete stuff, I sat down with Mathghaman after we'd gotten the watch set. "Something's weird here." He turned to look at me, but offered no comment until I elaborated.

"Everywhere else we've gone, whether it's the Land of Ice and Monsters, the corsair lands, the plains to the east… they've all been teeming with monsters. Haunted. Cursed. Here…" I swept my hand to indicate the woods where we sat and, by extension, the rest of the country we'd been riding through. "Here, even though we've seen merrows, eac uisge, the walking dead, and all sorts of other weird stuff over the last few months, everything seems, well… normal. Natural."

"Because it is." Mathghaman leaned back against a tree. "The Outer Dark may make inroads here, but it has not dominated this land or its people, not for nearly as long as it has elsewhere. This place is still relatively unscathed." He looked up at where the stars were starting to come out, through the branches. It had rained for most of the last day, and things were just generally getting wetter as we neared the coast, but the clouds had cleared just before we'd made camp. Some of the trees still dripped on us, but the wool of our cloaks kept a lot of the moisture off us. "The Galel have held the line for a long, long time. And while no man is immune to the wickedness that draws the creatures of the Outer Dark and their minions, such things have much less of a foothold here."

"But if the Empire has its way..." I trailed off. It wasn't so much a question as it was just me thinking out loud.

Mathghaman nodded. "Indeed. This has less to do with the Galel as a kingdom and more to do with keeping the Outer Dark at bay, if only for a little while longer." His eyes glinted in the dying light. "Tigharn guides all things, but he lets us do what we can. Since we cannot know all his plans or purposes, we can only fight the good fight and leave the rest in his hands."

I nodded. It was about as clear as it was going to get. And I didn't even think that Mathghaman was being deliberately obtuse. When it came to the metaphysical stuff here, he knew a lot more than we did, but even his knowledge was still limited, and he didn't want to overextend our perception of that knowledge.

We settled in for the rest of the night, as the wind whispered through the tops of the trees.

* * *

Edernon was massive. A triple outer wall was surmounted by a huge keep that would have looked like an H from above, with sloping walls and a squat, round tower rising from the center of the H. The stones were dark with age, and several places in the wall looked like they'd been repaired over the years.

We'd gotten the brief from the king himself before we'd left Cor Legear. Edernon was ancient, one of the first fastnesses of the Galel on this rocky shore. It had stood for generations while Cor Legear itself had been a stony hill in the wilderness, on the frontiers of the remnant of the Commagan Empire. And that was part of what made it one of our target sets.

The reason we were currently crawling into a crack in the rocky mount across an inlet from the fortress was that King Uven's ancestors hadn't always been the Galel kings. The scion of their house had taken command during one of the wars with the corsairs, or so the story went, when the old king had fallen in battle, and been proclaimed king by the lords of the kingdom. That had left the lords of Edernon playing second fiddle to younger upstarts.

According to the king, there had been some bitterness about that over the years. It hadn't erupted into open rebellion in a very long time, if ever, but that bitterness was nevertheless there, and the kings were conscious of it. Therefore, Edernon was suspect as a place that a pretender to the throne might see as a refuge. Even if the lords of Edernon didn't want to see what amounted to just another upstart on the throne, they *might* see an opportunity in a civil war. Let the upstart king and the rebels exhaust themselves against one another, and the rest might turn to ancient Edernon in the aftermath.

King Uven hadn't been convinced, when it all came down to it. We had this target mostly on Vepogenus's recognizance. He didn't trust anyone, least of all the current castellan of Edernon, Melcon.

With only six of us, it didn't make a lot of sense to go riding up and start making accusations or even just asking probing questions. That wasn't usually what Recon did, anyway. So, once Rodeffer and I picked our spot on that mountain, we set in, started to camouflage our position, and commenced surveillance.

A hide site is not a comfortable place. It's never large, because large means more easily spotted, no matter how carefully you camouflage it. It's also never particularly level, because if you're doing it right, it's situated in some kind of inaccessible terrain where no one is likely to walk on you. That was a lot more difficult in Syria, where most of the places we'd worked were both flat and extensively cultivated. Here, even in the oldest part of the kingdom of Cor Legear, we found ourselves a crack in the mountain with only one real approach, and that approach was easily covered by Santos with the Mk 48.

Camouflage was a little more difficult, since there was very little vegetation on that windswept crag above the sea. Most of the top of the hill was bare rock, and we had to find what nooks and crannies we could cram ourselves and our gear into, preferably without being visible to the fortress across the inlet.

That's the other part of hide site living that takes years off your body. Sitting in a hide is always a matter of moving from one pain to another, often for days. When you're in a small space, with six dudes who are not small—and everyone in that hide was a pretty big guy—then there's never room to stretch out, and you get steadily more cramped and sore as time goes on. Add in the fact that you're lying on rocks the entire time, and it gets worse.

There were just enough low, wind-twisted shrubs on that hilltop to conceal the actual observation post. We could only have one man up there on glass at a time, just because the slot that faced the castle was so narrow, but we couldn't have concealed any more than that, anyway, not without piling enough veg in the crack that it would be immediately obvious to anyone familiar enough with their surroundings to spot.

That's the thing about setting up in a rural area where people don't have technology to distract them. We'd seen it in places in Syria, where people walked everywhere, and had even before the civil war had started. They tend to know just about every detail of the environment where they live, even if they don't deliberately memorize it for tactical reasons. That means if something's off, they notice it even before they realize they have.

So, we hunkered down in the cracks and crevices, eventually settling on shift changes in the OP about every couple of hours. That was a calculated risk. A man can burn out quick if he's on glass continually for a long time. All the same, we had to limit the amount of movement in that crack, since it was still semi-exposed to our target.

We settled in to watch.

* * *

I can't count the number of hours I've spent in hide sites, watching a house, an intersection, or just a village, struggling to stay awake as nothing happens. The vast majority of recon and surveillance is crushing boredom.

There's a lot of work that can and has to happen during that boredom, however, and we had our hands full doing it. See, especially when you're looking for insurgent activity, it's not always going to be obvious. Sometimes it's subtle stuff that you'd miss if you weren't familiar with the area, just like you might miss a bush out of place that you'd see if you were a local who walked past that bush every day. So, you have to get acclimated, in a way, to the daily routine of the target.

We call it "pattern of life." Knowing nothing about the daily life of Edernon, we had to watch and catalog everything we saw, so that if something *was* off, we could pick it out more quickly.

That meant hours upon hours of watching people tending the fields, going down to the coast to fish and coming back up. We watched the guards on the walls and patrolling the roads and trails around the fields that surrounded the fortress.

Now, I might not have been all that familiar with Edernon and the ordinary manner of living there, but I recognized a heavy security presence when I saw it. Even during my two hours on glass, I saw that not only were there platoon-sized patrols constantly coming and going from the castle, along with what looked like a company stationed on the walls, but every common man and woman on the ground had at least a knife or an axe on them, even when what they were doing didn't seem to require it. Some even carried spears, even when the longer weapons would have gotten in the way.

The people of Edernon were nervous.

When I came back down to the main hide, I talked to Mathghaman and Bearrac about it. "I know that they've got to be worried about the Deep Ones this close to the ocean, especially after what happened in Lemmanonius. Word about that has to have gotten around by now. But they're not just watching the water."

Mathghaman nodded. "These are a people expecting war to visit them at any time." He rubbed his bearded chin as he looked up toward the slot where the OP was situated. "It certainly fits with some of Vepogenus's concerns. And yet…"

"And yet we haven't seen anything spooky."

Mathghaman smiled slightly at my choice of words.

"That would make me suspect that Melcon is not, in fact, in league with Tharain," he admitted. "However, it is no guarantee. It is possible that Tharain has fed upon his family's resentments and turned him to rebellion while still hiding his true allegiances and the depths to which he has fallen. Sorcerers are oft cunning and deceptive. It seems that many of Tharain's supporters in Cor Legear had no idea he was in league with the Empire and the Outer Dark until he unleashed those horrors into the hall."

I followed his gaze toward the OP. We were on the far side of the hill and couldn't see Edernon itself from our position in a depression in the rock. "So, how do we tell for sure? It's possible that Melcon is gearing up for war with his own king. Or maybe he's just right on the coast and he's worried about pirates and Deep Ones. Or maybe, with everything going on, he's just plain scared."

I scratched my beard. While I wasn't unused to being out in the field, it had been quite a few days since I'd managed a wash, and I itched a little, especially in the damper air this close to the sea. "How do we find out, shy of watching a full army with a Dullahan at the head riding out toward Cor Legear?"

That's always been an issue with surveillance from a distance. There's only so much you can tell just by watching through glass.

"We could go down and pay them a visit." Bearrac couldn't be comfortable, wedged between two boulders the way he was, but he didn't appear *uncomfortable*, either. He was Bearrac.

All eyes turned toward him, except for Farrar up in the OP and Santos, who was about two yards below, still holding the rear.

"How do you propose we do that?" I asked. "If they're so nervous that they're patrolling their own backyard with platoon-sized elements, how are they going to react when strangers with weird clothes and weapons ride up to their gates?"

He shrugged. "We would not ride up with rifles, helmets, and chest rigs." It always seemed a little odd, hearing a Tuacha say, "Chest rig," though the actual wording in *Tenga Tuacha* was a little different. "Two of us, dressed simply and with only our blades, might well pass as mere travelers."

I snorted. "A Tuacha isn't going to pass as a 'mere' traveler anywhere, much less here, Bearrac."

He smiled behind his massive hedge of a beard. "Perhaps not. Still, I am confident that the team can cover us from here, should we encounter trouble at the gate."

"I can go with Bearrac, if you wish, Conor." Of course Mathghaman would make that offer, though I felt a certain degree of chagrin that he'd even been able to read my reluctance and worry. Walking into a potential nest of bad guys with only two dudes, and them armed with only knives and swords, was not my idea of a good time.

I shook my head, though. "No, I'll go." I looked between them. "Who's going with me?"

"I will." Bearrac cracked his knuckles. "It *was* my idea in the first place."

He and Mathghaman traded a knowing look, and the King's Champion shook his head slightly. He definitely would have gone, but he wouldn't take this away from Bearrac.

The Tuacha are a strange people, sometimes. They are somehow more than human. They're faster, more graceful, stronger, and *much* longer lived, though I still hadn't figured out by how much. They tend to be more perceptive, wiser—in most cases—and to have a quiet depth of knowledge that puts the biggest eggheads I'd ever known back in The World to shame. And yet, all the same, they were still *very* human. Not only were they still corruptible, though it was harder, but they still had feelings and egos, and they could get prickly about their honor. The fact that a man of Mathghaman's stature could back down and leave a vital mission to one of his subordinates, simply because that man had thought up the plan and volunteered, spoke volumes.

With a shrug, I headed down to the lower crevice to give Santos our five-point contingency plan.

CHAPTER 19

IT was fortunate that I still had my "civilian attire," blue tunic and green trousers, in my ruck. Those clothes had gone from the Isle of Riamog, across the Western Sea, through the Kingdom of Cor Legear, across the plains of the northern marches of the Empire of Ar-Annator, and back again. They had taken up space and weight, but now I was glad I hadn't ditched them.

My boots were worn and dirty enough that they might not notice that they were Marine combat boots, instead of the buskins most people wore in this part of the world. The rest of my attire, tunic, breeches, cloak—even my belt—were all of Tuacha make. Fine but plain, and unlikely to attract too much attention.

Unfortunately, the same couldn't be said about the Sword at my side. Anyone with enough knowledge of the old stories would recognize that legendary blade. There was no helping it, though. I'd considered leaving it behind and just carrying my Bowie, but I hadn't been able to bring myself to set it aside, not for as long as this was likely to take. I was the Sword Bearer. The Sword of Iudicael was *my* responsibility. So, I tried to keep it under my cloak as much as possible and wore my Bowie in front of it, hoping that no one looked too closely.

Bearrac and I walked out of the trees and onto the beaten dirt track that formed the main road leading up to Edernon, only after taking a few minutes back in the shadows to watch and listen, making sure we didn't stumble upon a patrol or even one of the locals moving to or from the castle with his oxcart. Strangers on the road might be taken in stride. Strangers walking out of the woods, armed, might not.

The road was empty as we turned our faces toward Edernon. Maintaining a watchful yet somewhat casual air, we started toward the castle.

It was a nice day. It had stormed briefly the night before, which, while miserable, had actually made me somewhat glad that we were set up in the rocks. We ended up wet and cold, but at least we weren't sitting or lying in a sea of mud. The road had mostly dried up by the time Bearrac and I reached it, so the footing was firm without being soupy. The clouds were starting to blow in off the ocean, but the day's rain was still several hours off.

The woods loomed to either side of the road, the hills standing tall and dark off to our left. We wouldn't be where Mathghaman or Farrar could cover us with my M107—yes, I'd packed it in, and yes, it was a heavy beast that had slowed me down considerably on the hike up to the rocks after we'd left the horses picketed in a thick stand of trees beneath, but it gave us a long-range advantage that I wasn't inclined to do without—until we moved about another mile north. That was just the reality of the terrain, and so Bearrac and I were on our own for a while.

I'd done some sketchy stuff as a Marine, and in a way even more so since we'd traveled through the mists and come here. Singleton operations was not among the list of sketchy stuff I'd done, however. Not that I was alone, but I was still used to having at least a team at my back, if not a platoon. Bearrac's reassuring mass at my side notwithstanding, I felt downright naked with only two of us.

We'd gone maybe a half a mile before the woods to our right thinned out and we came within sight of a field. About a dozen people were out with scythes, harvesting the fall grain. All were armed, with two standing near spears that had been stuck in the ground with their back-spikes, or "lizard gutters," as the Galel called them.

Eyes lifted as we came into view on the road, and a voice was raised. We'd been spotted, and if I'd thought that these people were nervous from watching them in the OP, that was nothing compared to the reaction when they saw strangers.

One of the younger men ran for the house, while everyone else dropped their scythes and either drew their knives or pulled their spears. A moment later, a jangling alarm bell—or maybe it was a triangle—rang out from the house.

"Keep walking. We're no threat." Bearrac didn't miss a stride.

"We might not be." I eyed some of those spears, and the clearly practiced hands that held them. "I'm somewhat more concerned about them."

He chuckled. "They won't attack us. They're just on alert in case we're the vanguard for someone worse. That's all." He gripped my shoulder with that massive paw of his. "We're just travelers, Conor. Remember that. We have nothing to fear."

I nodded. My version of sneaky tended to be creeping through the woods or low-crawling through the weeds. This spy stuff was not my forte.

To be honest, it was a little surprising that Bearrac was slipping so easily into it. The Tuacha—most of them, anyway—were almost pathologically honest. This seemed a little bit too much into the realm of skullduggery for them. He later explained that it was less a matter of lying and more a matter of dissimulation. He would simply be confident, act as if he wasn't an enemy, and let them make what assumptions they would.

True to his word, the farmers watched us warily, but didn't come out to confront us. We kept going, even though the ringing of the alarm traveled ahead of us, as the next farm over took up the call, then the next after that.

About a quarter mile down the road, the nearest patrol intercepted us.

Twenty riders, mostly dressed in greens and blues, their helmets painted in the same colors—which made sense, I realized, living this close to the ocean; the salt air had to rust armor and weapons like crazy if they weren't coated—and spears in their hands. Those spears weren't leveled at us, not yet. The lead rider, a wiry man with a long, blond beard, reined in directly in front of us and sat his saddle ramrod straight, his spear pointed at the clouds and his shield on his arm. He was neither threatening nor welcoming. This was a man doing his duty, and his duty was to patrol the road and make sure no enemies approached. Until he determined which we were, he was going to be cautious.

I could respect that. Especially since I didn't currently know if we were enemies or not.

"Hold." His voice was steady, even as his eyes took in every detail of us before flitting to the woods and the road behind us, probably looking for any friends who might be coming along after us. "Who goes upon the road to Edernon? Name yourselves and state your business here!"

"We are travelers from the west." Bearrac looked around at the riders and the woods and fields. "It seems we find a land troubled by fear. What ails this place, that two men on foot are waylaid like an army of bandits?"

The man in the blue helmet eyed both of us carefully for a moment. Something had just changed his demeanor, and I wasn't sure what it was. I tried to keep myself from tensing up. With only the Sword of Iudicael and my Bowie, I was at a disadvantage if this got kinetic in the next few moments. I really, really wished I'd at least brought my .45. I probably could have hidden it under my cloak, somewhere near the small of my back. Bearrac had been insistent, though, that we bring nothing that might seem out of the ordinary, just in case.

I knew he was right, but that didn't make me feel any better about it.

The man in the blue helmet finally focused on Bearrac. "You are of the Tuacha da Riamog?"

Bearrac went completely still. I'd seen him do that before, usually just before some intense violence. The Tuacha might be possessed of great gifts of wisdom, beloved of Tigharn, but they are also warriors, one and all, and I had yet to see a regular man who could match one. Even as outnumbered as we were, I knew that he was going to put some serious hurt on these guys in the next few minutes if things got weird.

Needless to say, I was tense as a tripwire, ready to draw the Sword and go to work. I was probably a lot more obvious about it than Bearrac was.

"I am Bearrac Mag Osgar, companion to Mathghaman Mag Cathal, King's Champion of the Isle of Riamog." His voice boomed out across the road.

I looked from him to the man in the blue helmet. *There goes our spy stuff.* Still, Bearrac was no fool. He'd picked up on something I'd missed. He was not the kind who would simply announce our presence to all and sundry without good reason.

The man in the blue helmet seemed to almost sag with relief. Several of the other riders behind him did, as well. I studied them carefully, still tense and ready to move, my off hand hovering near my Bowie. I'd draw it first, then sweep out the Sword with my other hand. A Bowie isn't as ideal for blocking as the buckler affixed to the Sword's scabbard, but it'll do the trick, and I could still stab somebody while I drew the Sword.

Hanging his shield on his pommel and handing his spear off to the man beside him, the man in the blue helmet swung down off his horse and approached us, pulling his helmet off as he did so. His hair was relatively short, shorter than his beard. He was also older than he'd looked at first, with deep crow's feet around his eyes.

He bent one knee before Bearrac. I fought to keep my expression neutral and not raise an eyebrow. *That's new. Also far from what we expected from a castle in rebellion against King Uven. Something else is going on here.*

"Lord Bearrac, I am Olgudach, First Knight to Lord Melcon, Castellan of Edernon and heir of the First Clan." He looked up at my barrel-chested, black-bearded companion. "Since Tigharn has brought you here, would you help us? Would you come to Lord Melcon and speak with him?"

Bearrac glanced over at me with some amusement, but he didn't say anything about the Sword at my side. Maybe he was still feeling the situation out. "Show us to your lord."

* * *

Up close, Edernon was every bit as big as Cor Legear, the walls thick and dark with age. It wasn't a hot day, but once we passed through the massive gates and into the keep, it got downright frigid. It was a natural sort of chilly, though, born of the damp air from the sea and the fact that the sun never got all the way through those thick stone walls except in small windows, so the interior of the castle was always cold, with that sort of humid chill that cut right through your bones. It was no wonder that even on a nice day like the current one, there was a massive fire roaring in the hearth when we were brought into the great hall.

Unlike Cor Legear, or even Lemannonius, there was only one high seat on the dais, up against the back wall. Lord Melcon sat on that seat, and he struggled to rise to his feet as Bearrac and I strode into the hall, Bearrac walking in like he owned the place while I followed behind him, somewhat more cautious and ready to fight.

Melcon was a bent old man, skinny as a rail, his skin almost papery over his bones, his hair thick but snow white. He still sported a massive handlebar mustache, in keeping with Galel style, and wore a short, broad-bladed sword at his belt. Yet he was clearly not a well man.

He coughed as he took a step forward, then staggered before reaching back for a stick that leaned against the high seat, snatching it and steadying himself with it for a moment, though he still teetered alarmingly on the dais. Two of his men had already taken a semi-panicked step forward but he waved them off.

"My lord," Olgudach boomed. "I present Lord Bearrac, companion to the King's Champion of the Isle of Riamog. I found him and his companion on the road, and finding that he was of the Tuacha da Riamog…" He trailed off as Melcon raised a hand and waved at him to stop, just before going into a coughing fit.

When the ancient castellan finally got his wind again, he looked up as he leaned heavily on his stick. "What brings a Tuacha to my door, then?" His eyes moved to me and narrowed slightly. Olgudach hadn't explained me at all.

"We came seeking news, Lord Melcon." Bearrac was unbothered by the somewhat hostile greeting, in marked contrast to Olgudach's plea. "We had heard of trouble out this way."

That was certainly one way of putting it.

Melcon snorted. "Trouble we certainly have. And small assistance have we gotten from the upstart king who sits in Cor Legear!" He coughed again, then sagged back down into the high seat. The coughing subsided, and he seemed to shrink.

It was a beaten old man who looked up at Bearrac and me with watery eyes. "I am already under suspicion because of old feuds. Now I hear that Tharain is in open revolt. Monsters from the Outer Dark prowl the lands of the Galel." He folded over in another fit of coughing. When he could speak again, his voice was barely above a whisper. "Pirates raid us with impunity. They have a sorcerer with them." His voice dropped still more. "I know they are trying to force me into war with King Uven. It would be easy for a royal envoy to point to the sorcery that has haunted this place for the last month and connect us to the horror that I hear happened in Cor Legear." He looked up at us suddenly. "Did you hear about that?"

"About what, Lord Melcon?"

Good on Bearrac, I thought. Let Melcon tell us the version he had heard, and we would know a little bit more about where we stood.

The castellan leaned forward in his seat, as if he was about to whisper a secret, still leaning on his walking stick. "Lord Artbranan was possessed by a thing of the outer dark, and some winged creature burst through and took Tharain away. It is said that the possessed Lord Artbranan was as strong as seven men, and nearly killed the king!"

He stopped then, and leaned back, his eyes widening, gathering his cloak about him as if it were some sort of armor. He'd just put something together. He pointed at us with a wavering finger. "They said… they said that the Tuacha were there, with some other foreigners." His eyes moved to me. With my beard and my hair now well out of regs, I looked less like a foreigner than I had when we'd first come through the mists, but I wasn't a Galel, and I probably looked like it. His next words were in a loud whisper that was almost a hiss. "You knew all this! You came from Cor Legear!"

Everyone in the room had frozen. I eased my hand toward my Bowie, ready to go for the Sword in the next instant.

"Did you come here to trap me?" Melcon demanded.

"*Lord Melcon*!" Bearrac's voice boomed through the hall. He stood taller, somehow, more imposing. Melcon shrank back in his seat, and it seemed that most of the lords in the hall—except for Olgudach—took a step back.

Bearrac, for his part, stepped forward. "You know little about the Tuacha da Riamog, Lord Melcon, if you can honestly bring yourself to accuse one of us of such deception, especially for the sake of the politics of a nation not our own!" He folded his massive arms across his barrel chest. "I came here for answers, as did my companion, Conor McCall, Bearer of the Sword of Iudicael." All eyes turned to me, then.

For my part, I was trying not to lose my cool. This was hard compromise, if Melcon turned out to be hostile. However, I trusted Bearrac. He must have sensed that Melcon's fears were genuine, which meant he was *not* in rebellion, and therefore *not* in league with Tharain's sorcery.

So, in keeping with Rule One—Always Look Cool—I swept back my cloak and let them have a good look at the gold-accented hilts of the Sword of Iudicael.

You could have heard a pin drop in that hall for a moment. Then the commotion started.

It got so loud for a moment I almost drew the Sword anyway, unsure as to what we'd just stirred up. After a moment, though, as Melcon sagged in his seat, clearly trying not to sob, I realized that it was excitement, not hostility.

Olgudach was the one who took charge of the situation. "*My lords!*" His roar was almost as loud as Bearrac's bellow. "May we have quiet!"

The general roar died down slowly. In the aftermath, it wasn't Melcon who stepped forward, but Olgudach.

He knelt before Bearrac, looking up at the Tuacha warrior's impassive face. "My lord, I ask this without condition, as I would not besmirch the honor of a Tuacha." He glanced at me. "Or the Sword Bearer." He bowed his head slightly, almost as if he was apologizing for not knowing which of us to address first. Turning back to Bearrac, he continued. "You said you came here seeking answers. What answers do you seek?"

Bearrac glanced up at Melcon, who hadn't moved, though his rheumy eyes were fixed on my massive companion. "You have already guessed it. Sorcery has been unleashed in the kingdom of Cor Legear, sorcery aimed at overthrowing the king and paving the way for the dominion of the Empire of Ar-Annator." He looked back down at Olgudach. "Those minions of the Outer Dark who seek such power are our enemies. We seek to root them out, wherever they lurk." The look he shot toward Melcon made it clear that he still wasn't *entirely* convinced that the castellan's fear wasn't an act.

Olgudach bent his head. He took a deep breath, then stood. "If I offer myself as hostage, until such time as we can find and slay the pirates and their sorcerer, will that be sufficient to prove my lord's loyalty?"

Bearrac looked to me, then. Almost too late, I remembered that *I* had been the one the king had asked to help. That put me in the driver's seat here, and while Bearrac had steered things in his way, now he was handing me the reins, now that the situation was a little bit clearer.

Another man might have resented that. It was Bearrac, though. If there was anyone in the platoon I owed the benefit of the doubt, other than Mathghaman and Gunny, it was Bearrac. I'd play along, figuring that he probably had a lot better handle on the situation than I did.

"That would depend on your king." It seemed like the right thing to say, and while Bearrac didn't nod, I got the distinct impression that he approved, anyway. "I imagine it would work in your favor if I took news of such a thing back to him."

Olgudach bowed, then turned to Melcon. "My lord. I ask that you offer me as hostage to the Sword Bearer and his Tuacha companion." I knew that the Galel put a *lot* of stock in the Swords, but being named first, with Bearrac of all people as my "companion," was still a little odd.

Melcon sighed. I didn't think it was because he was upset, so much as he was backed into a corner and just tired. The man looked like he was pushing eighty, even before the rest of this had happened. It was still entirely possible he was much younger than that—stress can age a man quickly—but he was no warrior, not anymore.

"If they will have you, Lord Olgudach, I give leave." He looked at me, then. "I am no traitor, no rebel. If Lord Olgudach can find you the proof of that, he will."

The look he gave Olgudach was somewhat less confident than his words, and there was the implicit order that if the younger knight couldn't bring back some proof that his castellan wasn't in the Peruni's pocket, then he'd best not come back at all.

I wasn't sure what I thought about that. If he was desperate enough, would he resort to creating evidence where there was none?

We were going to have to step carefully.

Of course, Bearrac seemed to read my mind, and gripped my shoulder as we turned and headed out of the hall, Olgudach leading the way.

We'd keep our heads on a swivel and move cautiously. This was still recon. It was just recon on a level we hadn't done before.

CHAPTER 20

WE didn't set out right away. Instead, we went out on the battlements, and Bearrac waved part of his cloak toward the mountain across the inlet. I didn't need to ask what he'd done. Without comms, we were limited to visual signaling to let the rest of the team know that we were good.

Olgudach and several of the men-at-arms seemed confused, especially since we then headed down into the courtyard, out through the gate, found a log alongside the road, and sat down to wait. Olgudach stood there for a moment, frowning, then shrugged and found a seat of his own. The men-at-arms seemed much more ill at ease.

"What are we waiting for?" Olgudach finally ventured. We'd been sitting there in silence for over an hour.

Bearrac pointed. "Them."

Mathghaman came out of the trees, then, astride his horse, Rodeffer and Farrar right behind him, leading Bearrac's and my horses, with Santos taking up the rear. Several of the men-at-arms' eyes widened at the strange weapons and gear, but Olgudach maintained his equilibrium quite well. Maybe word about the strangers with their odd boom sticks had reached Edernon. There had certainly been enough time for just about every Galel in the kingdom to have heard about us, now that I thought about it.

Bearrac and I accepted our weapons and armor, geared up, and swung into the saddle. By that time, Olgudach had mounted as well and joined us, along with half a dozen men-at-arms, also mounted but not looking like they would be particularly comfortable fighting on horseback. I leaned on my saddle and faced him. Having Mathghaman and Bearrac at my back was simultaneously comforting and discomfiting. They were going to let me take lead on this, even though I figured both of them were probably better qualified than I was.

"So, where are we going?" I didn't make too much of a secret of the fact that I didn't entirely trust Olgudach, though he certainly *seemed* sincere.

He picked up on it, too. I could see it in his eyes. He was a professional, though, just like Fortrenn and Galan. He had responsibilities, and while his pride was pricked by my suspicion, he wasn't going to let it get in the way of doing his duty to his lord.

"We do not know exactly where their haven is. They come in the night, always in the night." If true, that certainly pointed toward the diabolical. If that was a term here. Most of the time, the monsters owned the night. Anyone who was comfortable moving around after dark, particularly in the borderlands where the Outer Dark was stronger, was probably in league with the monsters.

That never worked out well for them, but that didn't seem to stop anybody. *This time it'll be different.*

"However, my best guess would be the islands to the north." He pointed out to sea. "Pirates and outlaws have used them as havens in the past. They have been abandoned for at least a generation, but that is where I would begin."

I pressed my heel to Allon's flank and turned him toward the north. "Let's go, then."

* * *

The fisherman's hut was ancient and weatherbeaten, both the logs and the slats that formed the walls at the ends of the A-frame, topped with sod, turned gray by the wind, sun, and rain. Nets hung from a couple of tripods, and a boat was drawn up on the strand, but there was no sign of any movement.

We'd left our horses at the bottom of the hill and crept up toward the crest, easing our way through the coastal grass as quietly as we could, but from where we crouched, watching the hut, it didn't look like we need have bothered. No one appeared to be home.

Olgudach was ready to go down to the hut and set up an ambush, but I overruled him. We set in to wait and watch.

* * *

The day dragged on in slightly uncomfortable silence. The Galel fighters weren't Recondos, but they weren't unused to waiting, either. Theirs was not a society where everyone had to be occupied and enthralled every minute of every day. They were also used to watchfulness, and the men on watch were always alert. I didn't see the problem I'd seen more than once, working with indig in Syria, where the locals just went to sleep because there was nothing happening, when they were supposed to be on security. These guys were more on point than that.

The discomfort, I think, came from the fact that we were currently allies with the men of Edernon, but far from friends. We were foreigners—high-status foreigners, but foreigners, nonetheless—there in service to a king who held them in suspicion. There had to be some hurt pride there, even *if*, as Melcon and Olgudach both insisted, there was no treason at work in Edernon.

That doesn't make for great rapport-building.

Still, to their credit, they stayed close and traded off on observation and security, rather than setting up their own OP elsewhere. Part of that was simple necessity, since there weren't a lot of great positions where we could observe the hut and the shore. Part of it, however, I think was Olgudach consciously trying to overcome that mutual suspicion.

I had just woken up from my brief nap, ready to take my turn on security, when I heard a hissed whisper. Looking up toward the crest of the hill, I saw Farrar motioning to me. I rolled over and crawled up to join him, keeping low and as deep in the grass as I could. Farrar had clearly seen something, and he was down as flat on the hill as he could get.

He pointed through the coastal bunchgrass as I got closer. Any movement that I might make as I parted the stalks to peer through was easily disguised by the wind coming off the water.

Our fisherman hadn't been away, from the looks of it. He was just a really late riser. It was probably a good thing we hadn't tried to go down and set up in the hut.

Even as I set eyes on him, the shaggy man in an unbelted tunic stretched his back and spread his arms as he looked out to sea. He seemed utterly unconcerned with fishing, but scratched himself, glanced off to the northwest, then hawked and spat on the sand before going back inside the hut.

"What kind of fisherman stays in bed until the sun's been up for two hours?" Farrar whispered. "I know when I was fishing a lot, I tried to get out right at first light."

"Maybe one who isn't much of a fisherman." I kept scanning the ocean and the hills to either side of us, but nothing moved. The fisherman came back out with a pot and started a fire in a ring of blackened stones just outside the hut. "Maybe the nets are a cover, and he's here for something else."

We went back to watching and waiting.

* * *

The rest of the day was pretty boring. The shaggy man actually did go out to fish for a while, though he didn't go far, and we still could keep an eye on him while his little boat bobbed on the waves about half a mile offshore. He was casting his nets, so he *was* fishing, and I realized that as far as he knew, there wasn't anyone around for miles, so it seemed unlikely that he was putting on an act to build his cover.

Then, after a while, he leaned over the gunwale for a long time. I felt the hairs on the back of my neck go up as I watched him, and suddenly wished I could just knock him off with the M107 right then and there. It would be a bit of a long shot, but still doable, if tricky because of the movement of the boat.

Don't ask me how I knew, but I was sure that he was communing with some minion of the Deep Ones. Nobody just hangs over the side of a boat like that for that long. Given what we'd already seen of this guy, I suspected a merrow, just like the thing that had ensnared Achivir in Lemmanonius. That was big. If that was what was happening out there, it marked this guy as a bit of a lynchpin, *somehow*. Why else would the Deep Ones bother with him, when they could just pull him down and eat him?

That alone was reason to take this guy down, but we just watched. Because we really *did* have bigger fish to fry. And we hoped that he'd lead us to them.

Recon ain't fun. It's a truism. Most of it is boring. Sometimes, it's not so much boring as it requires to you sit and watch things that you'd rather do something about, because the mission requires it. Sometimes that works out. Sometimes it's bullshit, and you really *should* have done something about it.

I watched the fisherman, wondering if I really was making the right call. After all, if we offed him, his contacts wouldn't necessarily know it. Maybe we should cut this link out of the killchain right then and there.

I didn't, though, just in case. A .50 cal is *loud*, and the sound of the report would travel. Presuming the Deep Ones didn't pass word about his demise.

So, we stayed in place, avoided compromise, and continued to watch.

* * *

Night fell. The fisherman had come back in after several hours out on the water. As the sun started to go down, he stayed up and puttered around the fire outside his hut, but he kept looking up and out to sea, always toward the northwest. He was definitely waiting for something. Or someone.

About an hour after sunset, as the last of Early Evening Nautical Twilight faded into actual night, they came.

Three large boats, not quite longships—they were noticeably smaller than the corsairs' vessels—came out of the dark and slid up onto the shore.

The fisherman stood as the raiders got out of the boats. None of them were particularly remarkable. They wore simple tunics and breeches and not much else. It was getting cold at night on the coast, so several of them were wrapped in wool or oilskin capes and cloaks, but they wore no armor, though they positively bristled with weapons. Knives, short swords, axes, and short javelins predominated, along with a few small round and square shields.

The Galel fighters with us couldn't see more than their shapes in the dim, flickering light of the fisherman's fire, but we could see fine through our NVGs. Mathghaman and Bearrac could probably see even better with their naked eyes.

I couldn't tell whether these raiders were Galel themselves, corsairs from the north, or some mix of the two. Maybe they were the outcasts of several tribes. Either way, they approached the fire and the fisherman greeted them warmly.

The short, wiry man in the lead, who carried a pair of javelins behind a small, square shield, didn't seem to return the man's warmth, but still greeted him anyway. We were too far away to hear what was said, and that was deliberate. You get too close to an objective, and you're asking for compromise. Standoff is vital.

Several of the raiders moved around the hut and two of them ducked inside as others spread out around the beach. Clearly, these guys didn't exactly trust the fisherman, either. That might have been simply because they were outlaws.

After a while, as the wiry leader sat down cross-legged by the fire, watching the fisherman—who seemed entirely at ease, despite the fact that the raiders clearly thought he might be ready to betray them at any moment—the rest of them settled down as well. It almost looked like they weren't going anywhere that night. In fact, half of them rolled up in their cloaks and went to sleep in the next few minutes.

I eased back down the back side of the hill until I was well out of sight of the fisherman's fire and joined Olgudach, Mathghaman, Bearrac, and Santos. "Looks like they're settling in for the night. Maybe they'll try to raid in the morning?"

"Perhaps." Olgudach's hoarse whisper was a little too loud, but hopefully the wind and the waves would drown it out. "Or perhaps they are waiting until later in the night." He was craning his neck as if he could see over the hill, which he'd have to be a giraffe to do. "They almost always strike at night. The creatures they call upon prefer it."

Mathghaman looked at him carefully for a moment. I could almost see the wheels turning in the King's Champion's mind. Probably because I was wondering the same thing. *Is that the truth, or a cover for your castellan dabbling in things he shouldn't be?*

"So, what do you want to do?" I turned to Mathghaman rather than Olgudach. I still wasn't sure if I trusted any course of action Olgudach would suggest, and he accepted being shut out in a way, probably because he knew that he was there as a guide and backup. It was the only way he could clear Melcon's name. I think he knew that if he pushed too hard, he'd only increase our suspicions.

Mathghaman raised an eyebrow, and I could have sworn that I saw the shadow of a smile behind his beard as he turned to look at me. "Are you asking me what I would suggest we do?"

Once again, he was reminding me that I was the team leader here. Not because Mathghaman felt like being lazy. I don't think there was a lazy bone in his body, any more than there was in Bearrac's. No, he was doing what Gunny would do. He was guiding me, making me step into the role of team leader—and, probably, Sword Bearer.

I thought about it. We might find more out by waiting and watching, possibly trailing them when they did move. However, that went against the grain a bit. Would we be able to keep up? Would we be able to get into position fast enough to gain any useful intelligence and still be able to intervene if things got out of hand?

I didn't have Big Marine Corps looking over my shoulder, telling me to stay out of it because saving innocent people wasn't part of the mission. I'd justified letting the fisherman alone, even when I'd been pretty sure he'd been communing with the forces of the abyss, because there was no immediate threat, even though there was a considerable long-term threat.

Here, though, if I was really in charge, there was nothing to keep me from intervening, even if it meant we didn't quite get the intel we were after.

For some reason, the words *Evil may not be done, that good might result* echoed through my head, just then. And to just sit there and watch while raiders slaughtered innocent farmers would be an unmitigated evil, no matter what I hoped to get out of it.

Maybe it was just a lot of dismal missions in Syria that was making me think this way. Maybe it was all the time we'd spent with the Tuacha. Maybe it was the Sword at my side.

Maybe it was a little of all three.

"We'll give them a bit of time, then move in and hit them." I glanced at Olgudach. "The men of Edernon will be right there with us, night vision or not." If they wanted to prove that they were on the right side, I'd give them a chance. "We need at least one alive." While we'd done our share of "kill or capture" missions in Syria, those had always been against sleeping, unsuspecting HVTs in targeted houses, usually at about two in the morning. An actual attempt at a prisoner grab from active belligerents in the middle of a fight wasn't something that the Marine Corps had particularly prepared us for. One more example of something our forefathers, as regular grunts in World War II, Korea, and Vietnam, had done that we weren't allowed to do anymore because it was "too dangerous."

Mathghaman and Bearrac simply nodded. Santos's expression, as always, was a little hard to make out. His NVGs blocked the upper half of his face, and he'd gotten good at hiding his mouth behind his beard. My enormous ATL still buzzed his head—as much as he could with the tools we had—but his beard had gotten almost as big and bushy as Bearrac's.

Still, I knew Vince Santos better than anyone else in this world except Sean Bailey. I knew what he was thinking. It was risky as hell, but he was down for it. He'd never admit otherwise, anyway.

We started to prep, while the raiders settled down for their rest plan.

CHAPTER 21

IT was just after midnight when we closed in.

I'd debated just how to handle this. There had been no sign of either sorcerers or even bows, which meant the most ranged weapons they had were their javelins. They still had two men up on watch, one facing the shore, one the waves. I got the distinct impression that they were just as worried about the Deep Ones, this close to the sea, as they were about discovery from landward.

I hesitated to go in without setting overwatch, just in case. I finally left Farrar and Santos on the hill, Santos watching the beach with the Mk 48 while Farrar covered his back.

The Galel went first, with Rodeffer, the Tuacha, and me just behind and on their flank. Not that I didn't trust them, but…

We stayed low as we moved down the slope. We were coming in from the south, where there were a few more wind-twisted bushes and dunes to hide behind. Furthermore, the landward sentry was watching the east more than the south.

Rodeffer was a few paces ahead of me, watching the sentry. He was good at this, too good to stare fixedly at a target who was awake and alert. So, I was pretty sure it wasn't his fault, even though we were less than fifty yards from the sentry, when the raider suddenly got to his feet, his javelin in his hand, turning toward where we were crouched in the grass.

Mathghaman, Bearrac, Rodeffer, and I all froze. The Galel, immediately to our left, didn't. They might not have seen the sentry stand up. While they'd had time to let their eyes adjust, it was a *dark* night, and the fire had died down to embers. We could see well enough with our NVGs, but the Galel didn't have that advantage.

Which was why one of them stumbled a moment later, his spear knocking against his shield with a loud *clock.*

The sentry let out a yell, turning as quick as a cat and throwing a handful of something on the fire. The flames roared up, casting a bright glow over the beach, and the raiders started awake, grabbing for weapons. The sentry stepped away from the fire, hefting his javelin and searching for targets.

I shot him first, putting a bullet through his brain at fifty yards. It wasn't that long a shot, and the offset red dot had barely settled before my trigger broke. He was a much more immediate threat than any of the rest, who were still waking up and figuring out what the hell was going on.

Then the door of the hut burst open, and a much worse threat sprang out into the open.

The fisherman wasn't a man, after all. An eac uisge bounded out of the hut, a bone-tipped spear in its hands, its too-large, fishlike eyes gleaming in the dark.

Without missing a beat, the monster of the Deep Ones launched its spear straight at the man who'd stumbled, and as fragile as that thing looked, it slammed right through the Galel man-at-arms' throat, sticking a foot out the back of his neck. He stood for a brief moment, choking on his own blood, then collapsed, the haft of the spear forcing his body over onto its side.

I shifted my aim to the eac uisge and fired as soon as the dot crossed its torso, just as Mathghaman and Bearrac slammed four rounds each into it. The creature staggered, then took two more rounds to the head, at which point it collapsed into a gushing puddle of transparent slime.

The rest of the raiders were on their feet, and the Galel were starting to close into a shield wall as they moved forward, but before they could close the distance to the raiders, who still couldn't quite see what they were up against, Santos intervened.

The first burst stopped the Galel in their tracks, even as it cut three of the raiders down. Santos walked the rounds from the first man's feet up and to the right, ripping that first raider's guts out before punching about three sets of four ball, one tracer into the next two men, smashing them to the sand in a spatter of blood.

The rest bolted, realizing that they were outmatched. They were in the open, though, and Santos was solidly behind the gun and ready for the movement.

Six more raiders hit the sand, cut down by two more bursts, and then Mathghaman stood and bellowed.

"Stand where you are if you want to live!"

For a moment, it looked like they might surrender. But the eac uisge hadn't been alone.

A horrific screech came from the dark water beyond the edge of the beach. I let my eyes snap that way for a moment, just in time to see two green lamps gleaming just above the waves.

The fisherman had indeed been speaking with a merrow, it seemed. Except he'd been just as monstrous.

Even as the merrow surged toward the shore, its minions got ahead of it. With a storm of thrashing limbs and foam, a wave of sea trolls came out of the water, their eyes glittering in the firelight, saliva dripping from the mass of translucent fangs in their gaping mouths.

The raiders were caught between the monsters and the machinegun. They didn't fare well. As soon as the trolls started taking losses, they lashed out at anything warm blooded that came within reach, and that meant the raiders. Several were torn to pieces, fangs and talons sinking deep into unarmored flesh, and went down screaming.

Our Galel allies were being smart, and they had circled up on a dune, while those who had brought short bows started lobbing arrows into the mass of scales, teeth, and rubbery flesh.

I tried to get a shot at the merrow, hoping that killing it would throw the trolls for a loop. Nothing so far had stopped those things except killing them, but it was worth a try, especially as Santos continued to turn them into chum with long, chattering bursts of 7.62. Mathghaman, Bearrac, and Rodeffer were engaging trolls with single shots and controlled pairs, while I tried to get a shot at those green, glowing eyes between swells.

My first shot hit a wave, deflected harmlessly by the water. Bullets don't go far in seawater, losing their energy fast. And it takes a bit to kill a merrow, though Mathghaman had done it in one shot in Lemmanonius. The creature was staying low, with only ever its face out of the water, and that only when a wave had passed. It was a thing of the deep, and it didn't need to come all the way out even to direct the feral things of scale and teeth that were trying to rip us apart.

Some of the trolls had moved fast enough that they were closing on the Galel, getting near enough that Santos had to shift fire to avoid hitting any of our allies. Battle was joined a moment later, as one of the sea trolls threw itself on one of the men-at-arms' shields, snapping its mass of needle teeth at his face, just before Olgudach thrust his sword through its skull.

Meanwhile, I got a good shot at the merrow and fired again.

That thing hadn't moved since the fight had started. I didn't know if it was overconfident, or simply didn't understand just how far away I could reach out and touch it.

My next round smashed through one of those glowing green eyes, putting them both out forever.

Unfortunately, that didn't stop the sea trolls, or even give them pause. Apparently, killing the merrow that had thrown them at us was not the same as getting shouted at by one of the carved faces that the Fohorimans used as sentinels against the Deep Ones. They kept coming, two of them dying even as they tore two more raiders apart, the rest scuttling along the dunes on all fours, almost like crabs, moving faster than anything built like a man should when crawling like that.

More gunfire crackled through the night, but those things were hard to hit when they were belly to the ground and moving fast. I caught one by sheer luck—or maybe something else than luck—when it came over the dune, my bullet hitting it in the chin and blowing the top of its skull off. Then they were too close for rifles, and I slung my M110 and drew the Sword.

Mathghaman already had his out, and strode to meet the monsters, his blade flashing in the firelight. Two of them died with as many strokes.

Two more were coming for me, their heads up at an unnatural angle for a man, their mouths gaping and hissing as they scuttled forward like something out of a nightmare. I tried to sidestep as I stabbed at one of them, trying to get them lined up so they couldn't both come at me at once. They were too fast, though. That one dodged at the last moment, throwing itself to one side before lunging to its feet, while the other darted around and in, snapping for my ankle.

That one did get stabbed through the skull, pinning it to the ground, but then the first one was on me.

If I'd grabbed my buckler with my off hand, I might have been in trouble. Since I'd trained for that draw for weeks and months, I should have. Instead, though, I'd grabbed my Bowie, and so when that sea troll lunged for me, it got eight inches of razor-sharp steel through its gullet.

Those things were so ferocious that that didn't stop it, though. Even as it was dying, it was still trying to claw at me and snap at my face, though fortunately my mail kept its talons off.

I brought the Sword of Iudicael up and over, then, splitting the thing's skull as I yanked the Bowie free. Watery blood gushed from the wound as it twitched, then dropped, as I dragged the Sword's blade out with hardly a tug.

That Bowie was a McCall family heirloom. My father had carried it in Vietnam. His father had carried it in World War II. I loved that knife. But it was almost crude compared to the Sword of Iudicael, which never seemed to stick, never took a stain, and never needed to be sharpened.

When I looked around again, the fight was over. The last of the sea trolls was still thrashing, but it had been cut open from crotch to throat, its watery blood spilling out to darken the sand, even as the flames in the fire pit slowly subsided.

Sheathing the Sword and the Bowie, I brought my rifle back up and advanced on the hut, keeping my muzzle pointed at the door. One eac uisge had come out of there, but that didn't mean there weren't more nasty surprises waiting in there.

It took moments to clear it. It was a small room, low-roofed, and the furniture was ancient, rotting, and clearly unused.

The bones in the corner told the tale. There *had* been a genuine fisherman who had lived here. The eac uisge had probably killed him and eaten him before assuming his shape.

I let the rifle hang and ducked out of the hut. Nothing. No intel at all. Whatever exactly was going on here, it had died with the puddle of slime still soaking into the sand not far from the threshold. And even if we'd captured that thing, I doubted it would have talked. A glance at the bodies on the beach told me that we weren't going to get anything from any of the raiders, either. None of them had survived.

"So much for taking one alive." I spat.

"We've got boats now, though." Rodeffer nodded toward the raiders' craft. "If we assume that Olgudach is right, and they're staging off those islands, now we've got a way to get to them." He glanced at the sky. None of us were wearing watches anymore, but we'd gotten pretty good at judging the time of day by reading the positions of sun and stars. "We might even get there with a bit of night left."

I looked over at Mathghaman. He nodded slightly. It was as good an idea as any.

And I wanted to know why the Deep Ones were involved as well as the Peruni.

CHAPTER 22

THE islands were low lumps of darkness on the horizon ahead, limned with the faint white of the breakers crashing against the rocks in our NVGs. I could see no structures, no fortifications. Olgudach had said that there weren't any; the islands were riddled with caves that the pirates used in place of such easily identifiable target sites. Unfortunately, there was no map to show us where those caves were, which was going to make the next phase somewhat interesting.

I held up a hand, and the Galel men-at-arms stopped rowing. There hadn't been enough of us, all told, to man more than one of the boats. That did ultimately mean that this one was kind of crowded, and riding low in the water, but at least we had the guns to fight at a distance if we got spotted while still at sea.

The boat drifted on the swell as I scanned the coast in front of us. The eastern horizon, the coastal mountains still visible as a dark, jagged line, was starting to turn pale as dawn approached. We didn't have a lot of time.

If I hadn't been wearing my NVGs, I might not have seen it. But the PVS-15s amplified the faint, flickering glow coming from a cave about twenty feet above the water. I pointed, and Rodeffer nodded. He saw it, too.

It took a moment to find a suitable landing spot that might be shielded from the cave. We didn't want to alert the bad guys any earlier than need be, though on the other hand, if that disrupted whatever they were doing, so much the better. There was something about that glow, especially when I turned my head to try to see it around my NVGs—there's only so much you can tell through monochrome green—that put my teeth on edge. Something weird was going on in there, and the sooner it got broken up, the better.

There wasn't a beach, strictly speaking, anywhere on the near coast of that rock. There were spots where the cliffs weren't as high, but no beach as such. We drifted a few dozen more yards before Rodeffer plucked at my sleeve and pointed.

Another of the raiders' boats was tied up to the cliff, next to what appeared to be crudely cut steps hammered into the cliff. We wouldn't have seen it if we hadn't been right on top of it. This little cove was well hidden.

Fortunately, it didn't appear to be guarded. It almost looked as if all the raiders, except for those few that would fit on that boat, had gone ashore and gotten slaughtered.

That didn't mean we could relax, though. There was still something going on. That was becoming more evident with each yard we drifted closer.

A sonorous, droning chant was coming out of that cave, and I could *feel* the tension building in the air. I knew that feeling. If the sorcerer had stayed back on the island while the raiders had gone ashore, that probably meant he was conjuring something big and heavy, too.

We needed to get in there, quick, before the sorcerer or shaman finished. We weren't prepared to go toe-to-toe with a denizen of the Outer Dark. That usually involves lengthy vigils, even for the Tuacha. For four Recon Marines, not to mention Galel warriors of unknown degrees of virtue and loyalty, it was something else.

Since I couldn't see any sentries, I signaled for us to move in closer, holding a finger to my lips to order quiet. Olgudach mirrored my gesture. He didn't want to get compromised in this place any more than I did.

The Galel might be mostly farmers and warriors, but since Edernon was on the coast, these guys knew their way around boats, too. They steered our captured craft in next to the remaining raider vessel smoothly and quietly, the oars making hardly a splash, and brought us to a drifting halt, as gentle as you please. Hands reached out as they shipped oars, grabbing the docked boat's gunwale and helping slow ours until we sat still alongside.

There were iron rings set into the stone of the cliff, crusted with corrosion, and the raiders' boat was tied to one of those. It was the matter of a moment to throw two half hitches around another, securing our boat to the cliff.

Then I was stepping off, out of the bow, my M110 aimed up at the top of the cliff. Mathghaman was right on my heels, and I could hear Santos's whispered grumbling about stack jumpers.

The steps were slick, narrow, and uneven. We had to slow down as we moved up toward the cave, even as every nerve screamed at me that we had to get in there and put a bullet in that warlock *now*, before things got so much worse.

We reached the top after only a minute or so, as much as it felt longer. I was sure I was slowing Mathghaman down, but he stayed with me and didn't push or sweep past me once we got to the top. His own rifle leveled, we advanced on the cave side by side. The rest of the team spread out behind us, Santos grabbing Farrar and moving to the flanks to cover our six while Rodeffer and Bearrac stacked up with Mathghaman and me.

The glow coming from the cave was leaking around a corner; the entrance didn't lead straight in. We moved up carefully, muzzles and eyes moving to every nook and cranny as we passed under the damp rock overhead and into the cave system.

Turning the corner, the sonorous chanting got louder and more oppressive. There was something about it, even though I couldn't understand the words, that put my nerves even more on edge. Something that brought to mind blood and viscera and nightmares. The stench coming out of that opening in the stony cliff was nauseating, a combination of sulfur, blood, death, and something even more metallic.

The glow, which I could now see around the edges of my NVGs, was a lurid blood red. It got brighter as we got closer, though it pulsed and flickered. Not like a fire. Its rhythm was almost like the breathing of some massive beast.

Mathghaman gave me the squeeze almost as soon as I'd halted to stack on the chamber. There wasn't time to sneak a peek and see what we were about to get into. The chanting continued, but now there were shouted words, incantations separate from the chant. Whatever was happening, it was happening in the next few seconds.

We flowed into the cavern, and into a scene of horror.

A fire burned in the center of the chamber, and a man had been spread-eagled above it, hanging from chains set into the ceiling. He'd been flayed open like the man on the table in Tharain's house, and his skin was stretched out from his back like wings. He was clearly dead, but even so, *something* was stirring in the hole in his chest cavity. The dark robed man stood with his back to the opening, his arms spread wide and a nasty-looking knife in his hand, barking out harsh, guttural syllables that started a stabbing pain behind my left eye, while the half dozen or so raiders knelt around the fire, spattered with blood, continuing that sonorous chant.

Mathghaman and I shot the sorcerer through the skull from twenty feet away at almost the same time. Blood and brains splashed and hissed in the fire, but we were a split second too late.

The hanging corpse jerked and spasmed, almost as if the dead man felt the flames beneath him, but it was simply because of the thing clawing its way out of his heart.

Long, chitinous black limbs ripped their way out through the ribcage, cracking bone and cartilage as the thing tore its way free. It resembled a gigantic, black spider—in fact, it looked like a supersized black widow—far too big to have actually fit inside the dead man. The stench was nearly overpowering.

I shot it immediately, hammering half my magazine into it. None of the bullets seemed to do much. It hissed at me, spat something that sizzled when it hit the rock next to me, and then climbed the chains toward the ceiling.

Mathghaman shot it a fraction of a second later, even as Bearrac and Rodeffer moved in and shifted their fire to the raiders who were even then scrambling to their feet and snatching up their weapons. Their eyes streamed blood like tears and they screamed as they came on. It was a sound that was part rage, part agony, part fear.

They died quickly. Rodeffer was a hell of a shot, and he had practiced to the point he could drag that longer, heavier M110 across multiple targets as fast as he'd learned to do it with an M4. His shots blended together into a single, staccato rhythm, and men dropped as bullets punched through lungs and hearts.

Bearrac was even faster, and he was taking headshots.

I saw that only peripherally, as Mathghaman and I were still trying to kill the spider thing. I'm sure we both hit it multiple times, as fast as it was climbing toward the rocky ceiling overhead, but it didn't even slow down, and then it slithered through a crack in the rock.

I could have sworn that it was far too big to fit through that opening, which didn't appear to go anywhere, but then again, I'd just watched that thing claw its way out of a man's chest that was half its size.

With the spider creature vanished, we dropped our muzzles toward our more human adversaries, but the work was done. The cavern was quiet except for the crackle of the flames, the glow of the fire now a normal, golden hue instead of the hellish red it had been before.

I looked around at the carnage. "We need to burn everything in here."

Mathghaman had already moved to the sorcerer, turning the body over with his boot. There wasn't much left of the man's face, between two 7.62 exit holes and the fact that he'd fallen on his face in the fire. If he was Galel, Peruni, or something else, it was now impossible to tell.

"That thing wasn't one of the Deep Ones' creatures." We'd seen *some* cooperation between the Deep Ones and the other monsters and sorcerers in this world, but those relations seemed to be adversarial more than anything else. One thing I'd definitely noticed in our time since crossing the mists was that the forces of evil tended to hate each other at least as much as they hated anyone else. "But these raiders seemed to be working with them."

"Temporarily, at any rate." Bearrac nodded back the way we'd come. "It was hard to see in the dark, but there was a noose hanging down to the water off the point." His voice was grim. "They sacrificed a man to the Deep Ones for their assistance."

"Yet it would seem they did so only to keep themselves secure in this place and on the crossing." Mathghaman bent over the dead sorcerer and withdrew an amulet from within the corpse's robes. It made my eyes itch to look at it, but aside from the look of distaste on his face, it didn't seem to bother Mathghaman much. "You were right, Conor. This is no thing of the Deep Ones." He tossed it into the fire, where it cracked open with—I kid you not—a shrill scream. "This is old, dark sorcery. Worse than anything the Peruni wizards usually dabble in."

"Like Outsider stuff?" Rodeffer asked.

Mathghaman nodded as he turned toward the cavern entrance. The faint light of dawn had started to spill through the opening. "Like that wielded by the Dullahans, in the days just after the Summoner bound them to himself."

"I have seen that amulet before." I'd barely noticed Olgudach's entrance into the cavern. He stood nearby, staring at the flames as they ate up the evil bit of jewelry, which still seemed to writhe in a way not easily explained by the fire, that faint scream still wailing just behind the crackle of the burning. The look on his face was a stark mix of horror and fury.

"Where?" Mathghaman turned to face him, and I did the same, feeling a jolt of adrenaline. If this thing had been floating around the kingdom already, then the root of this corruption went deeper than the king had feared.

Olgudach's expression hardened as he put the pieces together. A killing rage blazed in his eyes when he met Mathghaman's gaze. "Killaros. It is a small hold, near the center of the kingdom. It has never been of great importance, as much as Lord Cemoyd might wish otherwise." Distaste twisted his mouth behind his mustache. "He is a small man, convinced more of his own sophistication and intellect than anything else. He has performed no great deeds, but he has collected many curiosities and displayed them about his keep to impress people." He nodded toward the fire, though he avoided looking directly at the amulet. "That was among his collection."

Mathghaman nodded. "We must make for Killaros, then. Whether or not the trail leads there, it touches there at the least. There is little left to follow here." A glance at the dead body of the sorcerer was enough to explain that comment. "And I fear that we are already well behind our enemies."

He strode out of the chamber, ignoring the bodies of the raiders and the sacrificial victim. "That thing was not here for anything on this island. It would not have fled otherwise. It was drawn out of the Outer Dark to do something on the mainland.

"We must make haste."

CHAPTER 23

THE first sign that things had gone very, very badly came as we neared Edernon again. Every man capable of bearing arms appeared to have been brought in to surround the castle. Knots of armed men and knights were clustered at all points of the compass, and if Edernon was not currently under siege, it looked like Melcon was expecting them to be at any moment.

Olgudach's face grew clouded as we rode closer. Something had certainly happened, and it didn't look like it was anything good.

For a moment, as we neared the northernmost warband, the knights prepared their lances and shields, and it looked like we were in for a fight. Santos shifted in his saddle, his Mk 48 across his knee. Letting rip with that pig from horseback probably wasn't going to go very well, but he'd at least take a good chunk of our opposition out before the frightened horse threw him. We hadn't trained as cavalry. At best, we were dragoons, riding to the general area of the battle before getting off and walking, like we'd trained for years to do.

The lead knight, a younger man with a green-dyed crest on his helmet and a green tunic under his battered scale shirt, beneath an orange cape, looked up as Olgudach kicked his horse closer and raised a hand to call a halt. "Lord Olgudach!" He reined in, quickly raising the point of his lance. "You have returned!"

Olgudach looked like he wanted to light into the man for stating the obvious, but he rode forward, his face thunderous. "What goes on here?"

The younger man gulped. He looked about old enough to be Olgudach's son, or maybe even his grandson. "Lord Fidaich's hold was attacked, night before last. The tracks led back here, and he rode out to confront Lord Melcon about it. Before they could speak, some many-legged horror came out of the earth and tore him and all but one of his men to pieces. That one ran, before the creature disappeared back into the ground." The young man gulped. "Lord Melcon saw it all happen and collapsed before it was over. He lies near death even now."

"Who commands, then?" If Olgudach had been angry before, that had given way to a sort of weary resignation.

"Lord Entifidich, my lord." The kid was obviously in some awe of Olgudach, and equally obviously reluctant to name the man who had taken over with Melcon indisposed.

Olgudach snarled silently. "Take me to him." He turned to Mathghaman and me. "This may take a day, but I *will* accompany you to Killaros. I *will* see my lord vindicated."

Mathghaman merely inclined his head. I kept my own expression stony. This might be everything that it appeared to be. It might still be an elaborate ruse.

If the men of Edernon thought they could string two Tuacha along for any length of time, though, I thought they were in for a disappointment.

We rode toward the gate, getting some odd looks from more than a few of the knights and men-at-arms. Most of them had only seen me in tunic and breeches. The armor and helmet with its NVG mount were odd enough; the chest rig and rifle must have seemed downright bizarre. They recognized our weapons as weapons, but we stood out as foreigners far more than if we'd just walked in speaking English.

Olgudach was on the warpath as he rode in the gate, swung off his horse, and stormed inside the keep. We sort of hung back, but he paused right at the top of the steps and turned back to us.

"Come. You should be here for this, since you saw what happened."

I could read into the subtext, at least a little. Olgudach's mission right then was to vindicate himself and his lord, and by extension, all the men of Edernon. To make it appear that he was trying to hide something worked against that, so even though we were foreigners, and not there *officially* in King Uven's name, he wanted it to be very clear that he *wasn't* hiding anything. The fact that two of us were Tuacha probably helped, too.

Mathghaman and I swung down, leaving the horses with Bearrac and Santos. "Keep your eyes open." I didn't need to say it, but all of my teammates nodded anyway, their attention already wholly devoted to our surroundings. This was a dangerous situation, and we all knew it.

Olgudach strode right into the great hall where we'd first met Melcon. A spare, slope-shouldered man in blue and green paced in front of the high seat, empty now, as Melcon probably lay unconscious in one of the rooms above us. About a dozen older knights lined the walls, all in armor and murmuring amongst themselves, but few approached the taller man, and they seemed to try to fade into the stonework as Olgudach came striding through the doors.

"Lord Entifidich!" Olgudach's voice boomed through the hall.

The stoop-shouldered man stiffened, and a momentary look of dislike flitted across his face. Clearly, these too men did not get along at the best of times.

"Lord Olgudach. I fear your investigation was too little, too late. The forces of the Outer Dark have already driven us to the brink." Entifidich's voice was slightly nasally, his words clipped.

"To the brink, but not yet over it." Olgudach's tone, as much as his expression and attitude, left no doubt as to who was in charge.

Entifidich seemed inclined to argue, though. "Fidaich was close to the king. What do you think is going to happen once word reaches Cor Legear that he was slain by a sorcerous abomination right on our doorstep?" He glanced at us but seemed to dismiss us. Probably not a great call on his part. He spread his hands. "Our hand has been forced, Lord Olgudach. We no longer have any choice. We can strike now and regain the throne for Lord Melcon, or else we can be crushed."

Olgudach stepped closer to Entifidich, inside his personal space. The Galel were easily as prickly about that sort of thing as Americans tend to be, except they were probably more likely to come to blows over it. The fact that Entifidich stepped back instead of challenging Olgudach said a great deal about both men.

"Your concern for your lord's welfare is noted, Lord Entifidich. However, your honor and your loyalty to king and kingdom—or lack thereof—are also noted." He looked like he was about to strike the stoop-shouldered man, but he restrained himself. "There is *always* a choice. And yours is telling. By striking out at the king now, you would put yourself—and Edernon as a whole—on the side of the Peruni and the sorcerers and monsters of our enemies. Is that what you want?"

For a moment, the tension in the hall seemed to get ratcheted up a notch. Even I understood just what kind of a deadly challenge those words represented. I also had little doubt, right then, that Olgudach would back them up with steel. Entifidich's life hung by a thread.

Entifidich understood it, too. In fact, from the look that flashed through his eyes, he hadn't even thought through that angle. The sheer horror that crossed his face told me that Entifidich wasn't really the threat. I hoped it told Olgudach that, too.

Unless he had other reasons to kill Entifidich and establish his own dominance.

As Entifidich backed down, bowing his head, however, Olgudach seemed to relax, ever so slightly.

"Forgive me, Lord Olgudach." The younger man seemed genuinely chastened. "I had not thought of that."

For a long moment, Olgudach just stared him down, his expression stony, his eyes cold. "To act without considering such things, especially as a lord and knight, puts not only yourself at grave risk, but it opens all those we are responsible for to the Outer Dark. You would do well to consider that gravely next time." He stepped past Entifidich and onto the dais, standing next to the high seat, and turned to face the knights in the hall. "Our enemies seek to drive us into open war with King Uven. Upstart he may be, but he is a Galel, and a faithful servant of Tigharn. I will be dead before I will side with Ar-Annator and their dark masters against even an upstart king!" His voice cracked across the hall like a whip. "And I will hang any man who would from the battlements by his ankles! Alive!"

If it was an act, it was a good one, and all the other men in the hall were either in on it or believed it to the core.

"We ride for Killaros." His tone brooked no argument. He stabbed a finger at a man with shoulder-length gray hair and a black mustache. "Lord Gede, I leave Edernon and Lord Melcon under your protection." His voice dropped slightly. "I trust I shall return to find both well."

CHAPTER 24

WE didn't head out immediately. Olgudach had some housekeeping to do, regardless of his impatience, and so did we.

Comms weren't something we'd messed with all that much since we'd arrived through the mists. For the most part, we hadn't had any higher headquarters to talk to over the radio, so the long-range stuff had been almost entirely neglected. Fortunately, we'd still brought the radios, even if they weren't the same PRC-150s that we'd sailed with off the *Makin Island.* These still looked like 150s, but they were from the *Coira Ansec,* which meant they were lighter, they worked better, and the batteries never seemed to die.

That could be a plus or a minus, if you were the comms guy.

Farrar had gotten off lightly so far. He had been the RTO, the team radio operator, when we'd left the *Makin Island*'s well deck. But since we'd only used the radios—and those the PRC-152s—for short-range tactical comms since we'd started using them again at all, he hadn't had to get a long-distance comm shot.

Even though the *Coira Ansec* radios worked far better than the original radios we'd brought, they still weren't magic. He still needed to actually work the antenna and get a proper HF shot, and that takes some skill.

The PRC-152 was the size of a big walkie-talkie, but it was capable of short-range VHF and UHF as well as satcom. We had no satellites here, so the last capability was completely useless. The HF operation was what we needed now, which was why we'd brought the bigger, boxier 150s.

High Frequency radio can bounce off the ionosphere, then the ground, then the ionosphere again, traveling, theoretically, almost all the way around the world. Some of that depends on signal strength and weather. Less so with these radios, but still.

So, while Olgudach gathered his forces and ensured that Edernon would be reasonably secure from raiders, pirates, monsters, and possibly Lord Fidaich's forces looking for revenge, Farrar crouched on the roof of the keep, an inverted-Y antenna pointing in the general direction of Cor Legear, and tried to get a link with Gunny.

I checked the sky. A few clouds were scudding across the blue, though there was a dark line over the sea that didn't bode well. From what I could see, there was a massive storm brewing, which would not only make travel and combat difficult, but it would also play hob with comms. Still, my primary purpose was checking the time. I was pretty sure we were within our comm window.

"Got him." He lifted the handset to his lips. We'd trained on Toughbook laptops, essentially texting, but we'd left those behind, going with voice comms instead. Perhaps a step back in time, but it required less hardware and showed less light. "Three, this is One. Calling for Five."

He handed me the handset. "Gunny's on."

"Five, this is One." I couldn't exactly stand up; the handset's cord was too short. So, I crouched by the battlements, getting some odd glances from the handful of lookouts up there, and put the handset to my ear.

"Tell me you've got something, Five, because right now we're looking at a whole lot of nothing." Gunny didn't sound exactly happy. That meant he and Bailey had both been chasing their tails.

"Looks like it." I gave him a quick but fairly detailed rundown of the fight on the beach and then the raid on the island. "Olgudach is getting his riders together now."

"You think this is on the level?" Gunny wasn't second-guessing. He wanted to know what my gut said.

"If it's not, then Olgudach is one hell of an actor." I thought about it. "They're not happy about having Uven on the throne, and he's made no bones about that fact, but they hate the Peruni more, and sorcerers an order of magnitude more than the Peruni. I think when he said he'd rather be dead than sink that low, he was being one hundred percent genuine."

Gunny didn't acknowledge right away. "Looks like Killaros is about a week's ride away for us. Probably a little more for Bailey."

"Olgudach thinks we can make it in about eight days." I eyed the horizon. That storm was getting bigger, darker, and coming on fast. "Hopefully. There's some weather coming in that might slow us down a little."

"Roger. Killaros it is then." He sounded slightly less frustrated, though there was a certain resignation in his voice. "We haven't found anything else except small-time bandits and the occasional minor monster. None of which are good things, but also none of which point us directly at Tharain. He's nowhere near our other target sets."

"We'll see you there, then." Gunny signed off, I handed the handset back to Farrar, and headed below to finish getting ready.

* * *

The storm hit hard, and actually delayed our departure by several hours. Rain and hail battered Edernon, and the waves crashed so hard against the cliffs that I was pretty sure that fisherman's hut where we'd ambushed the raiders was simply gone. Lightning split the sky every few minutes, and the thunderclaps were so loud that the horses in the stables were near panic. We stayed under shelter, some of us fuming at the delay—mostly the Galel—and waited out the worst.

Finally, though the rain hadn't stopped, we saddled up and headed out. Olgudach couldn't wait another minute. That man had blood in his eye.

Hunched under our cloaks, following the Galel, who were probably even more miserable than we were, we headed south.

* * *

That storm was only the beginning. For the next four days, we rode through rain and wind as belt after belt of storms swept in off the ocean, driving deep inland before spending their fury on the hills, fields, and woods.

I almost didn't need to ask Olgudach if this was normal. I was pretty sure it wasn't, especially not this close to fall. Thunderstorms tend to come in the spring and summer, when things are heating up. Not when they're starting to cool down. I'd seen some freak occurrences, even back in The World—thunder snow is a thing, as I'd discovered on one particularly interesting training op in the mountains—but this was a little too intense to be just a freak occurrence.

Something evil was stirring in the heart of the Kingdom of Cor Legear, and it was gaining strength. The nasty weather was just a symptom.

After the fourth day, the weather all seemed to be drawn south, away from us. Unfortunately, that was also the direction in which we were going.

Olgudach reined in at the top of a rise, peering into the dark line of clouds before us. His frown hadn't gone away since we'd arrived at Edernon.

"I take it Killaros is right around the middle of that," I said, as I reined in and pointed toward the mountain of dark clouds stacked against the sky.

He nodded. "Things grow worse."

"Pretty sure they've *been* this bad for a while." I kicked Allon into motion again, heading down the next slope. "It's just coming to the surface, now that things are in endgame."

Olgudach didn't say anything, but that was probably because he was thinking exactly the same thing.

* * *

We made camp on a hilltop on the border between holds that night. Olgudach wasn't willing, considering the circumstances, to seek shelter with any of the other lords. Determining who could be trusted would require time and careful observation, something we couldn't afford at the moment, particularly if Tharain was up to something particularly dark at Killaros. And from the looks of that storm, that was exactly what was going on.

Santos and I set our watch. Mathghaman had shown no interest in picking any particular time; the Tuacha barely slept as we understood it, anyway. He simply told me to put him and Bearrac on watch at the least convenient time of the night.

I couldn't quite do that. If I was going to be the team leader, I was going to put myself there. Right smack-dab in the middle, where I'd get maximum sleep disruption. I couldn't ask my guys—or our Tuacha allies—to take that while I was in charge.

There'd been a time. I'm somewhat ashamed to admit it. But that time wasn't now.

Being around Mathghaman was rubbing off on me.

I didn't get to sleep uninterrupted until my watch, though.

It wasn't Santos who woke me up, though he was already moving that way when a white flash of light, that I could see through my eyelids, jolted me awake. When I opened my eyes, though, there was no light. A faint red glow came from the coals in the firepit, not far away, but the white illumination that had jerked me out of sleep was nowhere to be seen.

I knew what it was. Or, rather, who. And that alone put me even more on alert.

Santos reached me a second later, as I sat up and grabbed for my weapons. He dropped to a crouch. "Something's moving out in the bushes."

I rolled to my feet, strapped the Sword of Iudicael around my waist, and snatched up my rifle. I'd slept in mail and chest rig, so I was ready to go.

Our campsite wasn't close to the woods. We had set up on a rocky hilltop overlooking the road, and the nearest wood line was over a hundred yards away. There were a few stands of bushes closer in, though, among some of the bigger boulders that studded the hilltop. Santos pointed to one of those, just beneath a massive finger of stone that jutted from the grass. "Over there."

I pulled on my helmet and dropped my NVGs, letting my eyes adjust as the world lit up in green. The slopes were empty. Nothing moved but the horses—which were getting restive, indicating that there really was *something* out there—Mathghaman and Bearrac, who of course were awake, and the wind in the grass. I turned back toward the bush where Santos had pointed, and the two of us began to advance on it, weapons up and ready.

We didn't get ten paces before the bush *stood up*.

Not like a man in a ghillie suit had just stood up out of the bush. No, the bush itself unfolded into a tall, gawky, vaguely humanoid figure, seemingly made out of branches, leaves, dirt, and thorns.

I couldn't see any eyes. That was almost a relief.

Santos and I both shot it a moment later, even as one of the Galel men-at-arms let out a shout, having just seen the thing unfold itself from behind the rock. I was sure we hit it, but our bullets seemed to just punch into it without doing much. Some of Santos's burst might have chipped off some bark and shredded a couple of leaves, but that was it.

In moments, the camp was in pandemonium, as one of the Galel threw more wood on the fire, our team was on their feet, already pouring more rounds into the walking bush monster, and Olgudach was bellowing, getting his men into a fighting formation.

The thing was closest to several of the Galel, and it struck out with long arms made of twisted, thorny branches, and smacked one of them off his feet. He didn't go flying, not exactly, but the way he hit the ground told me his neck had just been snapped.

Spears jabbed at the thing, but it snapped two of them in half with another almost leisurely swipe of that long, prickly arm and slogged forward, forcing the Galel back. Two more hammer blows smashed against shields, driving at least one of them to his knees, at which point the thing drew back a limb and stabbed it right through the man's face.

It was now too close to the Galel for us to shoot at it without risking hitting some of them, so we'd ceased fire. Our bullets weren't doing anything more than their spears were, anyway. I had a hunch, though.

This thing wasn't natural. Which meant it was time for me to draw the Sword and go to work.

Olgudach was somewhat ahead of me, though. Not that he had a blessed sword of his own, but he grabbed a flaming brand from the fire and strode forward, bellowing at his men to clear the way. He ducked under another swipe of that thing's limbs, which had to be easily six to eight feet long. Seeing how fast he had to move put the lie to the apparent torpor of the creature's movement. It was *fast*. It was just big enough that it didn't *look* fast.

He thrust that torch at the thing, and it jumped back, but Olgudach wasn't giving it an inch. He pursued, keeping low, jabbing the brand at the creature's midsection. He kept it off balance, as big and weird as it was, until he threw all caution to the winds and lunged.

That thing might have been constructed out of a living bush, but whatever was puppet-mastering it had seemingly dried it out just over the last few minutes. It went up like a torch.

Flickering light blazed across the hilltop, and the thing twisted and writhed, letting out a thin, whistling cry as what might have been a shadow darted up out of the burning bush as it withered in the fire. For a moment, everyone froze, until Olgudach bellowed, "Get some water and earth around that thing before it burns us all out, you fools!"

The Galel scrambled for the hide buckets they'd staged around the fire, and soon there was a line of men setting up a perimeter around the burning bush, which was now motionless, the fire quickly dying down, fortunately without setting too much of the grass on fire. There had been enough rain and hail lately that it seemed everything was still too damp to catch.

Olgudach joined us a moment later, after drawing Santos and me out of the bucket brigade line. I'd dragged my whole team in there, since we didn't want to get burned out any more than the Galel did.

"Such things in the heart of our kingdom." Despite Olgudach's pugnacious refusal to get stampeded and his single-minded, raging focus on getting to Killaros and punishing Tharain, he sounded downright haunted. Scared. "Such things should not prowl our lands. They never have, not since the days of the Summoner."

"Dark times are upon us." Mathghaman was sympathetic enough, but he was also the sort of leader who absolutely refused to sugarcoat anything. He'd been that way in the north, and he still was. "Whatever lies at the heart of Tharain's scheme, even if it is only Peruni wizards, the fight for the heart of the Kingdom of Cor Legear has only just begun." Even as he said it, lightning flashed brilliantly in the tower of storm to the south, over Killaros.

It took a long time for anyone on that hilltop to get back to sleep after that.

CHAPTER 25

THINGS were already looking ominous as hell when we linked up with Gunny and Bailey, about ten miles from Killaros.

The rain was coming down hard, and the thunder was an almost continuous rumble. Even the better *Coira Ansec* radios had struggled to get through the noise of the weather, and we'd had to get right on top of each other before we could conduct final deconfliction and move in to join forces.

Gurke and Gunny had been in place for a day, and with the exceptions of Gunny and Diarmodh, the entire team looked absolutely miserable. Bailey was only an hour ahead of us. His team was as wet as any of the rest of the platoon, but Bailey didn't put up with whining in his team. Even if it was nonverbal.

"Any movement?" I crouched under a tree with Gunny, Gurke, Bailey, and the Tuacha. The rain wasn't quite as hard under there, though water dripped steadily from the leaves overhead. Fortunately, our Tuacha cloaks had hoods, and they were very good at keeping the rain off. Even when they soaked through—which they did, eventually—the wool never seemed to let so much water through that we got too damp and cold.

"Not much is moving around the castle itself, so far. Just that storm." Gurke looked up. "It ain't natural."

"No shit, Sherlock." The acid in Bailey's tone gave the lie to his stoicism about the weather. He was just as miserable as anyone else, and it tended to come out in his interactions with other people. A glance from Mathghaman, however, made him look down, slightly abashed.

After all, he was a Sword Bearer now, and while I'd never gotten any brief on the duties and responsibilities thereof, there still seemed to be a certain *noblesse oblige* attached to the ancient, blessed weapons.

We were Marines, of course, which meant that decorum and manners were hardly second nature, but there was something about the Swords and our companions that made me feel like I should at least try. Bailey was still getting used to that.

"Whatever's going on up there, it's serious, and I doubt we have a lot of time to stop it." Gunny ignored the little byplay. "Orava's still six hours out. I think we're going to have to roll without him, and have Team Menninkai move into overwatch to play QRF for the rest of us."

"Go in as a platoon, or separate teams?" I glanced up toward the tower of Killaros, little more than a slightly darker outline barely visible through the sheets of rain sweeping down out of the black clouds overhead. Another flash was followed by a monumental *crack* a moment later.

"We did get some recon done while we were waiting." Gunny beat Gurke to the punch. "The main road appears to be heavily guarded, though we didn't get close enough in the weather to see whether they're Tharain's men, or someone else. Couldn't see much more than silhouettes. There also appear to be patrols in the fields." He chewed on his lip for a moment. "I think the full platoon is still going to present too large a footprint, at least until we have a better idea what's going on and what kind of opposition we're looking at. We'll continue to operate as teams up until it's time to move in and assault the objective."

He looked around at the lot of us and got nods in return. It made sense.

We got down to planning.

* * *

While we could just barely see Killaros from that position, we still had a long way to go, both as the crow flies and as the crow walks. We had observed the objective—as much as we could through the storm—from a hilltop, but we still had several hundred feet to climb before we even got to a spot where we could find our way into the high valley where the town sat beneath the castle. The tower itself stood at least a hundred feet above that.

Most of the Galel land we'd ridden through had been extensively cultivated, with only small stands and strips of woods between fields that stretched for hundreds of acres around the castles and towns that formed the heart of each hold of the kingdom. The land around Killaros, however, was much more like Cor Hefedd. The rugged hills were thick with woods and thickets, sometimes forcing us to divert for hundreds of yards when the brush was simply too dense to push through.

The storm overhead continued to rage, making comms difficult and our footing absolutely atrocious. I lost count of how many times my boots slipped in the wet just in the first mile.

If it had just been the storm, as unusually fierce and persistent as it was, we *might* have had some doubts about exactly how bad things in Killaros were. However, one thing we'd found over the last year and a half in this place was that when weird and evil stuff is afoot, it attracts spooky things.

They were just flickers at first. Movement seen out of the corner of an eye, gone when we turned to look. Whispers that might just be the hiss of rain on the vegetation and the rocks.

As we climbed higher and got closer to Killaros, though, we started seeing things.

We'd seen shadow people in the east, especially around Barmanak. I hadn't expected to see them in the heart of Galel lands, but once, when I looked up, I saw a near-perfect silhouette of a man, black as night even in midday—though the light of midday was more like twilight in that storm—standing on a boulder above me, like it was watching me. When I blinked, it was gone.

We kept seeing such things as we climbed higher. Sometimes they were solid shadows, like that figure I'd seen on the rock. Sometimes it was the glint of eyes, suddenly there, then just as suddenly gone. The spooks and monsters were gathering.

They didn't approach us or interfere with us, though. I wondered why. Maybe it was because of Mathghaman and Bearrac. Maybe it was because of the Sword of Iudicael at my hip. Maybe both.

Maybe it was *because* we were in the heart of Galel lands. As much evil as appeared to be gathering at Killaros, the things drawn to it were still small, weak. The Outer Dark had penetrated into every corner of this world, but there were some places that it still was only able to touch lightly. Despite how far some of the Galel had fallen, their kingdom was still more secure than many of the other places we'd been.

Even so, those shadow figures gave me the screaming willies, and the higher we climbed, the more often we saw them without being ambushed, the more creeped out I got. There was something deeply wrong here. Not just that there were spooks amid a never-ending storm. That was almost normal for this place.

It was the fact that nothing we'd seen *had* tried to attack us or otherwise interfere with our movement that weirded me out.

This is too easy. I know these things have to be watching us, and they can probably communicate with Tharain or his sorcerer in Killaros. So, why is this going so smoothly and easily?

What's waiting for us on the other side of this ridge?

Looking up, squinting against the sheets of rain, I signaled Rodeffer to halt. He kept going a few paces before looking back and seeing my raised hand, at which point he looked for a good spot to circle up. That ended up being a shelf about ten yards higher up, still a good two hundred yards short of the crest of the ridge.

It took some time to get everyone up there. I was just as glad that Olgudach and his men had stayed with Gunny, though Gurke was probably fuming. Unless it meant he could ride instead of humping a ruck over this ridge, in which case he was probably smugly thinking that he'd gotten the best end of the deal.

Gurke could be that way.

Still, without the Galel along with us, we could move faster, even in the rough terrain and the "Recon Weather." Not to say that we were moving *fast*, but still faster than we could have with Galel straphangers. They were horsemen, most of them. This was our element.

Mathghaman joined me in the center of our tight little perimeter, as Bearrac took up a position next to Rodeffer, watching the top of the ridge. Santos, as always, covered our six, flanked by Farrar.

There was only so much we could do with six dudes, so we did what we could.

"The spirits of the night gather." Mathghaman had already figured out why I'd called a halt, naturally.

"That's what I'm worried about." We were both speaking in whispers, barely audible over the rain, occasionally drowned out entirely by the thunder. That thunder was making me nervous. There wasn't a whole lot of cover on that ridgeline above us, and that meant we were going to be exposed to the storm in all its fury getting over it. Spooks, monsters, and men with bows and spears were one thing. It would *really* suck to get struck by lightning before even getting to the target. "Though not quite the same as the last few missions. These things are just watching. Not even trying to come at us."

Mathghaman's eyes glinted in the storm. "These are lesser creatures. Spies and pests that haunt the shadows and the obscure places of the world. Most of them would not dare come near the Sword of Iudicael."

"Or two lords of the Tuacha da Riamog," I pointed out.

Mathghaman merely shrugged.

"Anyway, while they might not be trying to drag us through cracks in the rock like that thing at the gates of Barmanak…" I saw Farrar shudder a little, though he didn't turn from his sector. Chambers had almost been horribly killed while we'd been focused on the road leading up to that ancient, haunted ruin, when a shadow man had slipped out through a three-inch-wide crack in the rock and tried to grab him. "I'm worried about who or what they might be reporting back to, though."

Mathghaman didn't answer right away, but just silently scanned our surroundings. The haunts that had hounded us for the last couple of miles seemed to have made themselves scarce, at least for a while. All I could see was the forest, the trees and bushes waving in the wind, lashed by the incessant rain.

I wondered, as I sometimes did, just what Mathghaman saw. He never spoke of it—none of the Tuacha did—but I'd always gathered that they perceived more than we did. They could see beyond that veil that lies between the physical and the preternatural. If there were still haunts out there, watching us, I suspected that Mathghaman knew exactly where they were.

"There is little we can do to stop it." His voice was low, and there was an echo of some anger there. "I cannot banish everything that might lurk in this storm. Especially as something dark stirs in Killaros itself." His eyes turned to the ridgeline above. "We must simply make haste, and hope that we get to our destination before what is being done cannot be undone."

There wasn't much more to say to that. I considered getting comms with Gunny, but I doubted he'd really have much of anything else to say beyond what Mathghaman already had.

Gunny's the man, but Mathghaman's got at least a generation's worth of wisdom on both of us, not counting the gifts Tigharn had already bestowed on him and his people to begin with.

We got back up and continued over the ridge.

CHAPTER 26

WHILE it meant a bit of a detour from our planned route, Rodeffer found a path through trees and tall, jutting boulders that gave us at least some cover from the storm as we moved up and over the ridgeline. It shielded us from prying eyes a little more, too, at least any natural prying eyes that might be in the town below and the castle right across the way.

Killaros wasn't a large castle. It didn't even have an outer wall, but was more like Cor Hefedd, being essentially a freestanding tower instead of a keep. It was taller and narrower than Cor Hefedd, standing probably ten stories tall, octagonal and tapering slightly toward the top. Instead of battlements, a peaked roof stabbed at the sky and the now-black clouds lowering above it.

It stood on a crag of rock that thrust out above the small, huddled town in the high valley like the prow of a ship coming out of the mountainside. That promontory probably stood a hundred feet above the highest roof of the town, and the builders of that town had been smart enough to avoid erecting any houses directly beneath it. It was massive and heavy, and didn't *look* like it was going to crack and fall off anytime in the next few centuries, but why tempt fate?

The terrain was important, but it was hardly the only thing we were looking at.

The town itself was tiny, a huddle of shingled roofs gathered about a central square, about a quarter mile down the valley from that blade of rock that formed Killaros's foundation. From where we crouched in the rocks above, almost even with that peaked roof of the tower, the town was little more than a cluster of darker gray blocks in the distance. The rain was coming down hard, even as lightning bolt after lightning bolt split the sky directly over the tower.

Strangely, none of them seemed to strike the tower or the hills around it. They danced around the clouds above the tower itself, forming forks of purple-tinged brilliance, but they stayed in the clouds.

I'd take it. I had no desire whatsoever to see if I could survive getting struck by lightning while wearing a mail shirt.

With the sky as dark as it was, we might have expected to see a few lights in the town below. Glass windows were rare in this world, but they did exist, and even where they didn't, animal horn was used in their place. The point being, we should have seen the glow of candles or fires down there. We didn't.

I was getting flashbacks to the Land of Shadows and Crows, the haunted village of the dead beneath Unsterbanak's castle. It would have been hard to disguise the kind of slaughter that would create a cursed place like that in the heart of the Kingdom of Cor Legear, but we'd seen as bad before. And the storm didn't bode well.

Hunkered down in a crack in the rocks, I shed my ruck, propping my weapons against a boulder, and dug the binoculars out. There wasn't a whole lot of light, but they were good binoculars. The limiting factor was going to be the rain, which was quickly obscuring the objective lenses with water.

I almost didn't need the binos, though. We were close enough to the first dark figure that I could just about make him out with my naked eyes.

One thing I'd noticed immediately about the Galel was their love for bright colors. There were no muted earth tones or pastels among these people. I'd only seen lighter colors because the fabrics had faded. These were people who would wear eye-searing orange just because.

So, there was something off about a figure dressed all in black, standing on a rock about three hundred yards from the base of the tower.

I tried to wipe some of the water off the binos' objective lenses and get a better look. That wasn't a shadow man, that was for sure. This guy was entirely physical, in a black-enameled mail hauberk that went nearly to his ankles, wearing a full-faced helm painted black, holding a forked spear in one gauntleted hand. No flesh showed, and he didn't move a muscle as the rain pounded down on him.

Nor did any of the soldiers gathered around the rock, though they were considerably less armored. We were still too far away to see much detail, especially through the dark and the rain, but something about them and their unnatural stillness told me that those men-at-arms weren't alive anymore.

Awesome. The walking dead. Seems that the parallels with the Land of Shadows and Crows are closer than I'd hoped.

Even as I thought it, the black knight or whatever he was turned his head. So, he wasn't a statue. Nor was he, apparently, a sorcerous automaton like the stygian suits of armor we'd faced in Taramas's catacombs. He moved like a living man. Unlike his retinue.

I kept scanning. He hadn't looked directly at me, so far as I could tell, and I was set far enough back in the scrubby bushes between boulders that unless there was a shadow man whispering reports into his ear—which was unfortunately entirely possible—he shouldn't be able to see me.

Continuing my scan, slowly and carefully since the storm was making it awfully easy to miss details, I spotted another of the black armored figures, standing below the promontory where Killaros sat. He also had a retinue of statue-still men-at-arms, though they stood behind and above him, while he surveyed the slopes above the town.

I found myself hoping that those men-at-arms were some kind of constructs, or even just men under some sort of spell. I'd fought the dead before, and I had no great desire to repeat the experience.

Finishing my scan, then sweeping back to double-check, I couldn't see any more of the black knights or their companies. That didn't mean they weren't there. I really couldn't see much past the tower, thanks to all the water in the air, even with the lightning turning everything white every few minutes.

Pulling back from the OP, I motioned for Rodeffer to take over. It was technically Farrar's turn, but I might need my comms guy.

Our radios were set for VHF, and I *should* be able to talk without needing a field expedient antenna. We'd have to see, though. "Five, this is One."

I had to call twice more before Gunny replied. The air was full of static, crackles that might or might not correspond to lightning flashes in the clouds above, and other noises that sounded disturbingly like voices where they weren't just unnerving noise that didn't sound like any radio frequency interference I'd ever heard before.

"One, go for Five." From the tone of his voice, it sounded like he'd heard me before, had tried to answer, and hadn't gotten through.

"We are in position, just above the west side of the objective. We have eyes on two targets. Both appear to be knights, dismounted, with roughly platoon-strength units of men-at-arms backing them up. They are situated at roughly two-hundred-yard intervals around the tower; they are the only ones we can see, but there might be more out of our line of sight. Be advised, while the knights appear to be living men, the men-at-arms aren't moving a muscle, and appear to be either enthralled or already dead. Can't tell from up here."

I had to repeat my rough SALUTE report—Size, Activity, Location, Unit, Time, and Equipment—twice more before Gunny had all of it.

"Good copy," he said, finally. "Two is reporting much the same from the other side." There was a pause, during which I could have sworn I heard another voice in the background noise. Not another voice on Gunny's end, talking while Gunny kept the radio keyed. Gunny wouldn't have done that, anyway. No, this was something else. Something separate.

Something that shouldn't have been on our net at all.

Mathghaman picked it up. "Turn the radio off."

I hesitated. Mathghaman knew his business, but without comms, we had no way to coordinate.

"Do it, Conor." Mathghaman rarely gave orders, but when he did, there was a great deal of force behind them. I was already reaching for the power knob when Gunny's voice came back over the net.

"Attention on the net. The net is compromised. Going comms black as of now. Rendezvous at Rally Point Victor."

I killed the radio, ripped my headset off, and stuffed both back in my ruck. Unfortunately, I didn't think that the worst part was the enemy listening in. I hadn't made out words, but something about that voice on the airwaves had given me the creeps, even though it had sounded like listening to a conversation in the next room with the door closed. No, it wasn't what *they* might hear that was the threat.

It was what *we* might hear. And what that hearing might let in.

I moved up and tapped Rodeffer. "Give me the binos, then get ready to move. We're heading down to Rally Point Victor." We'd identified several rally points around the castle, pinpointed by landmarks that we could make out on the maps. There were no grid coordinates to work with here. Victor was a wooded hill just south and west of the main road leading into the valley and the town.

I just hoped, as I stuffed the binoculars back in my ruck and got ready to move, that it wasn't already held by the enemy.

* * *

Things were getting weirder the closer we got. The shadows moved around us constantly, though they were rarely so defined as the silhouette I'd seen atop that rock. The wind swirled in strange patterns that almost seemed to defy the terrain we were moving over.

I could have sworn a cold hand that I couldn't see tried to grab me at least twice.

Still, nothing jumped out at us, nothing attacked us. If there were patrols out—and initial reporting said there were—they were nowhere near us. We didn't hear horses, or men, or anything but the wind, the thunder, the rain, and the creak of our own joints as we moved over rocky, rough hillsides toward the rally point.

I signaled Rodeffer to halt in a small but dense stand of oaks—or as close as this place got to them—about a hundred yards shy of the rally point. Without comms, this was going to get a little trickier, and I really didn't want to get shot by a friendly because we were all jumpy and couldn't see very far in the storm.

Taking a knee in the deep shadows under the trees, I searched the hilltop that was Rally Point Victor. Gunny and Gurke should have been there ahead of us, so I was looking for our far recognition signal.

A lot of this Sneaky Pete greenside stuff had sort of gone by the wayside over the years, even for us. We'd had to relearn it here, where batteries were hard to come by and so we had to find low-tech solutions for an awful lot of problems. In many ways, we were back to Vietnam or World War II levels of fieldcraft.

When we didn't get down to blades and go all Viking Age, anyway.

There. A flashy far recognition signal wouldn't be a great idea, either, without knowing the enemy's full presence and capability, so we'd decided on something simple. In this case, a pair of sticks, lashed into a rough cross with boot bands, was hanging from the crotch of one of the bigger trees.

Letting my eyes travel from the signal, I spotted the man right behind it on a rifle. We were close enough that he could probably see me if he was on his game. It had to be either Chambers or Franks. Probably Franks.

Lifting my hand, I held my position for a moment. The far recognition signal was pretty much on the guys who had reached the rally point first, but I wanted to take this carefully. We hadn't done a lot of team operations, so linkups were still a little rusty, and everyone was jumpy after all the weirdness going on. I didn't want to rush and get shot.

Friendly fire… isn't.

Since I was a little jumpy and not especially trusting, I braced my rifle against the tree and put my eye to the scope. Sure enough, that was Franks there, on a knee, behind his own M110, his ruck leaning against the trunk. He probably shouldn't have had his ruck off, but that was Gurke's business, not mine.

Even as I identified him, Franks put a gloved hand out and waved, carefully. He saw us, too, and had identified us. That took care of the near recognition signal, too.

I lowered the weapon and turned to Rodeffer. "Let's go."

He flinched ever so slightly as he stepped out from under the tree and not only got a face full of windblown rain, but another lightning bolt flashed by overhead, followed in seconds by an earsplitting crash.

We moved fast. The weather was one reason. The other was that we didn't want to be in the open for long, even as the darkness got deeper, the rain got heavier, and visibility got correspondingly worse. Even though the bulk of Killaros was on the other side of the low ridge we were paralleling, the peak of that tower was still visible, if only as a dim, dark shadow through the rain.

I didn't think that anything inside that tower at the moment would be limited by the rain. Neither did Rodeffer.

We hustled into the trees, moving past Franks and getting into the deeper woods, where the rain wasn't as bad. It was still wet, but we had at least a *little* shelter.

Gunny and Gurke were waiting under a pair of elm-like trees. I knelt next to Gunny, Mathghaman joining us as Santos got the rest of the team set in around us, joining Chambers, Diarmodh, and Franks on the perimeter.

Then we had to wait for Bailey.

* * *

"So, we've got at minimum four of these enemy security elements." Gunny apparently wasn't going to comment on the unnatural stillness of the figures behind the black knights. I'd described it over the radio, and that was enough at this point.

It wasn't that we were getting *used* to the weirdness. It was more like we were becoming hardened to it, accepting it as another obstacle to be overcome, a threat level that had to be dealt with. Once we knew something was weird, we just knew we were going to have to step carefully and be prepared to adjust our course of action on the fly.

It also helped if we kept our minds straight, and while I didn't think anyone had outright mentioned it, abject fear only seemed to feed some of these things.

"Expect five." Mathghaman's interjection was quiet, but it had all the force of every bit of the man's knowledge and experience.

Gunny nodded. "That fits with the geometries." He didn't specify *which* geometries, but I gathered that he was talking both the terrain, the castle, and the town, as well as the more mystical dimension of things. If there was sorcery happening within the tower of Killaros—which there certainly appeared to be—then everything involved would be tied into it, somehow.

"Do we need to take out the outer security first?" Gunny looked at Mathghaman, who peered down toward the valley below with a frown, stroking his mustache.

"Possibly. That alone might disrupt what is happening." He shook his head. "Without knowing more, however, it might only bring everything the enemy has to bear on us." He glanced at the storm. "It will be at least another day before enough of the men of Cor Legear can join us here. From the looks of things, I doubt we have a day."

"There might be a way in past one of those security elements." Bailey pointed to the shoulder of a hill on the far side of the tower. "The terrain up there gets pretty rough, and if I saw it right, there might be a narrow avenue through the rocks and the bushes that should take us almost right to the base of the tower, without having to cross any of those black knights or their fighters."

Gunny thought about it. There was a lot of risk involved. Olgudach was down the mountain, gathering what men he could, but he didn't have nearly the forces needed to storm Killaros. There should have been more of the Galel nearing the valley by then, but so far, they had enough to maybe take the town.

I wondered about that. We'd had next to no word from Cor Legear itself since we'd left for Edernon. Something was going on, if King Uven or Vepogenus, at least, couldn't gather enough men to storm Killaros, presuming they had figured out that Killaros was Tharain's hideout in the first place.

I was getting a very bad feeling about this. All the same, there was heavy-duty sorcery going on here, and regardless of the bigger picture, we were there, and sorcery was our enemy.

It was time to go to work.

CHAPTER 27

WE didn't move immediately, mainly because when Orava finally joined us, the time we'd spent snooping around the valley having given him and his team time to catch up, he reported that Olgudach was moving up the road toward the town with his knights and men-at-arms. That amounted to about two hundred men, which was probably entirely inadequate to the situation at hand, but it still meant we had to pause and coordinate. Gunny and Diarmodh headed down to meet up with him and figure things out, while the rest of us stayed in the rally point and watched.

The storm was getting ever more vicious. The wind lashed the rain and hail against our hilltop, the clouds got darker, and the lightning got even more frequent, if that was possible. Underlying the nastiness of the weather was a deeper, more electric tension. It was hard to make out over the howl of the wind, but there were other voices in that storm, dark and terrible. We really were running out of time.

Finally, just before nightfall—as difficult as it was to tell under those lowering, swirling black clouds—Gunny and Diarmodh accompanied Olgudach up to the hilltop.

"There is word of great disturbances to the east and north." Olgudach had, apparently, sent riders out to either scout or seek out news. "Vepogenus's forces are delayed, though I sent messengers to him as soon as we departed Edernon." He looked up at the dark shadow of Killaros, even as another fork of lightning backlit the tower starkly against the sky. "Time grows short. Whatever Tharain is planning, it is on the edge of success. We *must* capture him and present him to the king."

I wondered how much of Olgudach's intensity was over the threat to the kingdom and how much was over the threat to Edernon. He was determined to vindicate himself and the rest of his clan. Still, Olgudach's motivations aside, our mission was pretty clear, and the need to act quickly just as certain.

"We can get in there, but we're going to need some kind of diversion." Gunny had traced a crude sand table in the mud under the tree. "That's going to be where you and your boys come in, Lord Olgudach..."

* * *

With Rodeffer in the lead, we slipped down through the rocks toward the tower.

If the builders had possessed explosives, and been smart, they might have leveled that ridge as much as possible. There was just too much dead space that an enemy could use to get close to the tower, which was exactly what we were doing. Fortunately, they hadn't had the means, or else they'd been confident enough in the security of their high valley not to bother to try.

Of course, with the weird stuff in play, it was entirely possible that anyone inside that tower already knew that we were there, and that we were coming.

Rodeffer moved carefully from boulder to boulder. We'd left our rucks behind in the rally point, so we were moving light. That still meant we bristled with weapons, between rifles, pistols, swords, axes, and knives. Fortunately, we'd all gotten better at moving with the gear, so sword scabbards and axe hafts didn't knock against rocks as we slipped between them.

Of course, the storm was making enough noise that we'd be hard to hear even if we had hauled off and swung a weapon against a rock.

He put a hand up. It took a second in the gloom and the rain to see that he was putting up an open hand to call a halt, rather than a fist to signal freeze, so I hesitated for a moment before I moved up to join him.

I didn't need him to point out what he'd seen. We'd found the fifth black knight, right where Mathghaman had predicted he'd be.

He was standing on a rock, his forked spear in his gauntleted hand, looking off to the southeast, backed up by the same platoon-sized element of motionless armored figures.

From there, I could see his retinue more clearly. They weren't dead men. That didn't make it much better.

The figures were scarecrows, though wearing armor and holding weapons. Not as if spears had been tied to branches, though. Hands made of sticks and straw actually gripped the hafts of the weapons.

That wasn't the worst part. They might not be moving at all, except for the stirring of the rags that covered them in the wind and the rain, but they had eyes. Eyes that glowed a dim purple in the gloom.

While they had never been alive, whatever was going on in there had succeeded in binding spirits to these crude puppets. Which probably meant that killing them would require about as much effort as putting down an undead skeleton. Namely, a lot.

Still, neither the knight nor his retinue seemed to notice us. Not an eye nor a face—or lack thereof—was turned toward us. The knight was moving like a living man, his helm occasionally turning to one side or another, shifting his weight slightly from foot to foot, his grip shifting on the haft of his spear. But he was watching his sector fixedly, and I hoped he couldn't hear much inside that helm. He sure couldn't see that much. The eye slits were tiny.

I signaled Rodeffer to keep going. If we could stay hidden, it looked like we might be able to get past this position without a fight. If there *was* going to be a fight, from where I stood, we were going to have to start it, and that wasn't the mission. We needed to get inside, get Tharain, and put a stop to this.

We might have to set all those scarecrows on fire later, but that was later.

Moving with exaggerated care, Rodeffer resumed his route, making sure he stayed on the far side of the boulder from the knight and his escort. I followed, but not before making sure that Farrar, behind Mathghaman, knew to move very, very carefully.

* * *

It took almost another two hours of agonizingly painstaking movement, but we got past the knight and the scarecrows, and closed in on the base of the tower.

It was bigger up close than it had looked. The tower's foundation had to be a hundred yards across. Killaros was relatively minor, as holds went, but it was still a formidable fortress. That somewhat explained why they hadn't worried too much about that approach. There was no way in short of using a cratering charge anywhere around the bottom of the tower except for the gate, which stood twenty feet up from the rocky hillside, narrow stairs winding halfway around the tower itself to reach it.

That was a problem. We'd be exposed as hell all the way up, and there were clear lines of sight from those steps down to at least three of the black knights. We'd never get to the breach undetected, even in the dark, if a knight turned his head and looked back toward the tower.

We could *hope*, based on what we'd seen so far, that none of them would. However, hope is not a plan.

So, Gunny set Orava and his Menninkai in on overwatch, to engage anything that came after us while the rest of the Marines and Tuacha climbed the steps and attempted to breach the gate. Orava accepted the assignment with his usual stoicism. One of us might have gotten a little put out at not being on the entry team, but Orava and his boys were some of the more heavily armed of the platoon, as the Menninkai had early on showed a great affinity for belt-fed machineguns, mortars, and thumpers. We didn't have the mortars at the moment, mainly for the sake of speed and mobility. They had plenty of 7.62 link and 40mm, though, so they were best set up to hold the base of the tower.

From their position among the rocks, Orava's team could cover the road that led up from the town, the hills behind, and the ridge we'd come down to reach the tower in the first place. They had decent fields of fire, and they'd do a number on any of the hostile forces we'd spotted if they moved in on us. We'd still have to move fast, but at least we had covering fire if we needed it.

I still had my team in the lead. Gurke was clearly sulking about it a little bit, but we'd led the way down to the tower, and I wasn't about to relinquish that spot in the stack. Especially since I had the Sword of Iudicael and Mathghaman with me.

We didn't hesitate, didn't hang out at the base of the steps to do any last-minute planning. We were there, and we had to move. Rodeffer stayed on point—the steps were too narrow to climb in anything but single file—and headed up. I was right on his heels, Mathghaman following close behind me.

Even if it hadn't been pouring rain for the last several days, those steps would have been a nightmare. No two were exactly the same size and they seemed to slant out slightly. I wondered just how they got supplies up to the tower with that kind of a route to the gate. Definitely defensible, but it would make matters extremely difficult for any of the poor devils who had to carry food, drink, and firewood up there.

Maybe they just winched it up with ropes.

While we didn't make the best speed to the top, it was still noticeable when Rodeffer slowed, his weapon up and pointed at the gate. He stopped altogether just short of it. There was a bit of a landing out in front, just enough that we could sort of stack up.

We weren't going to need to breach. The gate stood open.

My hackles went up immediately. The rain didn't seem to have gone far inside, and the gatehouse was dark. It was almost as if the gate had been opened just for us.

That never bodes well.

I gave him the squeeze. We were committed. Hanging out in the open wouldn't do anyone any good. With a deep breath, his sights just below his eye, he hooked through the gate, clearing the short corner inside at the same time I crossed the gateway behind him, doing the same before sweeping my muzzle back toward the center.

Nothing. The gatehouse—not unlike the narrow passage where we'd slaughtered dozens of Dovos at the tor in the north, our first day in this world—was empty, still, and featureless except for the murder holes in the ceiling and the inner gate at the far end.

We swept forward, muzzles shifting to cover the gate or the murder holes alternately, giving the rest of the platoon space to make entry. The inside was strangely calm and quiet, and we were out of the rain for the first time in days.

The inner gate stood open, as well. A few flickering candles provided the only illumination in the reception hall beyond, and they didn't provide enough to see much, not from inside the gatehouse.

We made entry much the same way we'd entered the gatehouse, spreading out around the reception hall, adjusting the gain on our NVGs to see better.

I wished I could have skipped that part.

Five bodies, their skin flayed off them in much the same way as the man who'd been hanging above the fire in that cave back on the islands, as well as the victim in Tharain's house, hung from makeshift scaffolds, their hides pinned to the vertical timbers, set around the central high seat. Foul symbols had been daubed in blood on the floor, the walls, and the high seat itself, and flies swarmed them, making them seem to twist and writhe even as we looked at them.

For a moment, as the rest of the platoon entered, we just looked at the horror that confronted us, weapons pointed at the dead men, waiting for some many-legged abomination to come crawling out of their chest cavities.

Instead, a high-pitched scream echoed from somewhere up above, and the gates slammed shut.

CHAPTER 28

THE scream reached a high, quavering, fever pitch, then went silent.

For a moment, nothing moved except our muzzles, searching for the threat. I had a sudden, sinking feeling that we'd been played. Killaros had been a trap.

And Olgudach had led us here.

I left thoughts of a reckoning for Olgudach for another time. Right then we needed to survive the tower and get out.

A rustling, scratching sound began to susurrate through the hall as we spread out along the walls, moving toward the stairs leading up higher into the tower. The candles brightened while their flames turned a greenish purple. Muzzles moved toward the hanging corpses, even as the buzzing of the flies seemed to get louder.

I more than half expected the hanging corpses to move with the noise, but they were dead still, as if frozen. No long, black, chitinous legs pushed out through their chests or worse. Yet the sound got louder, turning from a rustling and scratching into a scraping, cracking sound.

I got it a moment before the floor in front of the high seat collapsed, almost directly in the center of the circle of flayed corpses, and the dead started climbing out.

The creatures outside had been scarecrows, but these were definitely dead men. The enemy must have emptied the crypts beneath the tower, generations of the dead providing the rotting meat or bone puppets for whatever spirits from the abyss Tharain had summoned.

They came at us with silent roars, some carrying weapons, others reaching out with clawlike fingers, even where some of them were missing.

Gurke opened fire first, slamming rounds into two of the shambling abominations, but with next to no effect. He may as well have been shooting at cardboard targets. A bullet passed right through a rotting carcass and smacked off a stone column just inside the door to the gatehouse, ricocheting with a nasty whine to shatter a window higher up the wall.

"Blades!" Mathghaman's roar echoed through the hall. The reasoning was obvious enough after that ricochet. Bullets couldn't hurt the undead hard enough, fast enough to stop them, and we stood a good chance of hitting a friendly in that enclosed, stone-walled space.

The enemy's timing had been impeccable. With the gate shut, we'd moved inward, intending to clear the tower, with the implicit understanding that we weren't getting out the way we'd come, so we had to eliminate the sorcerer. Unfortunately, that had put us in a position where the bulk of that decomposing horde was between us and the gate, and we had nowhere to go but up.

We closed ranks, swords and axes coming out, bristling and glinting in the dim, greenish, purplish light. The dead weren't moving all that fast, so we had a brief few seconds to form up before they hit us.

Then they were on top of us, and the fight really got going.

I snapped my buckler up to block a rusted, broken short sword wielded by a withered, dried out husk of a corpse wearing what looked like ancient, corroded ceremonial armor, and thrust the Sword of Iudicael through the dead man's throat. The faint purple light in the empty eye sockets went out like I'd just thrown a light switch, and the thing crumpled, the head coming off as the remnant of the neck disintegrated.

Confronted with a brief gap, I hacked at the dead woman trying to claw for Farrar's throat while he clashed with an axe-wielding warrior that was now little more than a skeleton clad in a deeply corroded breastplate and rotting baltea. I buried the blade of the Sword of Iudicael in her skull, past the wispy, rotting hair and papery skin, and the body collapsed just as quickly as the first, giving Farrar the moment's respite to pry the axe away from his throat and hack the skeleton's skull off. That didn't stop the creature, but my next thrust with the Sword did.

I didn't get a moment's breathing room then, since three more of the dead were lunging toward me in the next second. Fortunately, the undead couldn't stand the touch of the Sword of Iudicael, and they went down fast when I hit them. Unfortunately, Bailey and I were the only ones with blessed weapons, though the Tuacha's blades did seem to be more effective than any of the others. I suspect that had more to do with their wielders than the swords themselves.

Still, we were forced back a step, then another. The sheer weight of bodies coming after us was enough that we couldn't hope to hold our position, and Gunny saw it immediately. "Break contact, fall back to the steps!"

I shoved Farrar back behind me with my buckler, even as I blocked another blow from a dusty corpse swinging a sword in one hand and an axe in the other. I was a Sword Bearer. My place was in the front.

Slowly, step by step, Gunny drew the rest of the platoon back into the staircase behind us, leaving Mathghaman, Bearrac, Diarmodh, Bailey, and me to hold the line, slowly moving back to close the gaps as our front shrank.

It sounds more orderly than it was. We jostled together, fighting to stay shoulder to shoulder as we hacked furiously at the shamblers trying to kill us. Only the fact that they seemed slow and stupid, mindlessly reaching out for us, moving stiffly as if the spirits only had a tenuous grip on the physical forms, saved us from being immediately overwhelmed.

The sheer weight of numbers pouring out of the crypts continued to force us back, though, until Bailey and I were side by side in the stairwell, hacking and stabbing at the mindless bodies flailing at us. They were starting to stack up on each other, and the pressure of the mob was forcing them up the stairs at us.

Of course, we were striking undead down with every blow. It didn't seem to matter much if we hit vitals or not. One blow from either of the Swords and the spirits animating the dead flesh fled, with a faint, almost inaudible scream that was in marked contrast to the thudding treads of undead feet. They hit the floor with thumps and clatters of armor and weapons that seemed loud, even over the pounding of blood in my ears and the rasp of my own breath. The dead on the floor were getting in the way of the rest, but it wasn't slowing them down enough.

Step by step, we backed up the stairs. Gurke had, presumably, taken point with his team, clearing up the steps behind us.

For all its defensibility, the staircase on the inside of the tower of Killaros wasn't built like the steps leading up to the gate. They were even and straight, so we didn't trip going up, which was a good thing with that mass of supernaturally controlled dead flesh and bone gnashing and flailing for us, just past the reach of our Swords.

Over our grunts of effort and the clash of weapons, I could hear Gurke cussing from somewhere above us. Whatever was going on up there, it was not going according to plan.

Not that anything about this op had gone according to plan.

A shout came down from higher up. It sounded almost like a plea for help, but I was a little too busy at the moment, as a massive skeleton, its empty eye sockets burning, wielding a long war axe, had pushed its way to the front rank. That axe swung over my head with a whistle, only missing taking the top of my skull off—helmet or no helmet—by an inch as I ducked. If the thing steering those moldering bones hadn't telegraphed the hell out of the strike, it probably would have killed me in one hit.

Coming up under that axe, I brought the Sword up with me, the point going in under the missing jaw and into the skull's brainpan. For a second, the lights in the eye sockets flickered, as if the spirit was desperately trying to hang on, then they went out and the skeleton crashed to the floor. Even as it did so, three more rotting corpses lurched forward, smelling of decay, death, and embalming spices, and Bailey pulled me back another step by the back strap of my chest rig.

The shouts came more desperately from the upper floors, and then Gunny was right behind us. "Turn and go." He stuck his arm out past my shoulder, just far enough that I could see the frag in his hand. It probably wouldn't stop these things, but it should slow them down.

Bailey and I turned and ran up the steps, as Gunny let the spoon fly and dropped the frag at the feet of the lead undead before turning and following us. As steep as the stairs were, we sprinted all out, breath burning in our lungs as we did our utmost to get above and around the next turn in the octagonal staircase before that grenade went off.

The concussion was brutal. Focused by the stone walls, it rippled up the staircase after us, carrying smoke and some frag that skittered along the walls. The shockwave almost knocked me down. In the open, frags can be a little disappointing, coming across as little more than a heavy *thud*, but in that stairwell, it was magnified to the point that it felt like standing next to a meteor strike.

Bailey tripped as the concussion washed over us, and I grabbed his arm, hauling him to his feet and propelling him higher. I could hear the shouting and crying above more clearly now, even through the ringing in my ears. We kept going, though I glanced over my shoulder once, checking our six, only to see half a corpse clawing its way up the steps behind us. It was pulling itself along by its shredded arms, missing more than a few fingers, so it wasn't moving very fast, but it was still moving.

We kept climbing. The stairs ahead of us were clear, except for Mathghaman, Diarmodh, and Bearrac, who had apparently been reluctant to leave us behind. They backed up, weapons in hand, ready to leap down and join the fight if we got into trouble.

Hustling up the steps, we put some more distance between us and the tidal wave of animated dead, even as Gunny pulled the pin on another frag and tossed it down behind us. The concussion wasn't quite as bad this time, but it still rocked us.

Mathghaman and Bearrac led us higher, bypassing floor after floor. My legs burned and my throat was raw as I panted for breath. I'd already burned a lot of energy, just getting to the tower and inside, then fighting up half a flight of stairs.

Santos and Applegate stood at the door at the top of the steps, weapons in hand and poised behind what looked like full-sized Galel shields. It was interesting that Gurke wasn't there, but I imagined that either Vince or Applegate had shoved him aside, since Bailey and I were the guys down the stairs.

They parted to let us through, and then fell back inside as Gunny joined us, slamming the heavy oaken door shut and barring it.

Gasping for breath, I struggled to stay upright and not drop to put my hands on my knees. We weren't the only ones there.

The chamber wasn't as big as the reception hall, but it was still huge. Killaros was definitely larger than it looked at a distance. I couldn't tell what this place had been used for, but it wasn't a master bedroom or a guardroom. A raised dais stood at the back of the chamber, beneath the peaked roof, the beams darkened by years of smoke. A large brazier stood at the top of the steps leading up to that dais, though it was currently dark and unlit.

The main floor was crowded. There had to be at least fifty people huddled against the wall and the base of the dais, shying away from the Tuacha and the men in odd green and brown clothes and bristling with strange weapons. They seemed to be most nervous about the Tuacha, though.

Fighting to bring my breathing and heart rate back under control, I scanned the crowd. They were all Galel, and all nobility, at least going by their clothing and accoutrements.

One face stood out to me all of a sudden. Her hair was in disarray and there were dark circles of fatigue and fear under her eyes, but Derelei was there. She stood by herself, disheveled and scared. Yet, when I looked into her eyes, even though she didn't recognize me, I saw a mixed expression of relief and calculation there.

Gone was the coquettish young woman who had clung to my arm on the battlements of Cor Legear. All her pretense had been stripped away, and now I saw something almost feral.

There was no regret for running off with the rebels there, in that brief second when our gazes locked. No sorrow except for the suffering she'd endured since the trap here at Killaros had been set. Only fear for herself.

I turned away. With Cailtarni dead and Derelei's true colors shown, there was nothing there.

An older man, dressed in a richly embroidered tunic and cape, took a stumbling step toward us, but then stopped. As I scanned the crowd, I started to get a distinctly "out of the frying pan, into the fire" feeling.

A moment later, the brazier atop the dais burst into flame, its fires tinged violet, and a man in red and blue robes, his eyes wide, almost feverish, with a bloodstained dagger in his hand, stepped in front of it. Dead men in ancient armor stood to either side of him.

And the shadows behind him began to coalesce.

CHAPTER 29

THE manic figure in red and blue laughed, a high-pitched, tittering sound. "Oh, this *is* delightful! Both of those cursed Swords, right here in my grasp!" He let out another insane giggle. "Won't Tharain be jealous!" He suddenly sobered a little and shrugged. "Well, he *did* give me the task, after all. He should probably have known better. What I could do with such artifacts!" His eyes seemed to reflect the lurid purple and orange glow of the fire, even though it was behind him.

That wasn't all that was behind him. The shadows continued to thicken, like black smoke, and a pair of gleaming purple eyes like lightning loomed through the darkness above the sorcerer's head.

"There is no escape." The sorcerer tried to hold back another giggle, but it slipped out anyway. Even as he said it, the pounding at the door started. "I suspect my pets are filling the entire stairway now. Even with your cursed weapons, you'd never get through all of them before they pulled you down and tore you to pieces."

He waved at the utter darkness gathering behind him. It shifted and warped, a creature of shadow and smoke, sometimes appearing almost like a werewolf, sometimes like a bat, sometimes like a formless, shapeless mass of tangible malice.

"Even should you try, however, there is no escape from my friend here." He looked at it fondly, like he wanted to pet the thing, though I didn't doubt he would lose his hand if he tried.

"So, then." Gunny stepped forward, his axe held loosely in his hand. "I doubt you intend to just stand there and gloat about how we can't get out. What do you want?"

The sorcerer's face contorted. "The Swords, *of course!*" He pointed his bloody dagger at me. "Why else would I have drawn you here?" His sudden fit of rage gave way to another titter. "Olgudach was easy enough to manipulate."

He left it at that, which raised all sorts of questions. Did he mean he'd messed with Olgudach's head, or that he'd bought him off with the promise of a new dawn for the lords of Edernon? It did seem awfully convenient that he'd identified that amulet as coming from Killaros, which then turned out to be a trap.

"Where's Tharain?" I stepped up next to Gunny, the Sword clenched in my fist. I'd have to fight my way up those steps, but I'd do it, even against that shadow demon thing.

Again he gave that nutso titter. "He is not here, if that is what you are wondering. You really should be more concerned with your own fates." Even as he said it, the shadow thing put what looked like a massive, taloned paw down on the edge of the dais next to him, glaring at us with those electric purple eyes.

"So, what?" Bailey stepped up to Gunny's other side, his jaw set, as pugnacious as ever. "We're just supposed to lay the Swords down and let you have 'em?"

The sorcerer sobered, then. "Oh, no. That's simply not enough." A slow, malevolent smile spread across his face. His eyes moved from us to the crowd huddled against the walls, trying to stay away from both us and the dais. His head tilted to one side, as if thinking, then, still in that attitude, his eyes flicked back to us. "It would be fitting, I suppose, to make you kill them. All of them." He straightened and shook his head with a shrug. "But they are hardly innocent, are they? Rebels and traitors, all of them. Slaying them, one and all, would be a bit too much like the enemy's idea of *justice*." He sneered as he hissed the word, then spat on the stones in front of him.

His eyes roved over the platoon, even though there were now an awful lot of rifles and at least two machine-guns pointed at his face. I think the only reason nobody had shot him yet was simply because no one was sure what that shadow demon was going to do once he went down.

We probably should have just shot him, but Gunny was treating this like a hostage situation, and so we'd follow his lead. At least until things got really kinetic, at which point all bets were off.

I think he was also trying to gather some more intel. This was the closest we'd come to having one of the rebels to interrogate, so he was going to play this as cool as possible in the hopes that he could find out just what was going on. Gunny wasn't the kind to talk when it was time for killing, so he had to have his reasons.

Except there was something else going on here. As my fingers flexed around the grip of the Sword of Iudicael, I could suddenly feel it. A sort of pressure, building behind my eyes. A faint buzzing in my ears. A heaviness, a drowsiness that made everything feel harder, more hopeless.

My eyes moved to those electric points of purple. Strangely, they seemed to fade between that burning violet and a black so deep it hurt to look at. A black that was so dark it was almost bright, if that makes any sense.

I didn't think the sorcerer was causing this effect. That thing from the Outer Dark was doing it. It was weighing down our minds and wills.

I knew the feeling because I'd felt it before. Felt it in Vaelor's Throne. Only the fact that the "elder god" had still been trapped in its prison of otherworldly stone, while we'd been in a firefight with our former platoonmates, had kept it from crushing us entirely.

I hadn't known what I carried at my side, then. Even now, though, knowing that Iudicael, messenger of Tigharn, had brought this Sword from the heavens, I didn't think I had the strength to stand up to this monstrosity.

I shouldn't have looked in its eyes. They seemed to grow bigger, as the sorcerer laughed his aggravating, high-pitched laugh. I didn't need to hear him to know he was talking about making us murder one or more of our teammates, to defile the Swords so that he—and the being of pure malevolence looming behind him—could stand their touch.

By that time, though, his voice had faded to muffled background noise, as the battle became one between me and the creature of darkness that had pressed itself through the veil, laying claim to the place bought with the blood of those the man in red and blue had sacrificed to it.

Only then did I really begin to understand that Bailey and I were its real targets. It bent its thought on us, bearing down on us with all the awful weight of its unnatural, near-infinite hatred.

That weight, as ethereal as it might have been, was nearly unbearable, and as it laughed at us in the backs of our minds, it let us see.

I saw the black tendrils of the Outer Dark slithering through Cor Legear, men and not-men coming from the Empire and the sea, traveling through the wilds, cloaked in shadow, hidden by sorcery and the treachery of those who resented Uven's rule. I saw the more subtle forces at play, the wisps of talk and spell, feeding jealousy, greed, ambition, and resentment, even as the raiders and pirates penetrated deeper and deeper into Galel lands, raiding places they never would have dared go near only a year before, spreading the chaos and bolstering those who argued that King Uven was unworthy to sit the throne.

Even as the dark clouds closed in on the Kingdom of Cor Legear, I saw some of the Galel lords welcome it, and as they did, the dead stirred beneath their holds. The dead, and worse.

We knew from Mathghaman that many of the Outsiders had been buried and imprisoned, their power turned against them by rebellious servants who sought apotheosis themselves. Brought to this world by the Summoner, the Outsiders were the embodiment of otherworldly malice.

This thing was one of them, lesser though it was. It was no Vaelor, but it was awake and present in the waking world, whereas while he had been rattling the bars of his cage, he had not yet fully manifested when Cairbre's self-sacrifice banished him back into his prison.

It showed us how it had burrowed into the heart of the kingdom, influencing one after another to break their oaths, destroy their honor, and give it a piece at a time. It had been well on the way before we'd ever left for the east.

The rest of the room had faded, the brazier only a faint, flickering, noisome light in the distance. Everything was darkness, except for those burning eyes.

With a sudden, twisting pain, I realized I was on my knees, driven there by the sheer horror of that thing's full attention. Gritting my teeth, I got one foot back under me and forced myself back to my feet.

It was hopeless. I knew it. I couldn't stand against this thing. It was older than me, smarter than me, and so much more powerful that it could probably squash me like a bug without even thinking about it. It wasn't angered that I was trying to stand.

It was amused.

I stumbled, and a wave of despair washed over me. The Sword threatened to slip from suddenly weak fingers. I looked up and saw those eyes, like purple bonfires above the sorcerer's head, even as the sorcerer looked straight at me while he pointed at Farrar.

Like a man sleepwalking, Farrar stumbled forward. I could tell he was fighting, but against an actual Outsider, he was failing.

"Kill him!" The sorcerer was screaming, and the shadow thing let the order through the terrible muffling effect of its all-encompassing attention. "Kill him and sully the blade, that it may be wrested from the lying, dead pretender's grasp!"

I wasn't going to do it. This was Mike Farrar, my RTO, a man I'd been to hell and back with. Yet even as I thought it, my mind was flooded with every frustration, every time he hadn't quite measured up, every time he'd questioned, every slight, real or imagined. Every reason I might ever have to hate him.

As my fingers tightened on the hilt of the Sword, some part of me knew what was happening, and knew that I wasn't strong enough to fight it.

Tigharn. Iudicael.

That was all. Just those two names. I couldn't even give them voice. Only think them.

But in that moment, it was as if a brilliant flash drove away the darkness that had hemmed in my sight. I breathed suddenly, as if I'd been underwater, and my vision seemed to clear. The shadow thing was still up there, but it was diminished, and its blazing eyes had narrowed. Something had just changed, but it wasn't entirely sure yet what.

There wasn't time to charge the dais. I dropped my buckler, drew my .45, and shot the sorcerer, one-handed, from thirty feet away.

He let out a choking scream and staggered back, blood soaking the blue robe under his scarlet, spangled cloak, the bloodied dagger falling with a clatter from his fingers. The dead men to either side of him stiffened, then fell, one of them taking a header off the dais and landing on one of the richly-appointed rebels standing beneath, a man who hadn't been able to crowd his way to the far wall.

The shadow thing seemed to shrink. The purple flames in the brazier died. Holstering the pistol, I started up the steps, the Sword of Iudicael held in front of me, point directed at the shadow demon.

It recoiled with a deep, feral snarl that almost stopped my heart. The Sword—or, perhaps more likely, the beings who had bestowed the Sword on me—had driven it back, but it was still dangerous, could still be my death. I faltered for a moment, but then Bailey was beside me, the Sword of Categyrn pointed in much the same way.

The sorcerer gasped and choked, writhing on the stones. Bloody froth spurted from his nose and mouth. I'd hit him in the lung. He didn't have long. And as he looked up, that feverish brightness gone from his eyes, I saw only fear. Deep, bone-chilling terror.

Not terror of us. No, his eyes were only fixed on us because he didn't want to look at the dark thing he'd summoned, that even then was reaching for him.

Bailey and I stepped forward once more. The shadow thing seized the sorcerer in one misshapen, smoky paw, and vanished.

The sorcerer let out one final, earsplitting scream of utter despair before he was dragged across the veil.

CHAPTER 30

THE storm abated, at least outside. Inside the tower of Killaros, pandemonium reigned.

We had immediately turned our weapons toward the crowd of local nobility huddled against the walls, some of them still holding their ears. The .45 wasn't particularly loud compared to unsuppressed rifle fire, but it *was* still loud, and my own ears were ringing faintly—more than they always do after so many years in the profession of arms, anyway—and my hearing was slightly deadened. It would come back, at least most of it, but cranking off a pistol shot in close quarters is always a little painful.

It was more than painful to these people, because now they were scared. Not just traumatized by what they'd just seen—though there was certainly an element of that to it—but they were scared of *us*.

Which told me all I needed to know, really. If there had been any doubt that these people had, indeed, rebelled against King Uven and sided with the sorcerous abominations in league with the Empire of Ar-Annator, then it was now gone. Why else would they fear the men who had just banished a minor Outsider?

"Who's in charge here?" Gunny's voice wasn't loud, but it cracked across the room, nevertheless. The tower had gone deathly silent as soon as the shadow demon had disappeared. The pounding at the door had ceased as soon as I'd shot the sorcerer, though I'd been a little too preoccupied to notice at the time. I expected that the stairs were choked with the dead of centuries.

None of the locals seemed willing to step forward. That probably made sense. If we were Galel, loyal to King Uven, admitting to being in charge of a Killaros given over to the enemy was probably a one-way ticket to the headsman's block or the gallows.

And while we weren't King Uven's men, our grudge against the Outer Dark would probably allow us to expedite that process.

Gunny wasn't going to waste time. "Well, then, we'll shut you up in here and leave you with the dead. Since you seemed so eager to court them in the first place."

"You can't—!" The man in the embroidered tunic and cape gasped. He was the one who had almost spoken just before the sorcerer had stepped out of the shadows.

Gunny fixed him with that unblinking, basilisk glare that had made many a harder man quail. "I can't?" He stepped forward, and every noble in the room took a half step back, several of them fetching up against the wall. Gunny stabbed a knife hand at the man. "I might not work directly for your king, the man you betrayed, but by all rights I should *still* tell my boys to shoot all of you, since you brought *that* thing into the game." His knife hand pivoted toward the dais where the shadow demon had crouched. "I might not be much of a monarchist, but when the alternative is pure evil like that, I'll make an exception."

"Gunny." Mathghaman's voice was low, but it demanded attention. "If this was indeed a diversion and a trap, and the enemy moves on Uven even now, we do not have time."

Gunny frowned more deeply, but he nodded. Mathghaman was right. Killaros had been big, flashy, and ominous, but it looked like it had been a trap for the Swords as well as a diversionary demonstration to draw all eyes there while Tharain and his sponsors moved on Cor Legear itself.

"We can't just leave this bunch." Bailey was eyeing the lot of them balefully. "They already summoned up the dead and some demon from the Outer Dark. Who knows what kind of mischief they'll get up to next?"

"Olgudach and his men should be down below, provided we don't have to fight our way out past all those black knights and scarecrows," Synar pointed out.

That brought something else to mind, something that the sorcerer had said. About Olgudach.

"That presumes that he's really trustworthy." The confrontation with the shadow demon had taken most of our attention, but that little detail had been weighing on me. "The sorcerer, I'm sure, was a liar and in league with supernatural liars, but just how did Olgudach know he'd seen that amulet here? Killaros is a good long way from Edcrnon. How often could he have been here? How likely is it, given the size of the chip on his shoulder, that the lord of Killaros would have shown him that amulet?"

"You think he set this up?" Gunny glanced at me sharply. "So, Edernon really is involved in this?"

The trouble was, I couldn't be entirely sure. "Maybe. Maybe not. That sorcerer said he was 'easy enough to manipulate.' That might mean that they played on his hold's jealousies and ambitions, and got him to turn." I squinted at the rebels, none of whom—not even Derelei—could meet my gaze for long. "Something doesn't feel right about it, though. Either he's one hell of a good liar, or he really was manipulated. In fact…" I looked up at the dais, now in shadow but no longer the stygian blackness of that thing. "I wouldn't put it past the demon to have planted the idea in his head that he'd seen that amulet here. It showed me things. Some of them might even have been true. The Devil will use the truth if it gets him what he wants."

I had no idea where that phrase had come from, but it seemed to fit.

Gunny took a deep, measured breath, thinking things through. Mathghaman held his peace, sticking to his chosen role as advisor rather than commander. I kept an eye on the rebels, trying to ignore the stench of death and decay coming in under the door. Going back down those stairs was not going to be fun.

"You dealt with him before, Conor." Gunny fixed me with that unblinking stare of his. "I'll leave this up to you."

I sighed. "Well, let's go down and talk with him, then. But I want Orava and his boys to stay on overwatch.

"Just in case."

* * *

We ended up making the rebels—the men, at least—precede us down the steps, clearing the moldering bodies out of the way. The undead had all dropped as soon as the sorcerer had been dragged off into the Outer Dark, or wherever that demon had taken him, and they were stacked like cordwood on the stairs. This way, we didn't have to handle them ourselves, and we could keep an eye on the rebels and avoid a knife in the back.

It took a while to get all the way down to the gate. Then we kept pushing them outside. Until we had someone to turn them over to, we'd need to keep an eye on them. That was creating some planning problems, but security always needs to be one of the first considerations.

We came out the gate and headed down toward the town. There was no sign of the black knights, and the nearest group of scarecrows were now nothing but detritus littering the ground. Apparently, the departure of the dark forces that had animated the dead had also stripped the spirits that had animated the scarecrows.

That was fine by me. I hadn't been looking forward to trying to hack those things to pieces. As amazingly strong and sharp as the Sword of Iudicael was, a sword isn't made to cut wood.

"Four, this is Five." Gunny was on the radio, behind me.

"This is Four." Orava's *Tenga Tuacha* was accented, but still understandable, even over the radio. We'd had to sort of shift to the *Tenga* over English, because while the Menninkai were *starting* to grasp the language, none of them were that good at it. I reckoned we'd learned the *Tenga Tuacha* as quickly as we had more because we'd been subliminally learning it thanks to the mind speech since we'd first met Mathghaman and his companions, in the pits beneath Taramas's citadel.

"Maintain your position and hold overwatch. We'll let you know when to collapse." Gunny left it at that. He didn't need to elaborate. Orava was quiet and stoic—

Menninkai culture seemed to idealize that attitude—and he'd hold his position until overrun or told to do otherwise.

Gurke, grumbling quietly about it, hustled the rebels into the shadow of a nearby building in the town, while Bailey and I moved down to meet Olgudach, who had brought his riders—and our horses—up through the center of town. That alone—the fact that he'd brought our mounts with him—tended to make me think that he'd been acting in good faith. Either that, or he was *really* quick to adjust his plans once things had gone awry. That didn't seem likely, but it never paid to be too trusting.

"Lord Olgudach." I stood in the center of the street, about twenty yards away from him, my hands on my rifle. He still had a sizeable force with him, and we were outnumbered if this went wrong. Of course, Orava was—hopefully—well positioned to take out a good number of them in the first few seconds, but a bit of standoff was still good.

"Lord Conor." He looked around at the debris and the handful of locals who were starting to peer out from behind their shutters. That alone was a bit of a relief. It meant that the rebels hadn't killed the villagers to fuel their sorcery. At least, not all of them. "What happened here?"

"Well, you were right. There were rebels here, and they were working some pretty bad sorcery." I didn't relax, my hands still on my rifle, ready to snap it to my shoulder and open fire in a heartbeat. "It was a diversion, though. Apparently, they really wanted us to come here."

"Tharain?" Olgudach's face went hard. "Is he here?"

I shook my head, watching him carefully. My hunch was getting stronger that Olgudach had been entirely sincere so far. "No. He and the 'real master' have already left. Going after King Uven."

Olgudach's eyes flicked up to the tower. "Then we must ride. Now."

I took a step forward, then. "There's more. Something that needs to be addressed before we take another step." I saw his expression freeze. "You said that you'd seen that amulet here, in Killaros. When?"

He frowned, opened his mouth to speak, then shut it suddenly. His frown deepened, and his eyes got wide. His gaze slid away from me, staring into nothing as he tried to remember.

That answered my question, though I still waited for him to speak.

"I… I do not know." He finally looked up at me, horror written across his face. "I was sure I remembered seeing it, and seeing it here, but now…"

I nodded. "The sorcerer said something about manipulating you. If the thing it summoned was in the shadows on the islands, it might have planted the thought in your head."

That didn't appear to reassure him. If anything, the horror in his eyes only got worse. I could understand. Olgudach was a warrior and a leader of men. To think that he'd been played that easily had to be terrifying.

I let my rifle hang. I was convinced. There was still a slim chance that he was acting, but that would have put him far and above any Hollywood actor I'd ever seen. And acting wasn't a big thing among the Galel.

“You were up against a thing of the Outer Dark.” I stepped forward, looking up at him where he sat his horse. “That spider creature was minor compared to this. It’s old, it’s powerful, and it’s smart. Even if you’d known it was there, it would have been hard to keep it out.”

He seemed to take a deep breath, as if composing himself, but he was still shaken. “What do we do now?”

I jerked a thumb back toward the tower. “I’m going to have to ask for some of your riders to keep watch on the rebels. They’ve got a lot of work to do. A lot of corpses to re-bury. That should keep them out of trouble for a while. In the meantime, we need to ride for Cor Legear.”

CHAPTER 31

IT was a long, hard ride to Cor Legear. Even under the best of circumstances, it would normally take at least two weeks. Pushing the horses hard, we might make it in a week and a half. Without knowing exactly what kind of head start Tharain had—and even if he'd left Killaros only minutes ahead of our arrival, if he was riding that flying horror that had plucked him out of the reception hall at Cor Legear, he didn't *need* much of a head start—we had no way of knowing how far behind we were.

I could tell that Olgudach was thinking about it as we rode. Visions of the king and his loyal followers slaughtered and Tharain sitting on the throne danced behind haunted eyes. He spoke little and slept less, as we rode through the fields and woods, sticking to the roads and no longer bothering to avoid the other holds.

We were stopped at the border between Killaros and Cor Dathul, the road blocked by two large wagons, behind which waited nearly a company of locals armed with spears, pitchforks, and bows. A single knight sat his horse in the roadway between the wagons, dressed in orange and blue, his spear held with the butt on his stirrup. He looked like a kid; he was probably at least twenty, but he didn't look like he could grow much of a beard, and he just looked fresh-faced, young, and scared stiff.

"Who goes upon this road?" His voice cracked about halfway through, robbing his challenge of the gravitas he'd probably been going for. It didn't help that, while he technically had us outnumbered, that wasn't going to count for much if this came down to violence, especially since Bailey's and Gurke's teams had split off as soon as we'd spotted the roadblock, maneuvering to put the knight and his entourage in an L-shape between us.

Olgudach held back. I didn't know if it was shame for his part in leading us into the trap of Killaros—though as I'd said, he could hardly be blamed—or if he thought that being a lord of Edernon, this far from his hold and en route to Cor Legear, might work against us.

Mathghaman spurred his horse forward. Despite all we'd been through, the man still exuded an aura of command, a regal bearing that never really went away. "I am Mathghaman Mag Cathal, King's Champion of the Isle of Riamog. My companions and I have fought and bled for your king, and now we ride to his aid once more."

The kid still looked nervous and scared. "From Killaros? We have seen the shadow that has lain upon those hills this last week."

"Why do you think that shadow's gone, kid?" Santos muttered.

Mathghaman, however, was as much a statesman as he was a warrior. "We have come from Killaros after the Sword Bearers banished the evil that had been summoned there by rebels and traitors to your land, people, and king." He held his hand out to indicate me as he spoke, since Bailey was out on the flank somewhere. "We are not your enemies, provided you maintain your loyalty."

And don't go playing patty-cake with the forces of the Outer Dark.

The knight looked a little uncertain still, but as he rode forward, studying the towering figure of the King's Champion, he seemed to let go of a massive weight on his shoulders. Clearly, he hadn't been comfortable with the idea of holding the road to Killaros down by himself, and knowing that the Tuacha were there must have been a relief.

It was clear that the Tuacha had as much of a legend here among the Galel as they did among the corsairs, if for opposite reasons. The corsairs hated and feared the "oversea men." The Galel looked at them almost as demigods.

We might do the latter, given what we'd seen them do, but Mathghaman would have cautioned against it. They were gifted beyond most men, longer lived by far, and possessed of a serenity and wisdom that I'd rarely seen anywhere. They were not infallible, though. Not incorruptible.

We'd seen that with Bres. He had been the warning that we had needed not to revere the Tuacha *too* highly.

Right at the moment, though, I'd take the Galel's cultural awe of the Tuacha if it got us past this roadblock and on our way faster.

Finally, after studying Mathghaman for a moment, the knight in orange and blue bowed his head. "Whither are you bound, lord?"

"For Cor Legear." Mathghaman allowed some of the gravity of the situation into his voice. "Your king is in grave peril. For his sake, and that of all those who do not bow to the Empire and their masters, we must ride to his aid."

The kid looked over his shoulder, toward where the great stone block of Cor Dathul stood. "I would ride with you, but…"

"We have no time." It was one thing to deconflict with the locals—those who were loyal and trustworthy, anyway—it was another to take the time needed to raise an army. Such a force was undoubtedly vital, but we weren't the ones to do it, and with Tharain ahead of us, it might be far too late by the time such an army got within sight of Cor Legear. "We must ride, now."

Even as he said it, a new formation of knights came down the road toward the checkpoint, led by a much older man clad in the same orange and blue, though the colors were reversed from the younger knight's emblems. I guessed, especially given the resemblance as they came closer, that this was the young knight's father.

The younger man filled the lord of Cor Dathul in, while we sat our horses impatiently. We couldn't just force our way through, as pressing as time was. Sure, we *could*, possibly, but that didn't mean we *should*. It would only make an already delicate situation worse.

We still didn't know who was truly loyal and who wasn't. More importantly, we didn't have a solid picture as to who would stand against the Outer Dark, loyalty to King Uven or not, either.

The older lord of Cor Dathul, however, was pretty easy to read. Slightly overweight, with a good amount of silver in his hair and bushy mustache, he grew visibly more horrified as his son outlined the situation as we'd told it to him. The kid was talking so fast that I was missing some of it—the Galel language in general sounds much like a dialect of the *Tenga Tuacha*, which is how we were able to communicate with them, but it's not one-for-one all the time—but I could get the gist, which matched up with what Mathghaman had told him.

Finally, the older man looked around at us. "If you can spare a few days, my lords, I can gather a force of nearly two hundreds. More than that will take up to a week."

Gunny shook his head. "No time."

"By all means, raise your forces and follow after," Mathghaman said. "But we cannot linger. Dark forces are moving, and they have already lent our enemies unnatural speed."

That obviously didn't make the lord of Cor Dathul feel any better. He nodded sharply. "You have good conduct through all my lands. Be warned, however. We have been beset by ruffians and even monsters in recent weeks. We think they came from Killaros, though they have wandered through our hold, unchecked even by the strongest of our warriors. If they are in league with the dark forces you speak of, they might try to stop you."

Mathghaman spurred his horse forward grimly, as the Galel respectfully stepped aside. "They might try."

* * *

By nightfall, we were well past Cor Dathul, heading up into the hills to the south of Cor Legear. We still had a couple of days' riding left, even pushing as hard as we were, but we were making good time.

Naturally, that was when things started to go wrong.

The first indicator was when a flock of birds suddenly flew up from the woods uphill and about half a mile ahead of us. I couldn't see what might have spooked them, but we were well away from Cor Dathul, and as far as we knew—and as far as Olgudach knew—there were no farms or settlements up that way. The frontier with the Empire of Ar-Annator lay only a couple of leagues away, across that line of rocky hills, and the terrain wasn't exactly conducive to farming or even grazing, anyway.

Still, nothing revealed itself as we kept going. It was a warning, though. Even if we hadn't already been on the lookout, as tired as we were, our alertness would have ratcheted up a notch at that.

It's strange. Something like the movement of birds was rarely noticed in Syria. It was as if we'd gotten so used to the technological elements of reconnaissance that we'd lost track of some of the natural indicators. Here, for whatever reason, we'd gotten more attuned.

I thought a lot of it had to do with the fact that we were in the field so long in this place. There was no Big Marine Corps to look over our shoulders, sure, but there was also no Big Marine Corps to provide us with a nice, secure FOB where we could kick back for a while and reimmerse ourselves in movies, phones, and the internet.

Out here, getting attuned to one's environment was a matter of life or death. There was no relief from it.

We kept going, threading our way higher into the rocky hills studded with oaks and scrubby evergreens, the trees getting thicker the higher we went. It might have been easier going down in the valley below, but it also meant going almost twenty miles out of our way, so we were taking the rougher road.

I could see the clouds gathering ahead. Still days away, it looked like another unnatural storm was building over Cor Legear itself.

A rock rattled somewhere up ahead. My team was on point right then, and Rodeffer reined in, throwing up a fist even as he grabbed for the rifle hanging by its sling across his saddle bow.

I was already scanning the rocks and the woods around us. This was a bad place to get ambushed. We had two ways out—back, or through. Going back wasn't an option.

I couldn't see anything at first. Whoever—or whatever—was out there, they weren't being melodramatic like the son of Cinioch had near Cor Hefedd, all those months before. They were staying behind cover. Maybe they knew what our rifles and machineguns could do.

Maybe they weren't human at all.

The first arrow took Rodeffer's horse in the neck, and it screamed and started to fall as he cursed, throwing one leg out of the stirrup and leaping free, even as the rest of us swung down and darted for the rocks, looking for cover as we scanned for the enemy.

For a moment, there was nothing. The faint breeze whispered through the trees overhead, the air increasingly drawn toward the glowering mountain of dark cloud hanging over Cor Legear, but it was drowned out by the screams of the dying horse until Rodeffer, cursing quietly, turned and put a bullet through its skull to silence it and put it out of its misery. Nothing else moved, except for the remaining horses, shifting and stamping nervously where we'd hauled them into cover under the trees and the rocks.

I moved up behind a boulder and plucked at Rodeffer's sleeve, pointing up higher into the rocks, where a massive boulder had been split by the roots of a gnarled, twisted evergreen almost as big as it was. There was cover and a better position up there, and I didn't want to get us pinned down in the kill zone anyway. Better to maneuver and see if we could get on the bad guys' flank.

I didn't think it was a coincidence that we'd run afoul of hidden archers on our way to try to relieve the king at Cor Legear.

It was a rough scramble, keeping our weapons ready and still pointed in a safe direction as we clambered over the rocks and a few fallen trees that lay between us and our chosen vantage point. Another arrow whistled out of the shadows and shattered against a rock not far from Applegate's head, and he hammered a burst of machinegun fire toward where it had come out of the trees. Splinters flew and bits of rock were smashed into a shower of grit, and a high-pitched, keening scream of agony erupted out of the enemy's cover. He'd hit something.

Rodeffer paused about halfway around the boulder, though the only signal he gave was pointing his rifle. He leaned out a little bit farther to get a better shot, even as I worked my way around behind him, making for a slightly smaller rock shaded by a fallen tree that was still green.

His rifle *crack*ed and I thought I heard a grunt and then the crash of a falling body in the brush. A yell sounded, and I heard more crashing and cracking as someone tried to move quickly, scrambling uphill toward the very boulder I was headed to. It was a good thing we'd maneuvered uphill. We'd be in danger of being flanked otherwise.

I leaned around the boulder in time to see a man wrapped in a dun cloak, a bow in his hands, arrow nocked, moving around the nearest tree at a half crouch, looking for Rodeffer. I leveled my M110 and shot him through the chest from less than twenty yards away. He'd never even seen me.

There was a flurry of movement below us, and another arrow slammed into the tree above my head, fortunately far enough away that I was pretty sure that the shooter had loosed at vague movement or just a figment of his imagination. The ambushers had suddenly found themselves facing a far more prepared and formidable force than they'd expected, and they were on the verge of panic already.

Unfortunately, they weren't alone.

As I worked my way around the boulder and the nearby trees, scanning just over my rifle's sights for more of the raiders, movement caught my eye, off to my right and entirely too close. I pivoted toward it, just as a thing that seemed to be made of the very scrub evergreens that grew between the rocks lifted itself above the boulders and came at me.

Ten feet tall and roughly man-shaped, it showed pale wood through cracked bark where the spirit animating it had stretched and warped the branches to force the tree into the semblance of a man. Massive splinters hung from its arms like spines, and a sickly greenish glow marked its eyes.

I knew better than to try to shoot it. I'd smash some wood and some bark, but that would be about it. The spirit driving that thing had to be banished, and that meant I needed to close with it and use the Sword of Iudicael.

"Rod, keep those archers off me." I slung the rifle to my back, cinched down the sling, and drew the Sword, even as that thing stalked toward me, its long strides crashing through the undergrowth. Rodeffer glanced at it, clearly nervous about leaving it to me, but that's teamwork for you, so he wedged himself a little deeper in the rocks and started picking off archers wherever he could spot them while I dealt with the tree monster.

That thing had a lot of reach on me, so playing it cautious was not going to work. I had to get in close and hurt it, so, as best I could in that terrain and brush, I charged.

It can be hard to surprise something that isn't entirely physical to begin with. Their perception of reality is different from ours, and that often gives them preternatural reflexes. Sometimes, however, the fact that they are unnaturally puppeteering something that isn't supposed to move that way works to our advantage.

This thing was a lot like the bush monster we'd fought near Killaros, but clumsier. In some ways, it was almost as if the fact that sorcery had been condemned in Galel lands for so long, the creatures of the Outer Dark didn't have quite the foothold they did elsewhere. Like a lot of the possessed puppets we'd faced already, this thing's hold on the tree it was using as a body was tenuous, and as I ducked under a ponderous haymaker of a swing and hacked at the limb, a faint tongue of flame leaped up around where the blade bit into the wood, and the limb stiffened, shriveling and turning black. A faint keening sound came from the midst of the creaking, rustling construct, and then I went to town, determined to hack this thing to bits or at least banish the spirit before it could get a good hit on me.

I aimed my next blow at the other limb, which was a lot bigger, seemingly built of several branches twisted together. The first hit was a glancing blow, but again there was that little spurt of flame, and the limb started to go stiff. Two more strokes and it was useless.

Pulling back the Sword, I aimed the point at the center of those green, glowing eyes, but then the thing fled, a faint wisp of greenish smoke flitting out of the cracks in the wood and heading off to the east with the same faint, keening cry. The eyes dimmed and went out, the remnant of the tree stiffening before it tipped over and crashed to the ground with a hollow *boom.* I barely got clear in time.

The gunfire down below had gotten momentarily more intense as I'd fought that thing, but it was already tapering off again. As I sheathed the Sword, stepping around the now once again inert tree, and brought my rifle back up, I saw a flurry of movement through the trees. Snapping the weapon up, I canted it to bring my offset red dot up, but then I lowered it once more as I saw that the man in the dirty yellow cloak was running for it, crashing through the brush, his hands empty, the quiver on his back spilling its last arrows onto the ground. He wasn't a threat any longer.

There'd been a time when I might have shot him, anyway. Just to make sure that he wouldn't become a threat once again. That was before, though. Before I'd become a Sword Bearer. Something told me that shooting a man in the back while he's running away would make me less worthy to carry that blade at my side.

“Consolidate!” Gunny’s voice rang out across the hillside. A couple more sporadic shots chased our attackers, but as I stepped higher and got a better view of the battlefield, it did look like we’d taken the starch out of our ambushers.

I just hoped that we didn’t run into any more such checks before we reached Cor Legear.

CHAPTER 32

IT was two more days to Cor Legear. We weren't attacked again, but the storm clouds above the Rock of Guard got thicker and darker. Even with the lightning flickering in it, that tower of cloud started to look more and more like smoke and ash the closer we got. There was dark sorcery at work, and we pushed our animals as hard as we dared to get there in time.

Maybe we wouldn't. Maybe we were simply too late, diverted to Killaros as the enemy had planned, and it was all over but the shouting. Maybe King Uven was dead, or worse, and Tharain was even then handing the keys to the kingdom over to the Emperor of Ar-Annator and his dark masters.

What then? I couldn't help but think about it as we rode hard to the north. We'd fought Fohorimans, corsairs, monsters and demons from the Outer Dark, even the headless disciples of the Summoner. We'd fought for our own survival and in service to unspoken debts. Now, we'd fought in defense of the Galel kingdom, despite not being Galel and having no real loyalty to them. We had fought as allies, not auxiliaries or lieges. What would we do if the kingdom fell?

The obvious answer would be to pull out and head for the Isle of Riamog. We'd come here to answer Galan's and Fortrenn's plea to help find the Sword of Categyrn, not to fight their wars for them.

I'd been there before, though. Been in places where the "mission," meaning the decisions made by somebody in an air-conditioned TOC miles away, required us to leave innocent people in harm's way, targeted by savages who'd happily murder men, women, and children just for talking to us, for the sake of some "big picture" that never ended up materializing, no matter how often they invoked it and implied that we enlisted knuckle draggers were just too stupid and limited to see it.

Here it was different. Here, with Gunny and Mathghaman deciding our direction, we had more control over our fate and our course of action. We had nothing stopping us from fighting the good fight but ourselves.

Would we cut our losses and head back to the Isle? I didn't think so. Even though I knew it would be partly my decision at that point, I didn't imagine that Gunny saw things that much differently. We might not be Galel, but their enemies came from the deepest, darkest pits of hell, and without some flag officer looking over our shoulders through a Predator feed, the decision to fight was an easy one.

I hoped it wouldn't come to that. Better to reach Cor Legear in time and help Uven beat back his attackers. Better to nip this dark, unconventional war in the bud before we were running for our lives, fighting the monsters, those Galel lords who went over to Tharain, and the Empire of Ar-Annator and their own dark lords, all at once.

If that was what it came to, though, I didn't doubt that we'd do it. So would the Tuacha. To a man. It was their sort of thing.

With all that in mind, we rode into the storm.

* * *

Only a few miles from the town, we entered the murk. It looked like mist at first, but it stank of sulfur and was turning brownish before things got really dark. Marines and Menninkai flipped down our NVGs, though the Tuacha didn't really need them.

The NVGs soon seemed to be pretty useless, though. They couldn't penetrate the dark clouds, that now seemed more like smoke than fog. I left mine down, just because it was dark enough that I needed them to see for the whole twenty or so yards of visibility that remained.

We slowed considerably, weapons up and scanning the darkness. It might have been unconscious, but everyone moved a little closer together, forming a tightly packed and cohesive formation. The Galel in the rear bristled with spears and swords, eyes out and shields held high, just in case.

The sounds had been faint before we'd entered the cloud. Too faint to be sure that we were really hearing them. Now that we were in the darkness and the smoke—it was definitely smoke, the deeper we got into it, and it scratched at the back of my throat as I tried to breathe—they got a lot louder.

Screams echoed through the haze, accompanied by bestial sounds of rage and wild, insane laughter. The clash of weapons and sounds of fighting and struggle underlay the pandemonium.

Still, we couldn't see anything, even as the outer curtain wall of the city loomed out of the dark, only a blacker outline against the dimness. Guns came up, scanning the battlements for threats. If the enemy had already taken the wall, we could be in for a rough time.

There was no movement, however. Everything was still, in marked contrast to the noises drifting out through the gates.

The gates themselves stood open, though they were relatively undamaged. Almost as if someone had opened them, rather than an attacker forcing them or blowing them open, the way that the Lasknut had destroyed the gates at Vahava Paykhah.

I reined in. The Galel might be cavalry, but we weren't. We'd fought from horseback before, but that had been part of a wild breakout after killing a dragon and at least knocking a Dullahan's head flying. This was going to be an assault, and I didn't want to try that on horseback.

Gunny agreed, already holding his hand up to forestall our advance. Olgudach rode up next to us, looking concerned, though he could probably see even less than we. But he could hear.

"Why are we stopping?" He had to wonder if we were turning back, now.

"Because my boys aren't knights. We're footsloggers, and that's how we're going to fight. I suggest, if you and yours want to stay mounted, you keep to the center of the lane, and don't ride in front of any of us." Gunny didn't need to go into greater detail than that. Olgudach and his boys had seen us fight, and they knew not to ride directly in front of archers, anyway. They might be knights, armored and armed for close-in combat, but these guys knew warfare, including archery and every other dirty trick that their enemies might play on them, trying to use their sense of honor against them.

Olgudach got it. He nodded grimly, flexing his fingers around the haft of his spear. "Let us proceed, then."

Bailey was apparently tired of letting my team go first, and he essentially shouldered his way to the front of the stack, practically shoving Baldinus in front of him. Not because Thomas Baldinus was reluctant to get stuck in, but just because Bailey wanted him to move faster.

With Applegate holding security on the battlements above, Baldinus, Bailey, and Synar slipped through the opening in the gate, weapons dropping level as soon as they cleared the opening and each other.

The Tuacha had stayed spread out through the platoon, and Eoghain was right behind Synar, pulling Applegate through with him with a murmured, "Last man."

I wasn't going to let Gurke jump the stack, too. When he glared at me as we pushed through after Bailey's team, I just patted the Sword at my side. "Sword Bearer."

Petty, maybe. It probably counted against me a little. But it was true that I probably had a better chance against any weird stuff on the other side of those gates with the Sword of Iudicael than he did.

We flowed through the gates. It was just as dark on the other side, though a moment later a massive lightning bolt forked across the sky, lighting up the grimy haze without making visibility much better. Just enough to see the buildings on the inside of the gates, and the vague shapes of men crouched over bodies in the lane ahead.

A moment later, as the thunder crashed, loud enough to make a grown man wince, two of the crouching forms snapped their heads up to look at us. It didn't take much to see that they weren't friendly. Something about the way they moved was just *off.* When they surged to their feet and ran at us, snarling like animals, no one hesitated.

A dozen rounds each smashed them off their feet in a welter of blood, and they crashed to the dusty ground.

That was striking. Despite the storm that we'd watched raging over Cor Legear for days, that had initially looked like the thunderstorms we'd thrashed through to get to Killaros, the ground was dry. So was the air, as it crackled with the electric tension of the lightning overhead. The city felt hot, parched, and a lot like how I imagined the ground floor of Hell probably felt.

We pushed forward, moving in a split column along the sides of the road, guns up and watching every angle we could for threats. The chorus of screams, shrieks, laughter, and roars of hatred had only gotten louder as we'd moved through the gate.

Olgudach and his men came next, riding in single file up the road, simply because of how little space there was to maneuver. We kept close to the walls of the houses but stayed clear of the windows and doors as much as we could, each man pivoting to cover each opening as he passed it.

After what we'd seen of the bodies in the street, no one wanted to take the chance of being grabbed from a window or door.

That caution slowed us down, but it was unavoidable. With visibility as poor as it was, we weren't going to do King Uven or anyone else any good by charging in where angels feared to tread and getting ambushed.

It was a good thing, too, because if we'd pushed too fast, we might have stumbled right into the middle of the mob trying to batter down the doors to a good-sized house on the main lane, one owned by one of the richer merchants in the capitol.

They took no notice of us at first, but just kept screaming and raving as they banged on the door and the shuttered windows. We spread out, Applegate and Santos holding on the crowd while Farrar and Synar covered the side streets, just in case. Olgudach continued his advance, riding at the front of his column, his spear lowered and couched, his shield presented.

There were no weapons in evidence. The mob was tearing at the wood with their bare hands, leaving dark smears of blood as their fingernails tore away. They were out of their minds. There was no doubt about that in my mind.

Olgudach might have challenged them. Instead, he sat his horse for a moment, watching with narrowed eyes. He couldn't see as much as I could, and I wondered which way he was going to jump. If he tried to charge that crowd, we were going to have to wade in there with blades. We couldn't risk friendly fire, which would definitely happen if we opened fire once Olgudach and his men were entangled with the crowd.

I made a command decision at that point. We didn't have the time to try to sneak past them, and we were going to lose too many people—it was inevitable from where I sat—if we tried to fight them blade to hand. So, I nodded to Santos.

It felt a little like murder. I had to remind myself, as Santos leaned into the gun, playing the stream of red tracers across the mob as the suppressor crackled and the brass and links rained down into the dust with a faint tinkle, that they were a lethal threat, unarmed or not. We'd seen what those others had done. Seen the raw meat where they'd torn the skin off the man and woman lying dead in the street and *chewed.*

A dozen of them went down like bloody rag dolls in the first couple seconds. The rest turned and tried to charge us, confirming that I'd made the right call.

Applegate opened fire from across the street, as I shot a snarling berserker, the whites of his eyes completely dark in my NVGs, through the throat. He choked, spat blood, and kept coming until I blasted him through the skull, by which point he'd closed another six feet. His head jerked back, and he fell on his face, a good chunk of the back of his skull gone.

It took moments to gun down the rest, but we had to be thorough. Any that hadn't been killed outright with the first shots just kept coming. They didn't stop until we'd put a bullet through every single one's vitals.

Gunny moved to one of the fallen mob, kicked the body over, and flicked on his white light. In its sudden glare, the dead man's eyes weren't black. They were blood red. So was the sigil carved into his forehead.

No, it wasn't carved. The longer I looked at it—which actually wasn't that long, because the sight of it made my head hurt—the more it looked like the skin had split *from the inside* in that disturbing pattern.

He moved the light to another body. It was the same. The same blood-filled eyes, the same ugly sigil forcing itself out through the skin, though in a slightly different place.

"I'd say we need to burn the bodies, but we don't exactly have time." He looked up toward the hill where the citadel of Cor Legear sat. We could still hear fighting over the screams and shrieks all around us, along with bestial noises that sounded like things we'd heard in the north.

Including things that didn't belong in this world at all.

"Tighten up, watch your fires, but don't let anyone get too close." He moved in with my team, falling in behind me.

"There are still innocent people in this city," Olgudach protested. "Otherwise, these lost ones would not have been trying to break down that door."

"I know it." Gunny didn't look up at him. "If they've got an ounce of common sense, they've shut themselves up in their houses and aren't wandering around. That's why I said to watch our fires. We have to move fast and get up there. If we can kill the sorcerer behind this, maybe we can stop it."

That was a big *if*, from what I was looking at. This wasn't just some wizard messing with powers better left alone. This was a full-court press to take down Cor Legear before the Empire crossed the border, and I suspected that we hadn't seen the last of that shadowy thing from Killaros.

We pressed on.

I'd expected to get swarmed after that chattering burst of gunfire, but as we moved up the lane toward the base of the hill, we didn't immediately get attacked by another mob. The noises, getting ever more disturbing, continued to rave around us, and I could only imagine that those under the influence of that sigil were so absorbed in their own depravity that they couldn't be diverted easily.

Something the size of a large hound bounded through the murk ahead of us. Rodeffer stopped dead, snapping his rifle up, but he didn't fire as it disappeared. I thought I heard a *bang*, then a distant scream, suddenly cut off.

Madmen with eyes full of blood were not all we had to worry about in Cor Legear that day.

We got about another fifty yards before we found ourselves surrounded.

They weren't dogs. Not really. They were low to the ground, and they moved like dogs, but they had anything from six to eight legs, their heads were roughly reptilian in shape, what we could see of them, and their eyes glowed a hellish purple.

Eoghain, Mathghaman, and Bearrac didn't hesitate, but immediately started to chant in that ancient language they used for prayer and invocation. Several of those purple points of fire narrowed, squinting as if in pain, and the nearest of the creatures recoiled.

Knowing that bullets would do no good, I slung my rifle and drew the Sword. Bailey stepped up beside me and did the same.

Strangely, both blades seemed to flicker and reflect the light of nearby fires back twofold. The creatures looked even more discomfited. They shrank back as we advanced, both of the Two Swords held in a high guard, poised to thrust down into unnatural flesh.

Mathghaman, Bearrac, Eoghain, and Diarmodh flanked us, along with Gunny, as we strode forward. The dog-lizard things skittered back a few paces, then turned and scampered off into the dark, disappearing in the smoke and haze after a few yards.

We kept going.

All around us, even as the dark bulk of the hill and the citadel rose ahead, suddenly backlit by a titanic flash of lightning, followed a mere heartbeat later by the stunning thunderclap, we heard the cacophony of madness and fear get louder. We couldn't see much of what was going on out there in the haze, for which I am still thankful to this day. But it was there, and we knew it, and we had to keep pushing past it.

Remember what I said about the "big picture" and having to brush past a lesser evil to deal with a greater? I'd seen it used as an excuse so many times that the very concept made my jaw clench. The problem with that is that sometimes, you *have* to go for the Big Bad and ignore the rest. This was one of those times. And as much as I knew I was going to hear those screams in my sleep to my dying day, I knew, on a level I can't exactly describe, that if we didn't get into the citadel and end this, we wouldn't manage to save *anybody*.

I looked down at the Sword in my fist and gritted my teeth. The path up to the gate lay empty ahead of us.

I sped up.

CHAPTER 33

THE outer gates hung open, cracked and sagging on their hinges. Parts of the timbers looked almost *chewed.* The enemy might have gotten the curtain wall gates open without violence, but they had smashed through these. Dead bodies littered the ground before and behind them. Most appeared to be the royal guard, in their red tunics, horribly torn and smashed. One man lying on his face before the gates had been ripped open, his guts torn out, and his helmet and skull smashed flat by something massive. Still, he was surrounded by the corpses of more Galel soldiers in different liveries, several of the bloody-eyed men with demonic sigils forcing themselves out through their flesh, and three twisted amalgamations of bone, chitin, and ash. He had not gone quietly.

I still wondered at the numbers as we moved quickly but carefully through the gateway and up the hill toward the inner wall. Had Uven not called together all his armies? He'd called for a war footing months before, when the Imperial emissaries had used sorcery to attack Cor Legear from the inside, murdering more than a few of the guards and raising their corpses as meat puppets for things from the Outer Dark. Had the rebellion already begun back then, with his lords generally ignoring the call? Or had more of them gone over than we'd feared? There weren't enough bodies on the ground, and we hadn't seen much in the way of resistance out in the town below. We'd heard it, but there hardly seemed to be much of any organized defense left.

I shook off the worries. Those were for another time. Right then was time to concentrate on staying alive long enough to reach the king, or, if we were too late, to kill Tharain and his pet sorcerer.

We kept climbing the hill toward the inner gate, most of us covering inward and forward, though I made sure Farrar was still watching the outer wall. I wouldn't put it past our enemies to keep archers or worse up there, if they had control of the outer wall, to deal with any squirters, even if they hadn't expected someone to move in to attempt to relieve the king.

That narrow killing ground between the outer wall and the main citadel was still and empty, though, except for the bodies. They lay in attitudes of violent death all the way to the gates, some of them in multiple pieces.

The wounds they bore were not clean cuts or axe strokes, either. Many had been ripped to pieces with horrific force. If not for the fact that I had a pretty good idea what we were up against, I would have suspected explosives.

At least we hadn't seen anyone turned to black mist like Nelson-Hyde had been.

Yet.

Nearing the inner gate, weapons up, I tried to mentally prepare myself for the worst. The screams and clash of weapons all seemed to come from outside the gates, below us, in the town. The citadel itself was deathly quiet. It didn't bode well.

The gateway was dark. Rodeffer moved to one flank of the open portal, while Baldinus took the other. I was right behind Rodeffer, my rifle held at the high ready, the suppressor just above his shoulder. We'd flood that opening with guns and bodies, and hopefully whatever we faced first went down to bullets.

Mathghaman was right behind me, and Eoghain was right behind Bailey. That was a comfort, if a relatively small one. I gave Rodeffer the squeeze, and we flowed into the stygian blackness.

The gatehouse was worse than the yard between the walls. The bodies were piled deep across the whole gatehouse, a carpet of dead flesh and viscera. The stench was nearly unbearable. Once again, though, as we flicked on weapon lights, though only in brief flashes to avoid giving enemies—flesh and blood ones, anyway—a solid look at our positions, we saw that the carnage wasn't one-sided. King Uven's men had bought their sovereign time, and they had reaped their share of souls. There were a lot of rebels and unnatural monstrosities among the dead.

While the outer gates were shattered and hanging open by their hinges, the inner doors were shut fast.

That didn't bode well, either.

A rattling, skittering hiss traveled through the chamber as we worked our way toward the inner doors. Rodeffer stutter-stepped, almost tripping over another corpse as he flashed his light around the corners of the gatehouse. Nothing. There was nowhere to hide in that narrow space.

No, not quite nowhere. I looked up, flashing my own light onto the ceiling.

I had no way of knowing if that was the same spider thing that had crawled out of the dead man's chest cavity on the island off Edernon, but if it wasn't, it was cut from the same cloth.

Its limbs stretched from wall to wall, glistening in my light. It wasn't just the thing's chitinous hide that was gleaming, though. Dark, foul fluids dripped from the spikes that lined those limbs. Little imagination was needed to tell where they came from.

That rustling sound wasn't coming from its legs but its mouthparts, beneath a face that looked like a many-eyed skull with a split jaw. It was stalking down the walls like a climber in a chimney, moving with a leisurely anticipation that I could feel more than see in those awful, dead eyes.

"*Sssssoooo.*" The word, drawn out and sibilant, might have come from those terrible jaws, but it could just as easily have been in our heads. This thing appeared more physical than the shadow demon in Killaros, but it was of a kind with it. I could sense it.

"*I had hoped that the master would allow a few more morsels to come into my web. How thoughtful.*" The dry, hissing laughter was worse than the voice.

I knew that it probably wasn't going to help, and our ammo was limited, but I brought my rifle up and shot the thing between the eyes anyway. It was a gesture, little more, but a necessary one. It was my bit of defiance, and I was quickly joined by just about every other gunfighter in the gatehouse.

Of course, while the bullets tore through unnatural flesh, blasting through the thing's head and thorax to spatter frag and splinters off the timber ceiling, they didn't even slow it down. If anything, that slithery laughter only got worse.

It dropped toward us, and I drew the Sword.

Bailey was ahead of me, though. He hadn't wasted rounds on that thing, but had immediately drawn the Sword of Categyrn. Now, as the many-legged horror descended the walls, he was the first one within reach, and he struck quickly, aiming for one of those multi-segmented legs.

That thing was *fast*, though, and it snatched the limb out of his reach. He was practiced enough with the weapon that he didn't overbalance, but it suddenly dropped to the corpse-strewn floor and went after him.

It moved so fast that it almost blurred, evading his Sword and shooting out one long leg, sweeping his feet out from under him. He went down, rolling off the body of a man who'd been torn in half, desperately scrambling out of the way as one of those limbs—tipped with a scimitar-like talon rather than a spider's grippers—slammed down through the corpse and into the stone floor beneath.

Baldinus shot it, then, probably just to try to distract it, and it lashed out. That leg suddenly got a lot longer, and it bashed Bailey's pointman against the wall. He hit with a gasp and dropped to one knee, that enormous talon poised above his head.

I had the Sword of Iudicael out by then, and I darted in at its side. It caught me on the shoulder without even turning its grisly head to look at me, and while I avoided getting my head taken off, I still went sprawling as a corpse rolled under my boot.

Even as I fell, though, I slashed at that leg. It snatched it back, dancing out of the way. As formidable as that thing was, it didn't want to make any contact with the blessed Swords.

It hadn't been counting on Mathghaman.

He leaped forward and seized the thing by the front legs, his own massive arms holding its mouthparts back from his face. He stared into those multitudinous eyes without fear, despite the fact that they were windows into the Outer Dark itself.

"You do not belong here, child of the abyss." His muscles strained as he leaned in, his teeth gritted. "Go back to the pit you crawled out of."

The thing shoved back at him, but despite its unnatural strength and mass, it barely budged him. It snapped its mouthparts at his face, slaver dripping to the floor.

"*Your power wanes, younger child of the one we do not name. We hold sovereignty here, now.*"

"You are a liar and the child of a liar and murderer." The veins were standing out in his neck, every muscle corded as he strained against the thing. "Invaders and interlopers. I abjure you, in His Name, back to the Outer Dark!"

Bearrac bent and gathered a handful of my chest rig, hauling me to my feet, the chant already beginning. Eoghain, Diarmodh, and Fennean were joining in, as I got my balance back, hefted the Sword of Iudicael, and waded in. Off to the thing's other side, Bailey closed in with the Sword of Categyrn.

It flailed and lashed at us with those spiked limbs, and we each took a bit more of a battering, but it couldn't move away. Mathghaman held it in place, despite their difference in size.

Physical size, anyway. I had a feeling the son of Cathal outweighed this thing in the spiritual realm, mortal man or not.

He held it while we moved in on it. It knocked Bailey sprawling again, but I got a cut in on the limb that it tried to hit me with in the next moment, and the Sword of Iudicael went through it like a hot knife through butter. Oily smoke poured from the wound, and the thing let up an earsplitting shriek of agony and rage, shuddering and thrashing in Mathghaman's grip.

Bailey surged to his feet, coming in low, and got between two of those chitinous limbs to plunge the point of the Sword of Categyrn into its thorax.

The scream then drove me to my knees. Mathghaman was actually lifted off his feet as the creature convulsed and shrieked, thrashing around in its agony. The steel itself probably didn't hurt it. That it was the Sword of Categyrn, handed down by a messenger of Tigharn… That had to hurt.

I staggered in and started hewing at those limbs. They came away easily, dissolving into smoke and ichor as they fell. Mathghaman finally gave the thing a heave and stepped back, as it continued writhing and twisting, seeming to shrink away as he and his Tuacha companions continued their chant, calling on Tigharn to banish this thing back to the Outer Dark.

With one final, agonized scream of hate, it melted away into black slime.

We stood there for a moment, panting for breath despite the metallic, sulfurous stink that now overlay the stench of death in the gatehouse. Mathghaman straightened and reached out to grip first Bailey's shoulder, then mine.

"If that was the gatekeeper, then we can expect worse deeper in." He looked around at all of us, spread out around the narrow room, guns either pointed at the inner door, the open outer gates, or the ceiling. "Steel yourselves and reconcile your souls with Tigharn. This will, as you would say, get ugly."

"I've never been much of a religious man," Gurke said into the sudden silence. "But yeah. I'll say a prayer or two. I'll even promise not to drink, chase loose women, or even cuss… that much… anymore."

"I advise you to take this seriously." Bearrac's voice was back to his usual growl.

"Oh, I'm taking it seriously, Bearrac." There might have been a faint shake in Gurke's voice. He'd long had the hardest time adjusting to the weirdness here. He'd done it, but it had always been slightly grudging, like everything else Gurke did that wasn't his idea. "I just get a little flippant when I'm scared shitless." He was staring at the puddle of black slime that had been the spider thing.

Gunny was listening, but he was also getting ready for the next phase. He tested the inner doors. "Barred. We're going to need breaching charges."

"Good thing that Oncu brought explosives along with the ammo." Chambers was already digging in his assault pack. We'd brought a few things after we'd left the horses outside the walls.

With the rest of the platoon covering the openings, Chambers and Franks started to build the breaching charge, working as quickly as they could.

Outside, the screams and hellish noises continued. Inside, on the other side of that door, it was eerily quiet.

I'd all but forgotten my rifle. I gripped the Sword of Iudicael as I watched the door, praying silently that I could get through the next few minutes with my life—and my soul—intact.

CHAPTER 34

WHILE it was probably redundant, up against supernatural threats the way we were, Chambers didn't want to count down out loud, so he held up all five fingers on one hand twice, counting down silently as he pulled the igniter then sprinted away from the doors.

Chambers was a quiet dude, but he knew his stuff. Especially when it came to explosives. Demo was only a minor part of what we did in Recon—and we hadn't been able to finagle Demo Pay since the early two thousands—but those who went to the Breacher Course took some pride in it. After all, blowing stuff up is fun.

In this case, that meant he'd cut the time fuse precisely, and ten seconds after he pulled the igniter, the charges went off.

Most breaching charges in recent years have been designed to cut through locks or entire doors. Water charges were simpler, intended to simply fold a metal door in half and throw it across the room. Blowing open a massive, double timber door, bound in iron and barred with another timber, gets a little more difficult. In the end, Chambers had tamped a cutting charge with what we used to call a "ghostbuster," essentially a sheet of explosive with detcord wrapped in a donut around it.

We'd had to give up the gatehouse until the charges went off. There was no way we were going to weather that concussion in that small space. We hunkered down just outside, Santos and Applegate still covering the kill-zone around the citadel, until the breach went off.

The thunder was deafening even from outside the portal. Smoke, splinters, and bits of bodies and gear billowed out of the opening, as most of us either turned away or tucked our chins, just to keep the concussion off.

We were already moving into the cloud before it had settled. Visibility was terrible, and footing was worse, since the explosion had thrown quite a few of the bodies and body parts around, but we pushed through, driving for the shattered inner doors as fast as we could, moving to take anyone on the other side by surprise.

There was so much debris in the doorway that we couldn't quite flood into the reception hall as fast as we might want. One entire panel of the doors had been cracked in half, and the other hung from one hinge, the smashed remnant of the bar still hanging from its bracket. Smoking splinters and chunks of wood littered the floor in front of it, making footing more difficult even without the smoke and the darkness.

Still, Rodeffer and Baldinus shoved the doors aside, riding them until they stopped, while the rest of us rushed through, guns up and weapon lights flashing—there was no disguising our presence at that point, so we may as well go loud—looking for targets.

There were none.

The reception hall was dark, silent, and empty. The shattered window where the winged horror had snatched Tharain from our grasp was still open, visible as a slightly brighter grayish brown against the blackness of the walls.

At second glance, though, as we scanned the room with our weapon lights, it turned out not to be quite as empty as it had appeared.

Vepogenus, bloodied and battered, hung from the wall behind the high seat. There was no sign of what was holding him up, but he was pinned to the wall about ten feet up anyway. His head lolled, blood dripping from his face, but as I studied him, I saw his chest rise and fall. He was still alive.

He wasn't alone, either. Knights and lords lined the walls, held above the floor by some invisible force, none of them looking too good. At least one was clearly dead. He had probably died while suspended there.

Nothing else moved.

We spread out, moving along the walls, though everyone kept their distance from the men hanging from above. No monsters leaped out at us, nothing opposed us.

But I was starting to hear something.

It wasn't the sorcerous chant that I dreaded, but it wasn't good, either. Somewhere up above us, high in the keep, a fight was going on. And someone—or some-*thing*—was laughing.

Mathghaman took lead then, though no one had asked him to. Bailey and I might have been the Sword Bearers, but he understood and perceived what was going on here better than any of us. So, we didn't ask questions. Gunny didn't try to stop us and make a new plan.

The Number One Man is always right. Just flow with it.

He headed up the stairway behind the reception hall, climbing the steps rapidly, his rifle held high and ready, searching for targets. Bailey and I pushed up to join him, but even we couldn't get ahead of Bearrac, who was right on his heels, flowing like he'd been doing Marine CQB his entire life.

They led us past the first couple of floors, heading for the royal apartments near the roof. All the while, the sounds of clashing weapons, grunts, shouts, and that awful, hollow laugh got louder.

A half a dozen rebel warriors crouched at the top of the stairs as we reached the second to last landing. Two of them turned as we moved up, their eyes widening as they looked down four rifle muzzles, though they must have had a hard time getting them any wider than they already were. Every man of them looked scared stiff.

The first man immediately dropped his weapon as Mathghaman advanced on him. The clatter drew the rest's attention, and a moment later, several axes, two swords, and a number of daggers joined it on the landing. Hands were held up in surrender.

"Please." The man who'd seen us first, his beard shot with gray and his tunic worn and faded beneath his coat of mail, held out his hands in supplication. "We only served our lord. We never intended it to come to this. Not like this."

As if to punctuate his statement, an unearthly howl came from inside the royal apartments.

Gunny wasn't having it, though. "If you really didn't want this, then you should have quit when you had the chance, before your own countrymen were getting torn apart and eaten in the streets." He shouldered forward as we stacked up on the door. "Franks, Synar, get some flex cuffs on these punks."

It took a moment to get them partway down the steps, out of our way, and then Mathghaman pushed the door open, and we burst into the royal apartments.

The apartments were mostly one large room, with the king's massive four-poster bed near one end, several chests around the walls, a huge, stone fireplace in the center, and a table and benches on the near side of the fireplace. There was a small closet of wood in the far corner, draped with tapestries, almost out of view.

The table and benches had been smashed to splinters, and a dark shadow crouched atop the ruin of the table. The king and Queen Nechtudad stood at the bed, surrounded by what was left of the royal bodyguard, about two dozen battered and bloodied men who nevertheless held a shield wall against a line of dark warriors.

Those warriors were not human. Or at least, if they had been once upon a time, they weren't anymore. They were tall, none shorter than seven feet, and gaunt as skeletons. That was about the most detail I could see, as they were all wreathed in shadow like black smoke. The dark blades of their swords drank every bit of the light from the handful of sconces on the king's end of the room that lit the place. They even looked deep black in my NVGs, and that took some doing.

It was what stood behind them that arrested my attention, though.

Tharain was expected. Though this was ostensibly his moment of triumph, he looked scared. Almost as scared as his retainers whom we'd rolled up in the stairway. And the figure standing next to him explained why.

It was tall as Tharain, even though it didn't have a head. Well, it did have a head, but it wasn't on its neck. It hung from a strap over its shoulder.

And it was facing the door, watching us with a sadistic, leering grin, its long, gauntleted fingers flexing around the long whip crafted from human vertebrae in its hand.

"The three defenders of a lost people, all in one room." The head was speaking, though the voice seemed to come from far away and deep beneath the earth. Even as it spoke, the door slammed behind us, cutting us off from half the platoon that was still in the stairwell. The room darkened still more. "Excellent."

Then it struck.

That whip snaked out like it had a life of its own, and to this day I have no idea how I got the Sword in front of my face that fast. The whip wrapped around the blade, almost pulling it out of my grasp… until the part that had touched it burst into blue flame and dissolved to ash. The Dullahan snatched the whip back with a *crack*, the sconces went out, and the duel was on.

Darkness fell like a curtain, and then it was just me and the Dullahan. It had either dropped the whip and drawn a sword that looked like it was made of bone, or else the whip had changed shape. It stabbed for my eyes, and I parried almost too late. That ice-cold blade slid just along my scalp, under my helmet, cutting one of the chin straps. I felt the flesh over my cheekbone go numb, even as I forced the blade away with the Sword of Iudicael and tried to get my buckler into the fight.

My hand didn't close on the buckler, but the handle of my Bowie. Without the time or the space to try to fumble for the buckler, I yanked the Bowie out and tried to stab the Dullahan while our swords were still crossed.

It batted the blade aside with casual contempt and then shoulder-checked me into the wall.

I hadn't been hit that hard in a long time, and the blow knocked the wind out of me. I hadn't realized I was still that close to the wall, but I couldn't see anything in the room but myself and the Dullahan, and that by the greenish corpse-light flickering and fluttering around its severed head. I could hear, but only dimly, as the rest of the Tuacha, Gunny, and what I thought was at least Rodeffer, fought the shadow-wreathed warriors confronting the king. It was all muffled though, as if it were underwater and far away.

The Dullahan stood over me, leering, as I levered myself away from the wall, fighting to regain my breath. I kept the Sword pointed at it, but as evil as it was, it didn't seem as scared of the weapon as many of the other monsters we'd confronted.

I reminded myself that this was, if the tales were true, one of the Summoner's original disciples. A grim apostle of the Outer Dark, gifted by the Outsiders to an extent that would make the Fohorimans, who had rebelled against the Outsiders and stolen their power, look like children playing pretend.

It stepped closer and batted the Sword aside. Its own weapon didn't burn and smoke at the touch of the blessed steel the way its whip had, so it probably wasn't the same. I just hadn't seen the whip disappear and the sword drawn.

"Such pathetic instruments the great powers have to work with. That fool, Garnard, feared to touch that weapon unless it was defiled first." It laughed, a deep, hollow sound. "I have been blessed by the Elder Gods. I need only take it from your defiled corpse. It can be destroyed after."

I crouched and circled, but it turned to face me without seeming to move, its bone sword at its side, seemingly completely unconcerned. I lunged, and once again it parried easily, not even bothering to riposte.

It was toying with me.

It stepped closer with a sudden thrust that I barely knocked aside. It hadn't seemed to move that fast, but the blade skittered along my mail-clad arm, and I felt the same terrible cold even through the mail and the padded gambeson underneath. I shoved that awful blade away with the Sword of Iudicael as I staggered away, fighting the pins and needles sensation running through my arm.

It pursued me around the room with an awful slowness for the next several moments, easily batting aside my clumsy attacks and aiming leisurely, seemingly nonchalant thrusts and swings at my head, shoulders, and legs, all still so lightning fast that I could barely hold my own.

"So pathetic. You are going to die, you know that?" The head's demoniac grin had gotten wider and wider, its teeth like a shark's, its eyes blazing with a wavering, noisome green fire. "It will not be a quick or painless death, either."

"Let me guess, this is the part where you offer to end my suffering if I surrender the Sword?" I gasped as I ducked away from another swing that almost took my head off.

It laughed again, a terrible, hollow sound. "Why should I bargain with such as you? I need not lower myself. I will slay you slowly, and you will curse your feeble master before you die. Then my lords will hold your soul for me to torment for an eternity when I receive the reward for all my deeds."

This time, as it swung for my arm and I twisted the Sword of Iudicael to parry, it suddenly reversed the blade, flipped it over my head, and slammed it down onto my shoulder.

My mail held, just barely, but I still think that it pulled the blow at the last second. Icy pain ran down my arm and I lost my grip on the Bowie, the knife clattering to the floor. The Dullahan stepped forward, its movement a blur, and kneed me in the chest, slamming me backward as it stomped down on my family's knife, snapping it off at the hilt.

I staggered backward, my arm numb, knowing I was next to completely helpless now. I kept the Sword of Iudicael up, but every inch of my body ached, and my breath sobbed in my throat. It felt like I'd been fighting this thing for days, and I hadn't been able to land a blow, all while it had smacked me around like a cat with a mouse.

It stalked me, the head laughing cruelly. I still could see nothing but that headless demon that had once been a man. It was as if I'd been transported to a special chamber of Hell, not to fight this thing, but to be tortured and executed by it.

I was going to die. I didn't have a chance. As hard as it is for a Recon Marine to say that, there are things we simply can't kill by ourselves. Usually, back in The

World, that meant air support. Artillery. Even overwatch. Here, though…

Then I knew. Knew why I was losing. Knew why I was about to die, even as that thing lifted its bone sword and aimed it at me, leering in anticipation.

"*Tigharn. Iudicael.*"

I couldn't do this on my own. That was the lesson of the Sword Bearer who had come before me, who had lost the Sword and put it on its path through the hands of evil men until it had finally come to me. Iudicael hadn't brought it down, all those centuries ago, just to say, "Good luck."

I knew then, too, who my luminous guardian was.

He was there, suddenly, banishing the darkness with his sheer presence. The royal apartments were suddenly lit up bright as day, and the shadow-wreathed warriors with their black swords screamed, a high-pitched, staticky sound, and dissolved into smoke and ash.

The Dullahan froze, the head squeezing its eyes shut with a grimace and a grunt of pain. I felt a hand on my shoulder, and suddenly the pain and the cold were gone. I could move again, and I took a deep breath that tasted cleaner than any I'd taken since before we'd passed the outer gates.

Leaning into my forward leg, I lunged, stabbing straight out with the Sword of Iudicael. I might have aimed for center chest with any other foe, but I put the point right between those rotting green eyes.

Transfixed, the face froze. There was no scream. No explosion. The body simply went limp and crashed to the floor.

Circuitry kill.

Yanking the Sword free, I turned to face the shadow demon that was fencing with Bailey. No, not fencing. It had him pinned to the floor, leaning over him, its eyes violet lightning, the same corposant dancing around the elongated fangs that jutted from its non-face as it dipped toward him.

But Bailey wasn't out of the fight yet. Even as I charged the thing, he got it, too.

"*Categyrn!*"

Another flash. The demon recoiled, and Bailey hewed at the pseudopod of darkness that held him down. The Sword of Categyrn clove through shadow and smoke, and flames began to course through the thing, even as another shining figure advanced on it. With an earth-shaking howl, it leaped through the nearest window and disappeared.

Panting for breath, I looked around the room.

Baldinus was down. He'd given as good as he'd gotten, but he'd taken one of those death-black swords through the thigh, and he sat against the wall, pale, his legs soaked in blood, his eyes fixed and staring. Applegate was still desperately trying to stop the bleeding, but he was obviously gone.

Bailey let out a choked-off cry and ran to his point-man. Baldinus and Applegate had been the closest, but we hadn't lost one of the original platoon in months. It had started to feel like we might survive all this, those of us who were left.

No one survives indefinitely, though.

The king, still pale and moving stiffly from his wounds, physical and otherwise, limped forward, Nechtudad at his side, and put a hand on Bailey's shoulder. "He will be honored among the greatest of Galel heroes." Uven's voice was hoarse and tired, but he looked around at all of us. "As will all of you. You have saved Cor Legear this day." His eyes settled on me. "And slain one of the Dullahans. No man in recorded memory has ever done that."

No one else seemed to have noticed the blindingly bright figure who had stood beside me for that brief moment and made the Dullahan recoil. I could have taken credit, absorbed the accolades. But I knew that I couldn't. I looked down at the Sword in my hand.

"I didn't do it alone."

EPILOGUE

IT took time to get Baldinus and the other dead down to the cellars beneath the reception hall, where they could be prepared for burial. We debated trying to take him back to the Isle of Riamog, to lie in the Halls of the Dead beneath the Temple above Aith an Rih, but that would take a great deal of time, and when Gunny had pointed out that he'd be buried with just as high honors, and just the same sort of prayers here, in Cor Legear, Bailey had only nodded silently.

We weren't that involved in the cleanup. With the storm dispersed and the worst of the monsters fled, there were enough Galel warriors in the citadel and the city to systematically go through looking for any stay-behind elements. Vepogenus, recovering from his enchanted dangle from the wall, had Tharain well in hand and well on the way to the gallows. The rebel lord was apparently in shock, and he hadn't said a word or even blinked since the Dullahan had been slain and the Outsider banished. We could only clean our gear, reload our magazines from the remaining supplies Oncu had brought, and mourn Baldinus.

I stood on the battlements, having sought some solitude, watching some of the red-clad warriors search through the wreck of the town. There was enough still standing that they could rebuild relatively quickly, but the rebels' assault had still done a lot of damage.

I felt the presence before I saw the glow. I turned to face the tall, shining figure and, while it didn't seem that natural to me, I sank to a knee.

"*Rise, Conor.*" Iudicael's voice echoed in my head. "*I am but a servant, the same as you.*"

"I have to thank you." Even as I returned to my feet, I couldn't quite look straight at that luminous face. "It would have killed me. Or worse."

He might have smiled. "*You called. You carry my blade.*"

"It's not quite as simple as that, though, is it?" I glanced down at the Sword at my side. "King Marachar carried it, too, and he died, letting it fall into the enemy's hands for untold years."

Once again, that impression of a smile. "*You have learned much since you were brought through the mists. Good.*" He put a shining hand on my shoulder. "*We each have to walk the path. Stray from it, and ruin awaits. Yet there is aid, should you seek it. As long as you keep your honor clean and bear my Sword, I shall be always at hand to aid you.*"

It's hard to describe expressions on the face of a messenger of Tigharn, a being as bright as the Outsiders were dark, but he seemed to sober, then. "*Steel yourself now, Conor. Grave deeds await.*"

Then he was gone.

* * *

I didn't have time to find Bailey and ask if he'd had a chance to speak with Categyrn. I knew that was the other shining figure that had appeared in the royal apartments, just before the Outsider had fled. Before I could find him, a rider on a lathered horse that seemed near death came pounding up the steep road toward the main gate.

Something about the desperation in that rider's mien had me hustling back toward the keep, glad I had my weapons with me still.

I met Gunny on the way. He'd apparently been meditating the same way I had been. We didn't say anything, but ran together as we hustled toward the hall.

We reached the reception hall at the same time King Uven did. He was doing better, but still moving slowly and stiffly, and he tired easily. He wouldn't be fit for the battlefield for a while, and I could tell it was chafing on him.

The rider, almost as soaked in sweat as his horse had been, rushed into the hall and knelt before the king, even before Uven could take his seat. "My king! It has begun! The armies of Ar-Annator have crossed the border. Even now, they march toward Cor Chatha."

King Uven sagged in his seat. "Of course. It would be now." With an effort, he straightened, then stood. "Call those banners that did not ride with Tharain. We ride for Cor Chatha." He looked to Gunny and me, and bowed his head. "I cannot ask more of you, and yet I must. Our forces are split and scattered, distrustful of one another after what has been done in Tharain's name. The fate of our kingdom will be decided at Cor Chatha. Will you ride with us?"

Gunny didn't hesitate. He didn't need to. He knew we were with him.

"We're ready."

Peter Nealen is a former United States Marine who now writes full time for a living.

https://www.americanpraetorians.com/

Other WarGate Titles Available now:

Forgotten Ruin
Tier 1000

For Updates, New Releases, and Other Titles, visit
www.WarGateBooks.com